THE CONSEQUENCES OF LOVE

Sulaiman S.M.Y Addonia was born in Eritrea to an Eritrean mother and an Ethiopian father. He spent his early life in a refugee camp in Sudan following the Om Hajar massacre in 1976, and in his early teens he lived and studied in Jeddah, Saudi Arabia. He has lived in London since 1990.

The Consequences of Love is his first novel.

SULAIMAN S.M.Y ADDONIA

The Consequences of Love

VINTAGE BOOKS
London

Published by Vintage 2009

2 4 6 8 10 9 7 5 3 1

Copyright © Sulaiman S.M.Y Addonia 2008

Sulaiman S.M.Y Addonia has asserted his right under the Copyright,
Designs and Patents Act 1988 to be identified as the author of this work

First published in Great Britain in 2008 by
Chatto & Windus

Vintage
Random House, 20 Vauxhall Bridge Road,
London SW1V 2SA

www.vintage-books.co.uk

Addresses for companies within The Random House Group Limited
can be found at: www.randomhouse.co.uk/offices.htm

The Random House Group Limited Reg. No. 954009

A CIP catalogue record for this book
is available from the British Library

ISBN 9780099521143

The Random House Group Limited supports The Forest
Stewardship Council (FSC), the leading international forest
certification organisation. All our titles that are printed on
Greenpeace approved FSC certified paper carry the FSC logo.
Our paper procurement policy can be found at:
www.rbooks.co.uk/environment

Printed and bound in Great Britain by
CPI Cox & Wyman, Reading RG1 8EX

This book is dedicated with so much love to
my mother, my maternal grandparents and
in memory of my father

For a brief glossary, please see page 344.

WHATEVER DREAM I had for myself in the future, my mother was always central to it. But now that dream was escaping my grasp. She was sending me away: me, a ten-year-old, and my brother, only three.

We were in a makeshift café at the armpit of the river. At the side of the hill lay a bush and in the bush was a hidden route from our village in Eritrea to east Sudan; a route that was so narrow and arid that it could only be travelled by camel.

Some of the smugglers had already arrived. I watched the flickering oil lamps bounce against the flanks of their camels. There were many people standing around, but not everyone was there to flee the war. Some, like my mother and the other women who lived on Lovers' Hill were there to say goodbye. But most, like my brother and I, were there to escape. My mother was all I had in the world, and I dreaded the moment the oil lamps would be blown out and the camels would set forth in the bush to begin our journey. The world I had known and loved so much would be over.

I was standing next to Semira, my mother's best friend. My mother was just a few yards away buying warm milk for Ibrahim from the tea maker, with her back towards me. The tea maker scooped milk from her pot and put it in a tin cup and gave it to little Ibrahim.

More camels arrived. The men were walking behind the camels, hitting them now and then with a long stick. They were famous smugglers, Beja men from the Beni Amir tribe.

They all had knotted hair and were wearing white *jallabiyahs* with blue waistcoats; swords swung over their shoulders.

My mother came back towards where I was standing with Semira. It was strange that there weren't many tears now. Everyone – Semira, my mother and even me – seemed to have cried all day long and now the only thing left to do was say goodbye.

As I saw my mother approaching, I looked at her face. She was wearing a long black dress and her favourite red Italian-made shoes, a gift from Semira. My mother was tall but the shoes made her even taller.

When she came by my side, she gave Ibrahim to Semira and held my hand. Semira joined the other women who were waiting close to the camels and the light of the oil lamps, waiting to say goodbye to us.

Suddenly I heard a loud thundering noise. I looked up at the sky and saw an Ethiopian fighter plane over our village. I squeezed my mother's hand and pressed my head against her. I closed my eyes, and said a prayer, 'Please *ya Allah* make these planes go away for ever. Please *ya Allah*. Please *ya Allah*.'

When quietness returned to the sky, one of the smugglers came to my mother and said, 'The camels are ready, Raheema. Don't worry. Nothing will happen to your children.'

My mother picked up our oil lamp. She clutched my hand and started walking towards the caravan. But I pulled her back, planting my feet firmly in the sand. 'I am not moving, Mother.'

She stooped in front of me. Her earrings dangled and swung in the breeze. A beautiful odour arose from her neck like swirls of frankincense gum from an incense burner. I looked at her long black hair. I rested my head on her chest.

She wrapped her arms around me. I wished I could stay like this for ever.

My mother whispered, 'My sweetheart, I am doing this because I love you.'

I begged her one more time, 'Please, Mother, don't send us away. I want to stay here with you. Please, Mother.'

She gently pulled herself away, and said, 'I want to look at you, my sweetheart.'

She held my face.

'Let's make a promise to each other,' she said in a soft breaking voice, the silent tears rolling down her cheeks.

'Let's make a promise that we will always be like this wherever we are.' She wove her fingers between mine and bowed her head to kiss my hand.

The smugglers made their final call for our departure. I hugged my mother and her oil lamp fell to the ground, lighting her red shoes in the darkening night.

As the camels started walking, I looked up at her face. I wanted to see it for the last time. But the light at her feet died slowly and my mother disappeared from view.

PART ONE

THE BLACK AND WHITE MOVIE

THE EVENING OF the second Friday in July was an evening of departures. It was 1989 and Jeddah was about to be abandoned by all of those who could afford a holiday. I had left my window open to let the humid breeze into my room. I breathed in the spicy *kebsa* meat mixed with the spice of men's cologne; the smells of the day turning into night.

The phone was ringing. After six rings I picked up. It was Jasim. He wanted me to come to the café to say goodbye. He was off to Paris the following day. He regularly travelled abroad and always came back from his trips with presents; he claimed they would encourage sensuality in those he loved.

He also said that I needed to collect the latest of my letters to my mother. I had tried many times to send letters home but they were always returned to sender. I had used Jasim's café as my return address ever since I had known him.

At that time I lived in a tiny flat in a small two-storey building. It was all I could afford, given that I was earning just four hundred riyals a month at the car-wash. The flat was at the poor end of a long street that swelled at the middle, like a man with a big belly and long thin legs. At the roundabout it was surrounded by shops and restaurants, before it stretched thin again all the way to Kharentina.

By day, its rows of white-painted buildings glistened under the sun and men in white *thobes* outnumbered women in black *abayas*. The scene made you feel like you were in an old black and white movie.

I walked past the villas, where the breeze had turned the garden trees into slow-moving ballerinas. Peering down Al-Nuzla Street, I could see the tallest building of our neighbourhood. It stood out because of its nine floors and was well known for the rich people who lived in it.

In front of me, on the pavement, two young men were strolling, holding each other's hands. They made their way into the Yemeni shop. A few moments later I stopped to let a man past, dressed in *jallabiyah* and *tagiyah* and carrying a box full of plastic Pepsi bottles. I tucked my T-shirt into my tracksuit and continued.

The fragrance of musk filled my nostrils. It meant I was getting close to the biggest mosque in the neighbourhood. At one time I had been living with my uncle right next to the mosque; my new home was a few blocks away in the same street, but this mosque was still the nearest.

I saw a group of six bearded men standing outside. They stood so close to each other that they looked like they were joined at the hips and shoulders.

They stepped aside to give way to the blind imam who was leaving the mosque. It was because of him that I no longer attended prayers. He was clutching the arm of a tall man who was holding a black leather bag. Their long beards quivered softly in the wind.

I quickly crossed the road and bowed my head as I started to walk in the opposite direction to where they were heading.

Then suddenly, a familiar Jeep with shaded windows swerved towards me and screeched to a halt. I froze. Religious police. I wanted to run but my legs felt heavy. Three bearded men jumped out and came towards me. I couldn't move an inch. But they passed and entered the building behind me.

Seconds later, they came out of the building with

Muhssin. Although I had never spoken to him, I recognised him from school. Muhssin was unmistakable – he modelled his look on the romantic style of Omar Sharif, the Egyptian actor from the Sixties. I pulled myself back to the wall. Muhssin's mother followed them, weeping, begging them to spare her son for the sake of *Allah*.

'Please forgive him, he is my only son, my only bread-winner. *Allah* is merciful. *Allah* is love.' The religious police-men bundled Muhssin into their Jeep and turned to his mother.

One of them brandished a stick and ran towards her, yelling, 'Go inside and cover your face, may *Allah* curse you.' He hit her on the back and buttocks as he herded her inside the building.

A moment later the Jeep sped off towards Mecca Street. I hurried into the building to find Um Muhssin. Through the small window pane, I could see that she was sitting on the staircase weeping. Her hand was shaking when she tried to get up. I knocked on the door but she didn't look up.

When I reached the junction of Al-Nuzla and Mecca Street I paused to consider my route. I didn't want to pass Abu Faisal's villa and face the possibility of a chance meeting with Jeddah's most prominent executioner. He was the father of Faisal, my school friend; but when I looked down the road and saw the white Cadillac parked outside his house, I immediately went the other way.

Jasim greeted me, a smile decorating his face. His trimmed goatee curled upwards, accentuating his grin. He was wearing Saudi dress, with the sleeves rolled up, his hairy forearms resting on the counter.

Some of the customers craned their necks to look at me. The smell of *shisha* — smoky, sweet — was gradually overlaid with the smell of hot coffee prepared with plenty of cardamom. Jasim was busy, so I sat down and waited.

I scanned the room and got a glimpse of the new waiter. He was young and agile and he glided through the tight spaces between tables as if his lower half were made of jelly. He squeezed past me and I watched as other customers reached out to touch him. He brushed aside their hands as though they were soft curtains.

The tables were deliberately close together: Jasim wanted men to rub against each other and produce a fire. 'There is nothing sweeter than seeing two men caressing each other with their bodies,' he once told me. 'It makes me imagine that flames of love might be created.'

Back then, I hadn't understood. 'But if the men think for a second that they are touching each other for any other reason than lack of space, then surely they will burn down the café?'

Jasim shrugged his shoulders and laughed.

Jasim's café was full of colour. And his obsession with colour co-ordination extended from the walls to the tablecloths, to what the boy was wearing.

The walls were painted in two sections. The top half was a misty rose, and the bottom half, with sporadic wild flowers sketched by Jasim, was a warm grey.

At the table always reserved for Fawwaz and his cronies — their whispers muffled by their thick moustaches — the boy stretched across to clear the small coffee-cups. He put the cups on a tray and sped to the furthest corner of the room to seek the shelter of an air conditioner. He stood facing the wall and he slowly circled his head as he lifted the hem of his *thobe* to wipe his face. I could see his tight beige velvet trousers contrasting perfectly with the blue table-cloth next to him.

The men were setting up a game of dominoes. Fawwaz placed his chin on his hand and peered at the boy. His stern expression could not hide the lust in his eyes. He leapt to his feet and went towards the boy.

Fawwaz stood in front of the boy and held his hand. I stared through them. Memories were starting to come back to me from my time as a waiter.

Jasim was sitting at the table with Omar, one of his closest friends. I loved those early smoke-free hours of the morning, when the café was quiet and the warm colours of the walls wrapped you like a silk robe.

I was polishing the counter while listening to an interview that my *kafeel* – the Blessed Bader Ibn Abd-Allah – was giving on the radio. He was a police chief in the Jeddah region and he was talking about young people and morality. He suddenly broke off from the calm one-to-one chat with the interviewer and steered into a sermon, quoting from the Qur'an and the Prophet's sayings to warn youth against malevolent behaviour. 'But,' the *kafeel* said, 'we are working together with the religious police to combat immoral behaviour. *InshaAllah, Allah* will bless our important work.'

I shut off the radio, went to the kitchen and lit a piece of charcoal. Holding it with the clamps, I brought it over to Jasim's table and placed the burning coal on the edge of the clay bowl. I pulled up a chair and sat down. Jasim passed me the pipe. I put the mouthpiece on my lips and as I inhaled I moved the charcoal around using the clamps. Omar was talking about a local controversy: a teenage boy had been arrested by the religious police for receiving a note from a girl while walking to school one morning.

'To my knowledge,' said Omar, pinching his left cheek as he talked, 'it is mostly princesses and rich girls who go around and toss notes at boys' feet. They do it for fun and to ease their boredom. Then when they have had enough these girls disappear back to their hidden world as quickly as they came; leaving behind heartbroken boys.'

'So how come I never had notes dropped at my feet?' asked Jasim.

'Well,' said Omar, 'I am telling you that these are rich girls and princesses, and they have a fine taste.'

Jasim stood up, surrounded by smoke and shouted, pretending to be offended, 'Are you saying I am not a handsome man?'

Omar laughed and pulled Jasim down. 'Just sit. You know you're not. Plus, you're smart, and smart people don't risk the consequences.'

I was woken from my reverie when Jasim called my name. I looked up. He indicated that I should join him at the counter.

'I am going to miss you but you will get a great present from Paris,' he announced as he kissed me on both cheeks. His eyes were bloodshot, streaks of red crossing the white of his eyes.

'Don't you ever get tired of travelling?'

He thought for a moment and shook his head, giggling.

'How long are you going for?'

'Shush,' he said, 'you are like a fire-breather. You burn me with what you say.'

It was as if every word he spoke were saturated with

an expensive fragrance. I brought my face closer to his and inhaled deeply.

'Have you been drinking perfume?'

'An exclusive one from France,' he responded.

His eyes lingered on mine. Sweat started dripping from his face as if I was truly breathing fire on him. But I was only watching him silently.

He turned to the small stereo behind him, slipped in a tape and adjusted the volume. Um Kalthoum began singing one of her melancholy songs. A customer yelled at Jasim, begging him to turn the sound up. Some men were up on their feet, their eyes shut and their heads swaying.

I looked at Jasim, surprised. He was shorter than me but his shoulders were broader. As he softly swung his neck and head to the music of Um Kalthoum, his *ogal* fell slightly out of shape.

'Since when do you listen to Um Kalthoum?'

He didn't answer.

Instead he looked at the reflection in the mirror behind the bar. Our faces met. His deep voice was bouncing off the mirror, 'What a beauty you are, my dear Naser. I have watched you grow taller, your eyes swell into the size of oceans, your cheekbones rise, and ah, your neck ascend to the height of the sky.'

I followed Jasim into the kitchen and through the crowded corridor to his private room.

The room was full of the dreams and fantasies of the kind of life Jasim was after. Painted red, it had enough space for a single bed, a chair, a TV, a VCR and video cassettes piled on top of each other. The walls were lined with posters, photos and handwritten poetry.

He closed the door, then grabbed my hand and rested his head on my chest.

'Not a single beat,' he muttered. 'Maybe one day. Maybe?'

I didn't answer.

For a while we didn't say anything to each other. Then he gently directed my hand to his chest and placed it on top of his heart, and asked me, 'Can you feel?'

His voice trembled. 'If I were to put the whole earth on top of my chest, Naser, I would cause the greatest of earthquakes.'

He threw himself on his bed and rolled over to face the wall. He then rolled back and with his chin facing up, he looked into the cracked mirror on the ceiling. He sighed deep and long and said, 'Oh Naser, you looked beautiful when you lived in that mirror. You were free, sexy and sensual. It was your world. And what a world it was.'

He closed his eyes and said, 'Your mother's envelope is on top of the TV. Please leave and switch off the light.'

Outside the kitchen, I bumped into the new boy.

'Can you get me some mint tea?' I asked. I glanced down and saw the boxes full of perfume bottles. I helped myself to a few and went to find a table outside.

The cars were gliding down the hill and speeding along Al-Nuzla Street. I lit a cigarette and watched them.

The boy came out of the café.

'Here is your tea,' he said. He put the little tulip-shaped glass on the table next to me and poured the tea from the large pot.

'Naser?'

'Yes?'

'I've got something to tell you.'

I leaned closer and he whispered rapidly, 'I spent last

night over at Fawwaz's house. His parents are not here. He told me the usual thing: "What we are doing is *haram*. But in this country it is like we are in the biggest prison in the world, and people in prison do things to each other they wouldn't otherwise do." He asked me to be his boy until he gets married. Anyway, the café will shut soon for prayer time and so he will take me on a date to the shopping mall.'

Not waiting for a response, the boy went inside. Not long after, he and Fawwaz came out of the café and walked down the street hand in hand.

When I was sixteen, and had been working in the café for about a year, I was taken to the shopping mall in central Jeddah by a man called Abu Imad, whom I nicknamed Mr Quiet. He was about forty years old. When we arrived at the mall, there were lots of men strolling across the hall, chatting and laughing, holding hands or arm in arm.

The air-conditioned shopping mall was built to a foreign design. Its five floors were full of shops that sold Western products. 'This shopping mall,' Jasim once told me, 'is like the glossiest of shopping malls you can find in Paris or London. You can buy all European and American brands of electrical goods, designer shoes and clothes. You can even find Armani and Calvin Klein.'

Right outside the mall was Punishment Square. It was here that heads and hands were cut off and lovers were flogged, beheaded or stoned to death. This was the place where Faisal's father did his job.

Inside the mall, my companion bought us both a drink and we sat by the fountain. Two religious policemen strode past us. They were both holding sticks, and they were turning their heads left and right, calmly and deliberately.

'Look,' Mr Quiet said, 'they are searching for secret encounters between men and women.' Then he leaned closer to me and whispered, 'Only the other day I witnessed a scene where a young man and woman were caught by the religious police. Thanks to *Allah* you are a man. Otherwise, we would be heading towards that Jeep now and *Allah* only knows where to after that.'

The waiter and Fawwaz disappeared from view. My eyes panned to a woman in full burqa exiting a shoe shop just opposite Jasim's café. Just then the religious police Jeep approached slowly and parked outside the shoe shop, hiding the woman from view. It reminded me that I had been in this country for ten years, yet I had never talked to a girl or held a woman's hand.

The woman emerged again from the shadow of the Jeep, crossed and walked down the road. The Jeep remained parked with the religious policemen still inside it, no doubt observing the street from behind its shaded windows, making sure that Jeddah remained a world of black and white.

I drank my tea in a single gulp and opened the envelope. It contained all my recent letters to my mother and as I flicked through them I noticed how the black ink still sparkled. I felt the need to run, to run a long way from Jasim and the memories of his café.

I WAS TEN years old and my brother, Ibrahim, was three, when our uncle brought us to Jeddah from the refugee camp in Sudan. We had been living in the camp for five months. My uncle, the elder brother of my mother, worked as a chauffeur for a Saudi family in Jeddah. He had heard about us being in the camp because someone from our village had met him in a café where Eritreans meet and told him about us. The man had told my uncle where in the camp to find us.

When my uncle arrived and said he was here to take us with him to Saudi Arabia, I refused. I wanted to wait in the camp with my mother and stay as close as possible to her. My uncle argued that Jeddah was not so far away. 'You see, you will not be far from Eritrea, which is just opposite Jeddah, across the sea.'

He finally managed to change my mind when he said that Saudi Arabia was one of the richest places on earth and that I could earn mountains of money to send to my mother.

We were taken to Khartoum, the capital of Sudan, and from there we flew to Jeddah.

Our plane landed at Jeddah Airport, in the early evening just a few days before Ramadan, 1979. From the very start I fell in love with the city.

We took a taxi to our uncle's house. The roads were wide and well lit, and my eyes flicked from one building to another, from one street to the next. Back in the refugee camp, at this time of night, the moon and the stars would shine giving us just enough light to move around. But in Jeddah, there was no need for the moon or the stars. I peered out of the window and saw lamps that hung above the street from tall posts. They were like goddesses aiming their generous light towards the city.

'Oh *ya Allah*, and the streets are so smooth. There are almost no bumps in the road,' I said to my uncle.

There were tall buildings on all sides, much higher than the one-storey houses I had seen in Khartoum. As we drove alongside the coast road, I hung out the car window and inhaled the breeze that smelt of fish and salt.

The taxi entered a tunnel that went deep in the ground. 'Uncle, we are going under the earth,' I said. 'Only dead people go there.' When we exited the tunnel, I cheered, 'We are still alive.' My uncle smiled and rubbed my head.

When the car stopped at some traffic lights, I looked across to a plaza where there was a huge sculpture of a bicycle. In my imagination, I could see someone riding it. I closed my eyes for a moment and saw two feet on the pedals, wearing red Italian-made shoes; slim legs in blue jeans; and long black hair falling back from a woman's face.

As the traffic lights turned green and the car engine roared into action, I saw her head tilt slightly and she looked at me. Then a wink. That was definitely Mother, I thought to myself. I held my brother's hand and lifted him from my uncle's lap. I pulled him closer to me and kissed him on the cheek. But he leaned his head back against my uncle's chest: he had fallen asleep.

'Ibrahim?' I urged him to wake up. 'Look, look.' I was distracted by the street with its large villas, trees, and beautiful cars in different types, colours and sizes. 'Ibrahim, look,

look at these cars.' I pushed my head through the space in between the two front seats to take a better look. Then I retreated and whispered in Ibrahim's ear, 'We will have a car like that one day.'

As we continued driving, there was something that puzzled me. Alongside the men in their white *thobes*, there were figures in black which, under the street lamps, looked like the men's shadows thrown against the white walls of the houses. They reminded me of the stories about invisible spirits my mother used to tell us, only here, you could actually see them. I knew that Saudi Arabia was a holy country and miracles could happen all the time here. But because I hadn't seen any women in the street, I had worked out who these figures in black were.

'Uncle, can I ask you a question?'

'Yes, son,' he replied.

'That's a woman, isn't it?'

'What?'

'There, look, there.' I pointed to the shadows.

My uncle smiled and said, 'Yes. Oh, blessed childhood ignorance.'

'Why are they covered so much? It is not cold here.'

'The women are wearing *abayas*.'

'Uncle?'

'Yes.'

'Don't they get hot dressed like that? How do they breathe?'

'It's *Allah*'s request. But He, the Greatest, will reward them in heaven, *inshaAllah*.'

'So, will the girls in my school look like this too?'

'You will be going to a boys' school. The girls have their own school.'

I thought back to the small school in the refugee camp. All my friends there were girls. In fact the boys would beat me up because they were jealous whenever we played the wedding game because all the girls would choose me. I told my uncle the story.

'Oh *ya Allah* we ask your forgiveness. I will have hard work on my hands with this one. Listen, Naser, it is bad for boys and girls to mix.'

'Why?'

'It's *haram*, son.'

'Why is it *haram*?'

'Grant me your patience, *ya Allah*. Because –' He stopped and looked away. After a few seconds, he added, 'Because we are like fire and oil, and if the two of us come together, there will be a big flame and thus hell on this earth and in the afterlife. So you see, son, *Allah* is trying to protect us for our own good. OK?'

'OK,' I said, leaning against the window, not understanding a thing.

'Here we are,' my uncle said, as the taxi parked next to a tall white building. 'This area is called Al-Nuzla.'

It had only been a few days since we left our tent in the refugee camp. But it already seemed as though we were on a different planet.

My uncle opened the front door. When I saw the TV, the large black sofa with red stripes, the thick blue carpet, I turned to my uncle, my eyes wide. I kissed his hand and cried, saying, 'Thank you, Uncle, for bringing us to this beautiful city.'

But then I imagined my mother all on her own having to hide under her bed from the bombs, like we used to do whenever the fighter planes came over our village at night. 'Please *ya Allah* help her stay safe,' I prayed silently, vowing at the same time that I would study and work hard to bring her and Semira to safety.

★

But that night, as I ran away from Jasim's café, Jeddah felt different. It didn't feel like the same place any more.

In the old days, when the place was only an arid landscape on the fringe of the desert, the inhabitants had called the place Jeddah, the implication being that *Jaddah Hawwa*, the mother of humankind, was buried in their midst. But that night I thought this was nothing but myth-making.

I remember thinking how the modern city planners had continued with their ancestors' habit of burdening the city with an oversized name. They started calling Jeddah 'The Bride of the Red Sea'. And they dressed her accordingly with the most expensive things. There were bronze sculptures decorating every major street; the bride glowed with jewellery. There were the elegant bridges that cut across the city from all directions, like henna drawings on a bride's hands. And there were the tree-lined avenues that were the petals sprinkled at the feet of the bride.

But despite all this, I thought to myself, Jeddah couldn't be known as the Bride of the Red Sea. It lacked the overwhelming happiness of a woman about to be married. In Jeddah there were too many people whose days and nights merged into one long journey of sadness. I was one of them.

But back then I didn't know that my true love was waiting for me in the folds of Jeddah's wedding dress.

IT WAS ALMOST 8.30 when I got home from Jasim's café. I had arranged to meet my friend Yahya later. He was about to leave for a camping holiday in the mountains of Abha and we decided to spend his last night in Jeddah at our regular place, the Pleasure Palace.

I had some time before our meeting so I decided to do some reading. I sat at my little desk facing Jasim's sketch of my mother. When Jasim, who was trained as an artist agreed to draw a portrait, he sat in front of me with a large blank paper and a tin of drawing pencils. As best I could, I described every feature of the beautiful face I had missed so much.

I told Jasim that she loved the colour red so he framed the drawing in flames, which made her look like a speeding star. I never tired of looking at this picture.

As I was about to take out my book from the drawer, I noticed my diary. I put the book aside and took it out.

I opened one of the perfume bottles I had brought back from Jasim's café and sat on the floor. I put the diary next to me and took in a mouthful, holding it in my mouth for a while before I swallowed it. The sparkles on my tongue engulfed the back of my throat and my nose. I could smell the chemical in my nose, and my lips and tongue felt as if they were burning slightly. I grasped my nose and squeezed it tightly in an attempt to control the sensation. Slowly, I started feeling dizzy as I drank more of the alcohol.

★

Ever since I arrived in Saudi, I had been writing in my diary. As Mr Quiet once said, 'I feel you never want to say anything because you are waiting for a special person. Someone who will understand the trapped mutterings inside your chest. Until you find that person, you should write it all down. Diaries are made for people like you.'

It's true to say that I had no woman to share my life with, no woman to make plans with. In Jeddah there was only the unrelenting drudgery of a world full of men and the men who controlled them. My diary was a link to my hopes, the keeper of my secrets, a sacred place where my heart beat with a soft, hopeful murmur.

I opened it at a random page. The entry said, 'Spring, Saturday, 21st April, 1984.' I took another sip of the perfume and my mind travelled back to that day, when I was fifteen.

That Saturday I woke as usual at six o'clock and was getting ready to go to school when my uncle came into our room. My uncle was a religious man and a conformist who hated my mother. But he was also the only person in the world who cared enough to help my brother and me – still, living with him was only slightly better than our days in a tent in the camp.

'Is Ibrahim taking a shower?' he asked me.

'Yes,' I replied, with some weariness.

'You're not going to school today,' he said. I didn't know how to respond to the news. On the one hand, I hated school and was about to jump with happiness at the thought of spending a day away from lessons. But at the same time, it was too good to be true. My uncle hit me whenever I suggested to him that I would rather miss school than sit through some classes which taught me to hate others who didn't have the same religion or the same interpretation of Islam.

I was far more suspicious than joyous, and I asked him, 'Why's that? What's the special occasion?'

'Because –' He was interrupted by my little brother barging into the room, washed and dressed and looking just like a good Saudi boy. He already looked a lot older than his eight years.

'Ibrahim, wait outside. I am talking to Naser now.'

'OK, Uncle,' Ibrahim said, the good little soldier. As he turned to leave, he looked at me and shook his head as if to say: 'And what have you done now?'

Uncle continued, 'I want you to take our *iqamas* to our *kafeel*, the Blessed Bader Ibn Abd-Allah. He asked that you bring it yourself. We need to renew our residency permits.'

I had long known that every foreigner in Saudi Arabia has to have a *kafeel* – a Saudi man sponsoring their stay in the Kingdom in return for an annual payment. But it only became clear to me that day that the *kafeel* therefore has full control over the lives of those he sponsors. I found this out when I said to my uncle, 'Why don't you go? You always do it.' I was about to storm out with my schoolbag, when he pulled me by my arm. He began to sweat.

He let go of my arm and said, 'Please don't be stubborn, Naser. We have to obey our *kafeel* and do as he asks. I need you to renew our residency permits, please. He asked for you to go. If we don't do as he says he will be angry and that will be the end for us in this country. Please, Naser. I am begging you.'

I hesitated. He had never begged me like that before. My poor uncle, burdened with the sons of a sister he despised, working as a migrant in this rich country, yet barely able to make ends meet.

But then I thought to myself: Why am I resisting? When I come back, I will have the rest of the day to myself.

'OK,' I said to my uncle. 'I'll go.'

He handed me the *iqamas*.

'What about the money?' I asked him.

'Sorry?'

'The two thousand riyals that I need to pay him when we renew our *iqamas*.'

'I don't have the money. But he said he would overlook it this time, may *Allah* bless him.'

I tried to smile to please my uncle. But we both knew that nothing was ever free for a foreigner in Saudi.

I rang the bell of the villa and a smiling Eritrean servant named Haroon answered in Tigrinya. He asked me to use the back door because the *kafeel*'s wife and the daughters were about to leave the house. I nodded and walked slowly along the tree-shaded alleyway and knocked at the back entrance. Haroon opened the door, still smiling, and asked me to come into the large and spacious courtyard. He told me to cross the yard by the small path bordered with small fruit trees.

'*Ya* Ali,' Haroon shouted as he walked behind me, 'tell the Blessed boss that the boy is here.'

Ali came out from a room at the other side of the yard and told me to wait. There were toys and small bicycles lined up outside. The wall of the courtyard was painted with fine abstract designs against a bright turquoise background, providing a pretty contrast to the green plants. A strong smell of incense hung in the yard as golden light pierced the garden trees. I looked up and counted four floors. Where I was standing was just one tiny part of the *kafeel*'s palace.

Ali came back and told me that the *kafeel* was ready for me.

'You go,' he said, bowing his head.

'Where? Why don't you take me?'

'It's OK, just go, over there,' he said, his head still bowed.

I walked ahead, trying to figure out where to go. I turned back to Ali.

'Which of the rooms is he in?'

'There,' he said, pointing to the big door next to a lime tree. 'There, there. Enter.'

The door swung open and a large man dressed in expensive heavy robes was standing there on the steps like a statue. I had seen him a couple of times before when I was much younger, but this morning was the first time I had been to his house on my own. He looked at me with great intensity.

'Welcome, Naser,' he smiled broadly.

'Thank you,' I said as I bowed my head to kiss his hand.

I smelt the Arabian incense as I entered the *majlis*. There were thick mattresses against the wall, piled up with large cushions, and colourful rugs on the floor.

I waited until he sat down.

'Sit,' he said. He seated himself on the mattresses and as he rearranged the cushions behind him to sit more comfortably, he added, 'Have you got the papers?'

'Yes,' I replied, as I handed him the forms with our official photographs, and sat down.

He flipped through the *iqamas* and I looked up to see his portrait hanging on the wall behind him. He was looking down at us, wearing a gold-edged cloak over his sparkling *thobe*. His face looked calm and serene.

How does he manage to have these boyishly smooth cheeks at his age, I was thinking to myself when he asked me: 'And the money?'

'What money?'

'Yes. It's gone up, you know? It's three thousand riyals now,' he said in a low voice.

'I thought you told my uncle you would not charge him this time.'

'Look, son. I said that to your uncle because I feel sorry for him. He is looking after you and your brother even though you are not his children. Just think of the money he already spent bringing you to this country, the money he spends on your clothes and food. He pays all of this from a job that earns him only eight hundred riyals a month. In the name of *Allah*, he is a kind and a good man.'

The light coming from the courtyard made his cheeks glow. 'I don't understand,' I said.

'Let me be straight with you, Naser. I think you should pay for the *iqamas* this time. You are fifteen now. You should help your uncle and contribute, if not every time, at least this time.'

'But how?'

'Think about it. Don't you want to help your uncle?'

'Of course I do. But I told him that I will pay him when I finish school. I told him that as soon as I get a job, he will never have to work again.'

I paused. Why was I telling him these things? This was between my uncle and myself. I stopped talking and I looked at him, like I did when I prayed to *Allah*, begging Him to be merciful with me and answer my prayers, even though I was a bad Muslim.

He surveyed my face for a while and coughed. He rubbed the bridge of his nose with thumb and forefinger, and said, 'Naser? Think about it, after all, and as far as I know, your mother entrusted you to look after Ibrahim. Did you forget that?'

I didn't know what to say.

'Naser?'

27

I whispered, 'Yes, but I will repay my uncle when I get a job after I finish my school.'

'I am talking about now, Naser.'

'Yes, but I don't have any money.'

'You have *Allah*'s gift.'

I closed my eyes.

I was imagining that my mother was running towards me, and after every step she would fall down but then she would get up and start running again, only to trip once more.

'Naser,' the *kafeel* said. He was now closer to me and his hand running slowly over my shoulders. 'Naser?'

I felt strange. I looked up at him.

'Put it this way, you have something that could be worth the three thousand riyals.'

I closed my eyes again and prayed that my mother would come and take me with her. But she couldn't get up this time. I heard her say something and I murmured, 'It's OK, Mother. I forgive you.'

'Naser?' The *kafeel* called me over to him.

At around ten o'clock that same night, I was still awake, still shivering. By then I had lost count of how many times I had showered.

I tried to sit in the bath, but every time I sat down I shot up again as if I had just sat on burning coals. I went to my bed and lay flat on my chest, but the pain was fierce.

I turned towards my brother's bed. I crawled across the floor to his part of the room. I knelt on all fours beside him. He was asleep. I caressed his hair. He turned to the wall and continued sleeping. 'I love you, Ibrahim,' I cried.

'I am sleeping, Naser. Leave me alone,' my brother groaned.

'Ibrahim?' I nudged him. 'I am in pain, please help me.'

He sat up and called my uncle, screaming his name.

'Don't shout, I'll leave you alone. I'm sorry,' I mumbled, returning to my bed.

I lay flat on my front and bit the pillow, clutching the edges of the bed with my fingers. I couldn't sleep. I thought of my mother and I wanted to be closer to her. I got up and put my clothes on, crept past my uncle's bedroom and left the apartment. I was going to the Corniche and the secret place that even my friends didn't know about. It was an hour before midnight and I still had time to catch the last bus.

I paid my fare and shuffled to the back seat of the men's section, putting my hands under my thighs to support my weight.

I leaned backwards and inhaled deeply. Despite the pain I liked sitting there, because it was closest to the women's section and even though we were separated by a full-length panel, their scent drifted into the men's section through the small window above my head.

During those first months in Jeddah, when I missed my mother and her friends so much, I used to take long rides on the buses just to be close to the women and their world. At these moments, I believed that life in Jeddah could still be beautiful. That many things were possible. I especially liked it during rush hour, because they would be crammed into their tiny section and the mixed smell of perfumed hair oil, sharp incense emanating from their *abayas*, and the scents of meat and fresh herbs from their shopping baskets seeping through the window would be stronger.

A man once slapped me on the head when he caught me glued to the panel, looking through the window at the women in their black *abayas,* standing so close together. The man shouted down to the bus driver to stop and I was thrown off. That day, I got off lightly.

The fountain of Jeddah claims to have the highest jet in the world, and is situated near one of King Fahd Ibn Abdul Aziz's palaces on the Red Sea coast. My secret place was not far from there.

The plaza around the fountain was wide and full of restaurants and cafés. Normally I would stroll along the Corniche, enjoying the sight of families picnicking on the beach, reminding me that once I too had had someone who cared for me and loved me.

But that night I was closed to the world. I hurried past the lines of parked cars and ignored the calls of the African street vendors, people who had come from across the Red Sea like me.

Further down the street, where I needed to descend to the beach, I could see the singer sitting on his bench and playing his *'oud* as usual. I passed behind him quietly and walked down the steep steps.

Walking along the beach, close to the water, I had to step over empty plastic bottles and dead shellfish washed up by the waves. In my mind I was already on my rock, in my own world with my mother.

It was a big rock, one of many there. Another rock leaned against it and the top jutted out, giving shelter. As I sat underneath it, I listened to the song of the *'oud* player above me.

When I first saw him, even though he was wearing immaculate Saudi dress, I thought he was homeless because whenever I came to the Corniche, day or night, I would find him sitting on his bench. But I soon realised that he was a lover who took refuge in the arms of the sea. In his songs he would describe an Egyptian girl who had given him the happiest days of his life in a café in Cairo overlooking the Nile. But when he told his father he wanted to marry her, the father tore his passport in pieces so he wouldn't be able to travel. He would sing about how he was planning to go and see her, using his wooden *'oud* as a boat; his heartbeat would be the engine and his hands the oars to row.

I kept trying to erase the memory of the *kafeel*, but the pain in my belly and body wouldn't dissipate. Dawn had broken and I was still sitting on the rock, still staring out over the sea, towards Eritrea. The waves were breaking gently under the rising sun. Now and then, clouds would appear in the sky, hesitating as if lost, before resuming their journeys over Jeddah. Then the waves fell still and the sea reflected the colour of the sky – I felt as if I had supernatural powers like Prophet Moses with his miraculous cane. I squinted my eyes to compress the wide sea into a tiny stream that I could easily cross, and walk all the way back to Eritrea, all the way back to the tender embrace of my mother.

She was sitting on her stool in the compound facing the street, as she always did in the afternoon.

I watched her silently from inside our hut. She sat with one leg crossed over the other, dangling her right foot in the air, her red shoe floating above the yellow sand. She was leaning into the strong breeze. Her long thin face was black as if it was dipped in shining kohl powder; and her cheek-bones were like small hills, covered by a smooth skin. When she gazed into the empty space in front of her, her eyes seemed even darker than her skin, and when she blinked, her eyelashes were so thick and long that they spread gently like the feathers of a peacock.

I was seven. I was wearing my white T-shirt and yellow shorts with black stripes. My curly hair was as long as my little finger. I looked to the side of the hut and saw our chicken trying to stab a hole in a sack of grain with its beak. My mother had bought the sack from the market the previous day. I chased the chicken away, picked up the sack and brought it inside the hut and put it behind the door.

I went out into the compound to get a drink of water from the *outer*. I stretched my arms wide to embrace the wind, inhaling the scent of spiced meat. I turned in both directions to find out which of our two neighbours was cooking.

There were two other women living alongside us: Lumlim and Kamela. Each family owned the space on which their hut was built and what was left we all shared: the barn, the three large barrels for water, the rope to dry our clothes which we hung between three long sticks of wood.

There was hardly anything green in our compound except for the huge tree next to our hut, close to Lumlim's. We sometimes gathered under it to hear her stories and occasionally listen to music from her old radio that dangled from a branch.

I walked over to the *outer*. It was under a small shade we had built to keep the clay pot cool. I picked up the cup and lifted the iron lid. The wind suddenly whipped our wet clothes around the rope, making the sound of an Eritrean *krar*. I turned round to see my mother's long, thick hair rising up into the air like the wings of a departing black swan.

BACK IN MY small flat, with the chemicals of the perfume making my eyes run, I closed my diary. I looked at my watch – it was twenty-five past nine. I was due to meet Yahya at ten. I put the diary back in the drawer but I wasn't ready to leave. I gulped down the last drops of perfume, and pulled my knees into my chest wrapping my arms around them. I stayed like that for what seemed like a long time.

With five minutes to spare I ran down the street to my favourite tree, in front of my uncle's old house, where I had arranged to meet Yahya. It was the tree that had grown up with me in Saudi Arabia. About a year after I first arrived in Jeddah, our municipality started planting palm trees in our street. They planted one opposite my uncle's house. I swore to look after it so that it would grow all the faster and I would be able to hide underneath it in the inferno-like heat. I watered the tree after school with bottles filled from our tap. I watched its small branches grow larger, until it looked like an emperor with a huge crown.

Over the years, its branches became more than leaves shielding me from the sun. They became my companion. They watched over me as I sat underneath them wondering if the girl of my dreams would be amongst the women passing by. And even when the dream appeared an impossible fantasy, I still sat under the tree, because it was a good place to watch the never-ending black and white film of passing *abayas* and *thobes*. Repetitive though it was, it was the only movie in Jeddah that allowed me to imagine that behind the all-black clothes, one of the actresses might bring some colour into my life.

It was a quarter past ten and Yahya still wasn't there.

Something seemed to be going on over to the left, near the overflowing rubbish bin. I saw Hilal gesticulating at the Asian street cleaner. It was Hilal who had found me my job at the car-wash. He was a Sudanese friend of mine who made his living from commissions he earned placing foreign workers in low-paid jobs, a kind of unofficial labour broker.

I looked away. There was no point in following Hilal into an argument. It would last for a long time.

I looked at my watch, wondering about Yahya. When I looked up, I noticed two women striding out together. Both looked the same height and their identical *abayas* made them look as if one were the shadow of the other, a twin of night. Their heads turned in my direction. Their pace slackened. Was it me they were looking at or something on the wall behind me?

Abu Mahdi, an old man who lived in the nine-storey building, was coming down the street. He was followed by a woman in full veil. She could only be his wife, because he only had sons and they were all married and lived in other parts of Jeddah. I had seen him in the street for the last ten years. Wrinkles now spread all over his face like a spider web. I wondered if his wife had aged too.

I could hear a car coming. I thought it was Yahya's but it turned out to be the white Cadillac of Abu Faisal driving towards Mecca Street. When the executioner's car drove by, I shut my eyes until he had gone. I never wanted to see him again.

★

I had first seen him at work six years ago, two weeks after the *Eid al-Fitr* of 1983. I was on my way to the shopping mall to buy a new shirt with the fifty riyals I had received as a present for *Eid* from a visiting friend of my uncle.

I took the bus to Al-Balad district in the oldest part of Jeddah. From there I walked through the narrow lanes floored with large cracked stones. Most of the buildings in this area were centuries old and built from mud and cut stone. The colourful carved wooden balconies appeared unstable, but they never seemed to fall, as if they were resting on the shoulders of ghosts.

The smell of imported spices floated out of the small shops, which were lined up in front of larger shops famous for their silver Bedouin jewellery.

As I left Al-Balad behind me and approached the modern shopping centre, the streets got noisier. It was about an hour or so after Friday prayers, so the streets were packed with men dressed in clean *thobes* and the still air was saturated with perfume and musk.

Just outside the entrance to the mall, I saw a large crowd gathering in the square, forming a huge half-circle.

I needed to get through the crowd to reach the shops. As I tried to navigate my way past the big bellies of the men I focused on trying not to faint in the sweltering heat. The crowd shoved forwards and I was lifted off the ground, I found myself at the front, surrounded by a men-only crowd. I heard the announcement over the tannoy. An Indian man was going to be beheaded for drug trafficking.

Abu Faisal stepped into the centre of the circle. I stood motionless. I had never seen him at work before. The men around me shouted: '*Allah wa Akbar.*'

Abu Faisal was wearing a black overcoat over his white *thobe*. His *ogal* sat like a black crown over his red *gutra*. He was the tallest man I had ever seen. He was made tall, we used to say at school, so that *Allah* could pass to him messages of strength when he was beheading and cutting off hands.

Behind him a stocky man was holding a long sword that was glistening under the sun. The blindfolded Indian man was led to the square and made to kneel down. Three men surrounded him. One of them sat down and asked him to recite the *shahada*. After a while they hurried away and the man with the sword walked up to Abu Faisal, who was pacing up and down with his head bowed. When he saw the man with the sword approaching, Abu Faisal stood still, straightened up and stretched out a long arm.

With the sword now in his firm grip, Abu Faisal swung it in the air to warm up his arm and looked around at the crowd. His eyes caught mine and I remembered the time when his son, Faisal, broke down in front of me because he said his father was going around saying that his son was born to be a beheader; something he didn't want to be.

The crowd's muttering receded now. Abu Faisal's sword was only inches away from the kneeling Indian man. The moment Abu Faisal raised his sword above his head, I turned around and pushed my way out of the circle.

The crowd fell silent.

I was dashing away from the crowd when I heard a high-pitched scream, followed by a chorus of 'Allah wa Akbar.'

I ran inside the mall and sat next to a water fountain opposite the electronics store. I put my hands between my legs, hoping that if I squeezed them tightly together it would stop the shaking of my arms that was making my chest shudder.

The roaring of the crowd outside pierced through the walls of the mall. My eyes were shut and I put my fingers in my ears, wishing that I could get away from the mall. The roars faded and I knew the beheading was over. Some of the crowd drifted into the mall, bringing with them their mutterings and soft shouts of *Allah wa Akbar*.

It was only then that I knew I could go home. I no longer wanted a new shirt.

Yahya turned up about an hour late. He parked his car a few metres away from the tree and got out. I stood up and walked over to him. He was wearing his favourite tight T-shirt with the Al-Ahli football club logo and was holding a Pepsi can.

Yahya lived off his father's inheritance. Before he died, his father had been one of the richest foreigners in Al-Nuzla. Yahya was famous for touring the neighbourhood on his bike. He used to boast that boys from all over the world loved him, and that he was their number one choice because of his muscles. He was the only person in our neighbourhood who did proper weightlifting, and he was happy to face the heavy traffic and drive an hour every day of the week to get to the only club in Jeddah that had weightlifting machines.

'Sorry I'm late,' he said in his throaty voice. 'I was busy packing.'

'It's all right,' I replied, snatching the Pepsi can from his hand. 'Ready for your trip?'

'Yep,' he replied. 'Hani and his family are also holidaying in Abha this year, so I will see him but I will still be able to do my own thing, you know.'

Hani was a Saudi friend and like Yahya he didn't go to

school. He worked in his father's import and export business. Yahya had cut his studies short when he reached year eight, because, he said, he saw no point in continuing if, as a foreigner, he wasn't allowed into university. 'So, when are you and Hani coming back?' I asked him.

'Around mid-September,' he replied.

Just then, the door of the villa opposite swung open and Muhammad Al-Hyrania emerged, wearing his short *thobe* and *tagiyah*, with his *gutra* loosely over his arm. He stood there watching us with unwavering eyes. He spread out his *gutra* on top of his head and started reading verses out loud from the Qur'an. His head was rocking back and forth, his eyes staring at us.

'We are not Mecca, why don't you face the right direction?' Yahya shouted at him.

The nerd started reciting the same *sura* again, his eyes still fixed on us. When he finished reciting, he shut the door behind him and walked up the road, with his hands crossed behind his back, now and then glancing back at us.

The Pleasure Palace was an abandoned palace that had once been owned by King Saud Ibn Abdul Aziz. He had been deposed about twenty-five years previously in a coup staged by his own family and with the backing of religious scholars.

The palace was only a few minutes' drive from our street. It was a gigantic place, crumbling under the weight of its own loneliness. Yahya and I left Al-Nuzla and took the familiar shortcuts down to the deserted boulevard that led to the King's Palace. I was sitting in the front seat and could see the tall towers that stood equal in height to the columns of the surrounding mosques. But this grandeur was an illusion. By daylight, you could see the golden paint peeling off.

We knew that the government or the religious police didn't want to come near the palace because of King Saud's history with alcohol and women. It was deemed such an evil place that we could roam around it, drink our perfume and sniff glue confident that the police would not chase us there. When we arrived in the back street behind the palace, Al-Yamani, a Saudi friend of ours who lived in Mecca Street, was already there, waiting by his car.

We greeted one another, then Yahya said, 'You won't believe what I saw earlier today. Zib Al-Ard outside the mosque with the *mutawwa'in*. He was dressed exactly like them. Oh *ya Allah*, he is even growing a beard. How could this have happened? This is our friend Zib Al-Ard we're talking about. I am going to kill whoever made this happen.'

I walked over to the part of the palace wall that had fallen down and was replaced by a zinc sheet. My urine clanged against the zinc and splashed in front of my feet.

On my way back, my heart suddenly felt heavy. I fell to my knees. I vomited, but because I hadn't eaten all day, the vomit contained only fragrant fluid. My insides were growling. I breathed in and out, slowly. I didn't want to be ill. I just wanted some time with my friends before they left, because after that I was going to be alone for the rest of the summer.

'Are you OK?' Yahya asked, staring at me. 'You've got to stop drinking that perfume,' he said.

'We all have our habits, don't we?' I replied, looking him straight in the eye.

He rubbed his hands, as if suddenly remembering something. He turned his back to Al-Yamani, took out his wallet and pulled out a small photo. It was a picture of a light-skinned boy with a smooth face and soft smile.

'Where is he from?' I asked him.

'I don't know,' he replied casually.

'What do you mean you don't know?'

'He just moved with his family to our street and he can't speak Arabic.'

'How do you communicate with him then?'

'Arabic is the language of Islam, ah? Who said it was the language of love?' he chuckled.

Yahya turned to Al Yamani and said, 'Come on, tell me what made Zib Al-Ard change. You are the one who knows him best.'

Al-Yamani started explaining between puffs on his cigarette. 'He was changed by the blind imam and Basil.'

'I know the blind imam, but who is Basil?'

'He is the blind imam's guide.'

I interrupted, 'I have seen him a few times with the imam in the street. But he is not from the neighbourhood, is he?'

'No, Basil is from Kharentina. You know, he used to be one of the bad boys there, a boy who was into drugs and owned a fleet of motorbikes. But everyone knew his main weakness was pretty boys and he had his fair share of them. But one day he had a serious bike accident and the boy who was sitting at the back of his bike almost died.'

'Which boy?' Yahya asked. Yahya stretched out his arm and leaned on my shoulder. I didn't like it when he did that.

'Don't worry,' Al-Yamani said, 'there are still some boys out there you haven't managed to sleep with.'

Yahya looked at me and said with a sly smile, 'A few perhaps. But it's only a matter of time.'

Al-Yamani continued, 'So when Basil returned home from the hospital, he decided to go to his local mosque to pray his thanks to *Allah*. That day, the blind imam was the invited guest. Everything changed during a speech in which the imam described hell so vividly it was as if he had seen it himself. Basil was so gripped that he threw his past behind him, including all his friends, lovers, and even members of his family, and dedicated his entire life to the imam and *Allah*. He is trying to make up for his sins in any way and as quickly as he can.'

Al-Yamani paused to take another drag.

'So, all Basil thinks about is collecting rewards. He is on a mission to build steep mountains of good deeds. Things like converting a bad boy to become a *mutawwa*, or sending a man to Afghanistan.'

'So how did he change Zib Al-Ard?' asked Yahya.

'Well, I don't know exactly,' replied Al-Yamani, 'but it must have happened at the prayer service to his martyred brother.'

'Khalid is dead?' Yahya and I asked in unison.

'Yes. Martyred in Afghanistan a few months ago during the heavy fighting between the communists and the mujahideens. The news of his death arrived recently. You would have wept if you had heard Basil's speech at the funeral. All the men were crying. Basil praised the martyr Khalid through beautiful poems,' said Al-Yamani. 'As Basil described what awaits martyrs in heaven, he was staring at Zib Al-Ard as if to tell him that he should be jealous of his brother's martyrdom. And I think he was. A few days later, Zib Al-Ard was dressed like a strict *mutawwa* and started acting like one. He stopped wearing *ogal* over his headdress and shortened his *thobe* to show his ankles. He threw away all his music tapes, pornography magazines and films. He even broke his TV and destroyed all his photo albums. "Pictures", he said, "are forbidden, because angels do not enter a house full of pictures and whoever takes them will be punished on Judgment Day, and will be challenged by *Allah* to give life to his creation." Only *Allah* creates, Zib Al-Ard said.'

'So why is Zib Al-Ard going to Afghanistan? I thought the war was finished,' remarked Yahya.

'Yes,' replied Al-Yamani, 'but according to Basil the mujahideens are involved in another equally important jihad against the pro-Moscow regime of Najibullah. That's why, Basil said, the Arab Afghans need more recruits to defeat the traitors and apostates. And Zib Al-Ard is answering the call.'

Al-Yamani paused. He mumbled, '*Astaqfirullah, Astaqfirullah.*'

'Why are you asking *Allah*'s forgiveness?' Yahya asked, irritated.

'I've just realised that now that he's became a *mutawwa*, it is *haram* to call him Zib Al-Ard. We must call him by his real name, Murad.'

'Oh, come on!' Yahya barked at Al-Yamani. 'He is still a midget and as far as I know his long dick still touches the ground when he walks. He will always be Zib Al-Ard.'

Al-Yamani shook his head and walked away, still mumbling, '*Astaqfirullah, Astaqfirullah.*'

There was a part of me which thought Zib Al-Ard was a perfect name and I wanted to yell it in every corner of the city to get back at him for following the blind imam and becoming Murad, but then there was another part of me which still liked him and couldn't forget that he and I had been good friends for a long time.

Who would be next to fall into the hands of the blind cleric and his Basil? Not me – or at least that's what I thought that night as I watched Al-Yamani leave the Pleasure Palace.

★

Yahya and I went to sit on the pavement outside the Palace. He passed me the Pepsi can. I put my fingers around the can, closed off one nostril with my finger, leaned my head forward and stuck my open nostril in the tab of the Pepsi can. I shut my eyes and breathed in the glue deeply. I held my breath for a while and as I breathed out, I slowly tilted my head backwards. I stayed like this for a while.

I put the can between us. The evening breeze caressed my legs. I looked over to the palace tower, the crumbling walls and the only palm tree still standing in the midst of the dry grass.

I felt sick again. I turned to Yahya: he was almost breathing on my neck, his eyes gleaming. I slid away from his hot breath.

Yahya stretched out on the pavement, lying down on his side with his legs pointing towards the grass. He put his hand on my thigh.

I pushed him away. He laughed.

I wanted to punch him, but I knew he was stronger than me. So I just looked away. My gaze settled on the palm tree again.

I felt Yahya's hand on my chest. I grabbed the Pepsi can and bashed it against his arm. His eyes widened. I closed mine, waiting for his retaliation. He stood up and picked me up by the shoulders and threw me across the pavement. I kept as still as the palm tree.

Yahya looked at me and screamed, 'No one hits me, you understand?'

I said softly, 'And I have told you a million times not to touch me.'

'Why?' he asked, as he came towards me.

I got up, and we looked at each other as I dusted the dirt off my arms and legs.

'Yahya, we're supposed to be friends.'

'I know you have been playing around,' he said.

I leaned my head back, closing my eyes, tensing my jaw.

'Is it because I am not a Saudi?' he asked.

'I'm off,' I said. 'Have a nice time in Abha.'

As I walked past him, he grabbed my arm and pulled me back. 'Answer me,' he said. 'Is it because I am not a Saudi? Don't I have enough authority or prestige for you?'

'No, Yahya, it has nothing to do with all that.'

'What is it then?' he yelled. 'Come on, tell me.' He let go of my arm. He spat on the pavement, pulled up the sleeves of his T-shirt and flexed his pumped-up muscles. 'How about these?' he barked at me. He then kissed his biceps and added: 'Do your men have anything like this?'

'Yahya, you are not listening,' I insisted, 'I am waiting for a girl.'

He started laughing like a hyena. He couldn't stop himself. 'You are becoming like Hani. You know he is going around with a magazine photo of an Egyptian actress, saying how deeply in love he is with her. He talks about her as if she is real. He talked about how he will spend nights with her in an apartment overlooking the beach, and how he will buy her anything she wants.' He paused and calmly took out a packet of cigarettes, put one in his mouth and lit it. 'Be careful and don't lose your mind as well.'

He took a long drag and then offered me one. 'Where do you think you will meet this girl? In a cinema? A theatre? That happens in other places, like Egypt, or Beirut, but not here in Saudi. Look, we live in a separate world, until we meet when we marry. In the meantime, I say, let's enjoy each other's company. Just like what you got up to in Jasim's café. That is your real destiny, you just need to accept it.'

I pushed him aside. I left him standing next to the palm

tree and didn't even say goodbye as I walked to the bus stop to get a ride to the Corniche.

I must have stayed for a few hours sitting on my rock, accompanied by the nostalgic voice of the Saudi singer. I envied his tears of love, his sadness for a woman whom he said was his sweetheart as well as his best friend. I wanted to join him singing so I could just taste the yearning of his heart.

But, as always, I chose not to bother him. Instead, I just dreamed along with his songs, my heart wandering to somewhere in the future where *Allah* would bring a miracle to me and a girl would hold my hand and I would tell her all the things lovers say to each other.

THAT DAY, AT the end of the night, I took a shower and retired to my bed.

My body ached for a female touch. I closed my eyes and imagined the world of my past where I lived with my mother and her female friends. I started visiting this world many years ago to stop the burning pain in my stomach whenever I feared I might never see my mother again. But later on, when the pain became less strong but still there, dull and persistent, it became the only place where I could meet women. My mother's world was now a refuge for my growing desires.

In order to earn a living, my mother braided women's hair and made henna drawings on their hands and feet. She worked from our hut, and used to sit on a stool next to her bed, which was in front of my bed. Her clients, many of whom were her friends, came to our hut whenever they liked. Her busiest working times were before weddings, *Eid*, Easter and Christmas.

Lying on my bed, I heard them talk. I listened to their stories about love, their husbands, and about what made them happy and sad. And whenever women came over to spend the night with my mother, I would pretend I was asleep but I would catch glimpses of them in unguarded moments. Semira, my half-Eritrean, half-Italian godmother, was the one who came most to our hut.

And now, with my eyes closed, I saw Semira in front of me. She wasn't the godmother I had known, lending me wisdom and advice, but she was a goddess of love and desire. She was the only woman I had ever seen naked and the memory of her curved body made me feel alive.

I remembered one evening, when I was nine years old and I was sitting on Semira's lap. She was chewing gum, which appeared between her red lips now and then. She was wearing a white shirt, tightly wrapped around her upper body and low-cut, revealing the place where her breasts sprung out of her chest. It was my favourite shirt. I was looking at the movement of her hands as she combed her hair. 'Can I have your chewing gum?' I asked her. She nodded, pushing the gum to the edge of her lips with her tongue. I reached with my fingers to her parted lips and collected the warm gum that had been in her mouth. The gum didn't taste sweet any more, but was full of the taste of her mouth. As I slowly chewed, my eyes wandered down her long neck and along the golden necklace that complemented her light brown skin. They stayed on the raised curves of her breasts, transfixed. She smiled and looked away.

THE NEXT MORNING, I got up at five o'clock and made my way to the car-wash. It was my last day at work before I started my two weeks' annual holiday.

The car-wash was in a small road off Al-Nuzla Street in one of the neighbourhoods populated by Chadians. It was right next to a makeshift school where a Chadian man taught French and English.

Our main clients were wealthy Saudi families who lived in the affluent Al-Nuzla Al-Sharqyhya. Their cars were brought to us by their chauffeurs.

But since most of these families were away during the summer holiday, mainly in Europe, we had fewer cars to wash. So that's when my fifty-year-old Chadian boss let me have some time off. He gave me two weeks holiday per year, which was a lot compared to some of the other jobs that were available to foreigners like me. In a way I was lucky, but I had to work extra hard during the year, working from the early hours until late in the evening, and in case a client needed to travel to meet someone important I had to be on hand to make the car look brand new.

So by late afternoon, after I had cleaned a Rolls-Royce and two Mercedes, my boss informed me that I could start my summer holiday.

It was my time to spend long uninterrupted hours under my palm tree with the warm memories of the past.

PART TWO

SUMMER LONELINESS

JEDDAH WAS EERILY quiet in July after the summer departures. Al-Nuzla Street was deserted, even during the cooler evening time. The streets which had been so busy a week or so before were now empty.

Nearly everybody I knew was away from Jeddah. My friends Faisal and Zib Al-Ard were fighting in Afghanistan. Jasim was in Paris, buying presents and probably searching for new ways to decorate his café. Yahya was camping and no doubt looking for love on a hillside somewhere. There was no one around, just me. I gave up thinking about my brother and my uncle – there was no point trying to be with people who didn't want to be with you. Besides, they would never talk to someone who worked in Jasim's café. Those who knew, knew. And what my uncle didn't know, which was a lot, he assumed the worst of. That was his religious way.

In our neighbourhood, there were only four kinds of people who didn't go away during the summer vacation: those who didn't have the money, those who didn't have any relatives to visit, those who thought of holiday as a forbidden, vulgar pastime, and those who preferred Al-Nuzla when it was quiet. Although I had some money saved from my time at Jasim's café, the only thing I would want to do is visit my mother and Semira. But they were in a country where the war never seemed to end.

Although I sometimes could find happiness by myself, shadowed by memories, I could not bear the searing heat and heavy silence in the empty streets of Jeddah during the holiday season.

The days seemed longer than usual and time was passing slowly. There was nothing to do, so there was nothing to write in my diary. With every minute I spent stuck in Jeddah, I felt myself sinking further.

On Tuesday afternoon, three days into my holiday, I decided to go outside and sit under the shade of my tree to take a break from reading.

I stepped into the hazy afternoon heat. I looked in both directions before crossing the road, but there was nothing moving. The street was deserted. With my sandal I scraped away the dirt on the pavement and sat down. I wanted to take a long rest. It was beautifully still at that time of the day. It was so quiet you could imagine a tumbleweed from one of those old cowboy movies rolling its way through Al-Nuzla. There was not one sheriff or religious policeman to stop it.

As I lay down, I noticed a woman — covered head to toe in a full black veil — walking briskly from the corner of the street. I wondered why on earth she was rushing around in this heat. I stretched out on the cool pavement, with my face turned to the street.

The sound of hurried footsteps was coming closer. I lifted my head. The woman was heading towards me, so I sat up.

She stopped, looking left and right. She was inches from me, looking at me through her black mask, her nose marked through her veil. She tossed a crumpled piece of paper into my lap and scampered away.

I quickly unfolded the paper. It was a note for me. I read it and the few words imprinted themselves in my mind.

I shook my head and sat back on the pavement and looked around to see if anyone was watching. What sort of trick was this? I folded the paper so that it was even smaller and pressed it deep inside my pocket.

The street was deserted again. I lit a cigarette and tried to look calm but thoughts and questions raced through my head. What a mad thing to do. Did the woman not know that the religious police watched our every move? And how could she possibly trust me? What if I were a traditionalist, a conservative; someone who would detest her actions as being un-Islamic? I might have followed her home and informed the man of her household on her. I didn't even dare to think what men, whose only concern it is to honour their honour, might do to her. *Ya Allah*, I thought, she must be a crazy, crazy woman to take such risks.

But despite that, I was still excited by the fact that I was sitting there with a girl's note in my pocket. And at some point, still sitting on the pavement, I started seriously considering the girl's proposal.

'Why not? It's going to be a long summer anyway,' the devil inside me said. I stood up and re-read it as I walked home:

> *My dear,*
>   *I am writing to you in secret. No one knows about this except me and Allah. I just want to say that I like you and I would like to write to you again. I will look for you at the same time tomorrow under this tree.*

I closed my eyes and tried to remember what she looked like: covered in a wide black burqa, and wearing black gloves and black shoes she looked like any other woman in the street. Underneath, though, anything was possible.

She might be the daughter of one of the royal families or one of the wealthy Saudi families who lived up the road in Al-Nuzla Al Sharqyhya. But if she were rich or a princess, why wasn't she away like everybody else? Maybe she was a servant or the daughter of a religious man? Could she be the wife of a man who had gone on holiday with his male friends, leaving her behind with their children? Was she a girl, a woman, or a widow? Was she one of the neighbours? She might be the sister of one of my friends? But my friends never talked about the women in their households.

I remembered what Omar had said that morning at Jasim's café about the girls who threw notes at boys' feet. Maybe she had written similar notes to other boys. Maybe she had already broken many hearts and was looking for her next victim?

Even if I did pursue this, just one careless moment could have me arrested by the religious police and that could lead to Punishment Square where lovers are lashed and sometimes even killed. How dare this woman put me in danger? Life in Jeddah was hard enough without being teased by someone with nothing better to do. Who wanted this kind of terror wrapped up in a scrap of paper?

I tossed the note into a bin and returned to my room.

That summer, in the absence of anyone to keep me company, I spent my time reading books, and re-reading my diaries and letters to my mother. Often also thoughts and memories would come back, from my time as a fifteen-year-old boy, trapped in Jasim's café and forced to accept the passion of sex-hungry men. I didn't need a diary as a reminder; the memories of those days stayed with me in the skin of my body.

*

It all started a few weeks after the incident with my *kafeel*, the Blessed Bader Ibn Abd-Allah. I was still having nightmares. Once, I woke up in tears in the middle of the night. I was crying and screaming for my mother.

My uncle came into our room.

'Be quiet,' he shouted.

But I continued to call her name. It was enough to set my uncle off in flames.

'I told you not to mention the name of that sinner, may *Allah* burn her in hell, *inshaAllah*.'

I jumped off my bed and pounced on his chest. I hit him in the face. He pushed me back on the bed, holding me by my neck with both his hands. He was sweating, his upper lip bleeding and his eyes staring at me, fixed as if they belonged to a lifeless doll. I was wheezing and struggling for breath.

As he turned his back, he shouted, 'Get up and leave my house. You are ungrateful, you don't even pray. You are an apostate and I don't want to waste my money on someone like you. I want you out by tomorrow.'

I protested, I cried, I pleaded, but my uncle was hearing none of it. He closed the door and the next morning he watched me as I packed my bags. He told me there was no hope in me becoming a good Muslim because I was brought up by an irreligious woman. 'But look at Ibrahim,' he said, 'I am his father now and you can see the difference. He is already showing signs of becoming a blessed Muslim.'

I didn't know where to go. I begged him one last time to change his mind. 'I am only fifteen,' I pleaded with him, 'I don't have any money. Where do you want me to go?'

'Go back to your bad Muslim friends, the glue-sniffers,' he replied, pushing me out of his house and shutting the door behind me. I sat outside the house for a while not knowing what to do next.

The only friend who could help me was Jasim.

By then I had known him for three years. I met him when I went to his café for the first time one morning when I was twelve. When I approached the counter to pay for my tea, he said there was no need to because I was his youngest ever customer who read a newspaper as he drank tea. 'And you are reading my favourite paper too,' he said, pointing to my *Okaz*. He told me that he admired people who liked reading and that instead of buying a newspaper every morning I could come to his café and borrow his.

We got to know each other better over time and as well as lending me his daily paper, he also started to give me presents, mainly novels and poetry collections. But it was when he painted my mother, based on my description, that he became very dear to me. With his beautiful painting of her, he made me miss her less because she was now within reach, because her face, ingrained in my memory, was turned real again, her smile colouring everything on my path, and because whenever I wanted her warm love, I would hold the drawing and embrace it tightly.

'You are my best friend,' I told him on the day he finished the portrait. 'You are my best friend.'

When I arrived with my bag, Jasim immediately took me to the kitchen away from the customers. I persuaded him to let me live in the small room at the back of the café, the one with the mirrored ceiling.

'Look, Naser,' he said, 'I can let you live in this room. But you have to understand that to me it is more than just a room.'

I interrupted him, 'Jasim, don't worry. I will beg my uncle to take me back. I am sure he will agree. Trust me, I will move out before long.'

'No, no, don't worry about moving out so soon,' he said, 'I want to help you. But I want you to help me too.'

'What do you want me to do?' I asked him.

'Work in my café. I will sack the waiter. The boy is so unreliable. I feel you will be a better one. And don't worry, I will pay you the normal wages.'

It didn't take me long to agree. Because, I thought, if I had had money I would have paid our *kafeel* in cash for the renewal of our residency and not with my body. 'I can now save enough money for me and my brother,' I mumbled.

'Are you OK?' Jasim asked.

'Yes I am,' I said, smiling and feeling happy that from now on I was going to take responsibility for myself.

'I love it when you smile, my dear,' Jasim said. He held my hand and looked at me with gleaming eyes.

I turned my head away.

He let go of my hand and warned me, 'But you know working here means you will have to leave school?'

In return Jasim promised me that I could read whatever I liked from the books he smuggled from abroad. He smuggled them on request of people who wanted to read books banned by the authorities. They were banned either because they challenged the government or because they were thought to be un-Islamic. His customers' favourites were books by the Saudi writer, Abdul Rahman Munif, who was stripped of his Saudi citizenship because of his political writing, and lived in exile in Syria.

★

I thought that my stay at the café would be short because I was convinced that my uncle would take me back if I offered him most of my wages as a contribution to the household. But a few weeks after I moved to the café, my uncle's boss relocated to Riyadh and he moved there with my brother. I found out only when I visited the caretaker of my uncle's building. He was a Sufi from Pakistan – an outsider like me – and he kept me up to date about Ibrahim and how he was doing.

But that morning, when he opened the door, he lowered his head and said nothing. Then he embraced me and said, '*Allah* is now your only companion in life, my son.'

I thought something terrible had happened to my brother. I shouted at him to speak up, begging him to tell me at once. But Ali firmed his grip around my hands and said, 'Nothing happened to him. But they left. They left you for good. But you are not lonely, son, *Allah* is with you.'

'What do you mean they left? Where? Which neighbourhood? Have you got their new address?'

'No, Naser, they left for Riyadh. For good.'

'Why didn't they at least say goodbye?' I cried.

'I am sorry,' he said, 'I am sorry.'

From that moment on, the café became my life. I woke up at six o'clock and worked until ten at night. After a full day's work, I didn't have any energy left to venture outside the café. I ate the food our Yemeni chef cooked in the café and it was Jasim who bought me new clothes. I started living a life completely opposite to the one I had lived with my mother: instead of women, I was now surrounded by men.

★

One morning, a few months after I arrived in the café, Jasim asked me to wear tight beige cotton trousers under my *thobe*. 'It is your new work uniform,' he said, as he sipped his coffee. It was early morning and we were in the back room.

'Look, Jasim,' I protested. 'I can't even zip up the fly. You got the wrong size.'

'No, I am sure they will fit. Just pull them up harder. Let me help you,' he said. He held my trousers by the waist and grabbed hold of my briefs.

I shivered at the warmth of his hands on my body. His eyes caught mine. 'Sorry,' he murmured. Then, 'Here, ah, you see, my dear. Perfect!'

He lit a cigarette and I could see his gaze running over my body.

'Look, Jasim, I can't wear this to work. It is bad enough wearing a *thobe*, I can't imagine what it will be like wearing something as tight as this. I'm tired of customers pinching my bottom all the time and promising gifts if I agree to their propositions.'

I could smell the cardamom on his breath as his face came closer to mine. 'Don't worry, you will wear it under your *thobe*. But can you blame them, Naser?'

'What?'

'My dear, in a world without women and in the absence of female glamour, boys like you are the perfect substitute. 'Why hide your attractiveness and your tender physique like a veiled woman? You are the closest my customers have to a beautiful and sensual person roaming freely in their world. So why sit on your beauty like a bird without wings, when you can fly?'

I sat on the bed not knowing how to respond.

'Naser, I want to make my café like a paradise, where

59

everything one desires, one gets. They can lock women away, but they can't cage our fantasies. I want to find other ways to set passion free.'

For a while, we didn't say anything to each other. And I did what I always did in Saudi when there was nothing else I could do. I closed my eyes.

Rashid was always watching me around the café, as he smoked the *shisha*, as he drank, and ate, and even when he talked to his friends. Although he wasn't the only person who glared at me, he was the most persistent. He was the man known in the café for having a big meal every two hours, a routine he kept despite having been warned by his doctor to lose weight.

'What are you wearing today, handsome?' Rashid asked me one day.

'A *thobe*, of course. Are you blind?'

'Come on. You know what I mean.'

'Just leave it, please,' I said. 'The usual?'

'Yes. Don't forget to make the beans swim in oil,' he said, winking at me.

On my way to the kitchen to get his order, I grumbled to myself.

'Naser?' Jasim called. He was behind the counter, doing some paperwork. 'What's wrong?'

'Him.' I pointed to Rashid with my head.

'Try to be calm,' he said, reaching for his handkerchief and wiping his forehead.

'I am tired,' I said in a low voice.

Jasim put his other hand on my shoulder and patted it softly. 'My dear, whenever you feel it is too much, always remember what I told you the other day. Be proud of who you are. Share what you have with others.'

I would stop complaining and do what he asked me to do because I felt I had no real choice. His café was where I lived too. And now that my uncle had deserted me taking my brother with him, Jasim was all I had.

The next morning another customer, Mr Quiet, lifted his ring-filled hand to get my attention. I smiled. He was one of the few men who had never tried to touch me. He always sat at the back of the room, the only table with one chair, which was always reserved for him. His face would disappear behind the haze of his smoke, his sunglasses and his own silence. I would serve him his usual: basbousa cake with coffee. He never spoke to me beyond saying, 'May *Allah* enrich you.'

Jasim was the only person he would speak to, and their conversation was always brief. He was tall, had a thick grey beard, and always wore a blazer on top of his *thobe*.

'Never ask him questions of any sort,' Jasim had warned me about the man. 'He likes to be on his own.'

'Not even his name?'

'I'll tell you his name. He is called Abu Imad.'

I laughed. 'He is even hiding behind his son's name.'

I hurried to Mr Quiet's table. '*Assalamu alaikum*,' I greeted him.

'*Wa 'alaikumu salam*,' he responded in his melodious voice.

'Anything else besides basbousa cake with coffee for you today?' I asked him.

'No, thank you,' he replied. 'May *Allah* enrich you.'

Moments later, Rashid walked in and sat at his table as usual.

'*Ya* boy?' he shouted.

'Oh, *ya Allah*,' I muttered, walking to his table.

'You are very slow today,' he said.

'If you want a faster service, maybe you should go to another café,' I responded.

'Just clean the table, my friends will be here soon.'

'I cleaned it a moment ago.'

'It is not done properly,' he said. 'Look, here, here and here. Didn't Jasim teach you that you should never talk back to the source of your living? Now shut up and keep cleaning.'

I shook my head, and as I leaned over the table he slid his hand under my *thobe* and slipped his hand between my thighs.

I threw the cloth on the table and stormed off to the kitchen.

In the kitchen, I washed my hands and started grinding the cardamom with the coffee. The Yemeni cook, holding the coffee-pot by its sharp curved spout, stood next to me waiting to add the spicy grounds.

Jasim burst into the kitchen and asked what I was playing at.

I ignored him and snatched the coffee-pot from the cook and poured some water inside it.

'Naser, I am talking to you,' Jasim said loudly.

'Just leave me alone.'

He asked the cook to leave us for a moment.

At that moment, Rashid entered the kitchen, yelling, 'Jasim, all I did was to ask this boy to wipe the table properly.'

Jasim turned to Rashid and said, 'Rashid, I know that as a healthy man you have your needs, but you have to be gentle with Naser. If you need anything from him, just ask him.'

I hit my fist on the table and shouted at Jasim, 'If you want to sell my body, you will have to be a man and tell me to my face.'

I looked at his eyes to see if he was feeling ashamed. There was nothing. I pushed him out of my way and hurried to my room. I took down my mother's picture from the wall and sat with it in my lap. I wanted to cry, but I shouted to myself not to. Instead I sat on my bed looking at her in silence, clenching my teeth.

Jasim barged into my room. He looked at me in a way that made me uneasy.

'Jasim, please forget it,' I begged, as he came closer. 'Please leave me alone.'

He sat next to me and whispered, 'Naser, it is hard for me to ask you to do this not least because . . .' He paused, sighed deeply and then he said, 'Naser, Rashid likes you. He said he must have you because he wants you to . . .'

'Let me guess. He wants me to be his boy until he gets married. I have heard it many times before but I am not going to do it.'

'Naser, we can't refuse Rashid. He might not look it, but he is a very important man for this café. I didn't tell you this before, but for me to keep my business open, I have to do certain things, obey certain rules. I am a foreigner like you; I could be kicked out from this country any minute if I don't follow the rules. You are very dear to me, I will only ask you to do things for a reason. If this shop is shut, where will you go? Who will open their house to you? Naser, your uncle and brother are living in Riyadh now. They will never have you back and soon you will have to renew your *iqama*. Where will you get the money for the renewal? If you don't pay and your residency is terminated, you will be deported. Is this how you want to repay your mother?'

'Leave me alone,' I yelled at him.

'Naser, listen to me. If you give Rashid what he wants, you will have nothing to worry about. *Allah* gave him everything but looks and manners. I'll offer him etiquette lessons and you will have to give him some of your beauty. And I can assure you that we will get some of his wealth.'

'Just stop it, Jasim,' I said, putting my mother's portrait aside.

But he must have sensed I was breaking, because like a killer peering at his victim, Jasim twisted his knife inside me: 'Think how much your mother had to go through to send you away from the war to safety. And now you want to go back to the war zone, to death. I am sure she misses you, if she is still alive.'

I jumped up and started punching him, screaming, 'I know she is alive. She is waiting for me!'

He didn't fight back. 'Hit me, Naser,' he said, 'but you must realise that we only have each other. I have no family and you have none. I swear to you I don't want him to touch you. But let's support each other. We have to do what is necessary to live.'

I left the room and ran out of the café.

I ran past the shops, the big mosque and the nine-storey building, I took the bus to the Corniche and ran to my secret place. A storm swept across the sea and the beach, and blew for a long time. I felt closer to my mother here, there was only the sea to separate us.

Sitting on my rock and staring at the dark water, I began to wonder why it had all gone wrong. I had no words to describe the feeling inside me. I slowly walked towards the sea. Would things have been different if she hadn't sent me away? Was she still alive in her hut at the foot of Lovers'

Hill? Maybe Jasim was right. Maybe she was dead. But if she were, I thought, then she must have died a long time ago, the day she sent my brother and me away. Because she had sung to us so often that we were her only reason to live.

That evening, I decided to leave Jeddah. I didn't care where to. I had had enough. I had no reason to stay. I had made up my mind, and the only way out was to make a lot of money fast so that I could leave as quickly as possible.

I fell asleep on the rock, my rage spent. I returned to Jasim's early the next morning, wet, dirty and hungry.

I opened up the café and the warm wind flooded the entire place, bringing with it the scent of drains and sewage. In the street, the potholes were filled with water. The school, just down the road from the café, had been forced to shut because of structural damage caused by the storm. We'd also heard that a restaurant belonging to an Egyptian man at the top of the hill had been brought down in the winds. The blind imam of our local mosque praised the destruction of the Egyptian restaurant during his morning sermon. As I laid out the tables and chairs I could hear him ranting, on and on. He started as usual, denouncing the enemies in this world and dedicating the majority of his speech to reminding worshippers of their duties towards their families. Then, after what seemed a deliberately long pause, he seemed to stray off his usual speech.

'We have new forms of evil lurking amongst us,' he said. 'This new evil is manifest in a foreign man, a man who came to destroy our morals and values. This man sells satellite dishes.' I shook my head. 'Now, oh *ya Allah*'s worshippers, we have a man who is going around selling these dishes and our people are swayed by this evil and now they are erecting these ugly things on their roofs like minarets. And do you know why? They want to watch prohibited Egyptian films and corrupt our youth. But last night, *Allah* spoke. He sent his anger and flattened the restaurant of a man who claims to have opened it to feed people's stomachs, but is only filling their minds with lust and immorality. This was a message from *Allah* to our government too: if they don't act, He, the greatest, will.'

The 'evidence' of *Allah*'s vengeance was still visible in the street. Soon after I had opened up, the customers started arriving. The Yemeni cook was in the kitchen and Jasim was counting the money. He said nothing to me.

I saw Rashid spit before he stepped inside, then announce, as if I was his wife, 'I am here, get me coffee.'

He sat at his table. A few men followed and scattered around the café, greeting each other. Suddenly Rashid stood up and shouted at his friend, Gamal, sitting in the opposite corner, 'Do you see what's happening to our city? Our government bombards us every day telling us how rich we are, yet look what's happening – one bucket of rain and Jeddah is drowning. They should install a proper drainage system with the money they have.'

Gamal laughed, and Rashid sat down, pleased with himself.

'Your coffee,' I said, putting it on his table.

At the counter Jasim held my hand and looked at me askance.

I stared back at him.

Taking my hand from Jasim, I turned around saying, 'I will be in my room.'

*

The air was heavy in the back room, and my eyelids were getting heavier by the second. Only the shrieks of the men as they played dominoes kept me in a conscious state. They banged the tables, but I blocked them out. I longed to hear from my mother and Semira that things would be OK.

I turned to the wall. I thought about Mother, about Semira, and about their friends, the sex workers, on Lovers' Hill. I thought about the countless years they gave their bodies to hungry men. I thought about the lonely nights they spent in the arms of men they didn't know; men who arrived under darkness; men who waited around the hill like wolves to avoid other men and wait for the signal that a woman was free. I thought of my mother and Semira, and how they had raised me and Ibrahim, helping each other with the little money they had earned. I wondered what they would say if they could see me here, in Jasim's back room. There was a knock.

I drew a deep breath. 'Come in,' I exhaled.

Rashid entered the room, closed the door and hung his *gutra* on a hook. He patted down his *thobe*, looked at his shoes and then, without saying anything, he turned off the light.

In the dark and just before he held my hand, Rashid whispered, 'Jasim said you will be my boy until I get married.'

One early morning, four weeks after Rashid started coming regularly into my room, I was smoking a cigarette outside the café, numb to what was going on around me. I saw Mr Quiet about to enter the café. He must have noticed that something was wrong because he came over to me.

'Naser, how are you today?'

I shrugged my shoulders.

He whispered, 'Please let me know if you want to talk. I can assure you that quiet people are good listeners.'

He lit a cigarette and walked inside the café, bowing his head.

I was too shy to talk to Mr Quiet about Rashid. It took me a while before I approached him.

As I served him, Jasim peered over at us from behind his counter just yards away, and Rashid watched from his usual table in the front of the café. I whispered that I would like to talk to him but that the only time I was free was before I opened the café and before Jasim and the Yemeni cook arrived.

He nodded and said that he would come the next day after early morning prayers.

Mr Quiet came to my room at exactly half-past five the next morning.

He said he knew what Rashid wanted from me in return for the safeguarding of Jasim's business. I wasn't the first boy that had happened to, he comforted me. He knew someone who could find me a new job quickly. His name was Hilal, from Sudan, and he promised he was a good man and would look after me.

It took a while after Mr Quiet promised to help me for Hilal to finally find me a job at a car-wash, and a small flat to live in.

By the time I left Jasim's, I had been working in the back room for six weeks.

On my last day, when Rashid had just left me with a

hundred riyals, I looked up at the ceiling. Jasim's pressure and my dream to leave the country had led me to accept life in the mirror. But not for much longer. I took one of my shoes and smashed it hard against my reflection.

For one last time, I looked up. My image was cut in two. Then I walked out, leaving my broken reflection behind.

Jasim begged me to come back when he found out where I lived. I told him to leave me alone. 'OK,' he said, shrugging his shoulders, 'but I am your only friend. No one will support you like I did.'

'Just leave me alone,' I said.

My friendship with Mr Quiet continued even after I left the café, and we would meet to talk in the shopping mall, or in the Corniche. I started feeling more comfortable around Mr Quiet. Ever since I arrived in Jeddah, I had never had a friend I could trust, and this was the first time I felt really safe with someone.

He was an illegal resident in Jeddah. He had been deported countless times before, but he'd always come back. Last time, he had learned his lesson, he said. Since smuggling himself back into Jizan, Saudi Arabia's main port in the south, he had covered his face with a long beard and dark glasses, and dressed like a typical Saudi. He also stayed away from other foreigners to avoid suspicion.

I also tried to get to know Hilal better, but he didn't have the time for friendships. Hilal, who shared a room with three Sudanese in a tiny flat in Al-Nuzla Street, worked hard in his job and he never had any time for leisure. 'I am in a rich country,' he used to say, 'so I am going to take the opportunity and work hard to save as much as I can.' He wanted to save to go back to Sudan and set up a bus service between Port Sudan and the capital of Eastern Sudan, Kassala, where he was born.

Even if I didn't have many friends, things looked up for me. I felt excited that I could build a new life on my own. I don't need my uncle or Jasim, I thought.

But no sooner was my smile returning to my face than Hilal brought me the sad news that wiped out the little happiness I had started to enjoy.

One Thursday morning, he came to my flat and told me that Mr Quiet's flat had been raided by the immigration police and that he was now awaiting deportation in a prison in the centre of Jeddah.

'I can't believe he was caught,' Hilal said. 'Abu Imad is the most careful illegal migrant I know, and believe me, I know many of them. I just can't understand how it happened.'

As soon as Hilal told me the news, I hurried to the prison to try to see Mr Quiet one last time before he was deported.

The prison used to be Jeddah's old airport before it was converted. From the outside, it looked enormous, fenced off by high white walls with windows only on the very top floors. When I arrived, I saw a statue of a small plane just outside the entrance, its rear tyres firmly on the ground but its front tyres slightly lifted, ready to soar. It was ironic that an object like a plane, modelled on a free bird, now stood at the entrance to a building where people were detained because they brought their dreams to the wrong place.

An armed policeman was standing outside the gate. I knew I didn't stand much chance, but tried anyway.

'*Assalamu alaikum*,' I greeted him.

'*Wa 'alaikumu*,' he replied coldly, stopping half-way off saying the full greeting.

'May *Allah* prolong your life,' I said. 'Would it please be possible for me to see a friend awaiting deportation?'

He stretched his sleepy face into a mocking smile. 'Are you a foreigner?' he asked.

I nodded.

'Where is your *iqama*?'

I handed it to him. He flicked through it, and then threw it back at me. I caught it against my chest.

'Leave. You can't visit anyone. The prison is closed,' he said.

'But he is the only friend I have left in Jeddah. Please let me say goodbye, just for once . . .'

'I said, go. *Yallah*, what are you waiting for? Do you want to join your friend in prison?'

I bowed my head and walked back home, to my lonely room.

Just as I arrived home, Jasim called. 'Naser?'

I put down the phone. But as I lay on the bed, I began to realise that once again he was the only person I knew. I switched off the light and cried.

PART THREE

THE WIND FROM THE RED SEA

IN THE DAYS following, I didn't really think much more about the note, and whenever I did, I tried to suppress the thought. Because there was no point. Where could it take me?

Friday evening, three days after the girl dropped her note, I decided to go to the Corniche to clear my head. I would stay the night in my secret place.

I woke up on Saturday morning, my back aching from sleeping on the hard rock. I closed my eyes, trying to rest for a bit longer, but the bright sunlight was shining through my eyelids. I sat up and yawned.

I walked to the sea to wash. As I bent double, I caught a glimpse of my reflection wobbling over the surface of water. It was as if it was trying to flee, diving to the depths of the sea. The cold water shook up my thoughts.

Why did I allow Jeddah, with its rules and prejudices, to make me passive and afraid? Why was I not out there looking for the girl in the street? I should be chasing her instead of hiding. Maybe there was nothing special under her *abaya*: yes, she could be a phantom, a madwoman, or a silly girl with too much time on her hands. But wasn't this still a chance worth taking in a country with such a high wall between men and women?

I looked over the water towards the Red Sea. I prayed that the girl was genuine and hoped that she would come looking for me again.

★

Back in Al-Nuzla the black and white movie was still playing, but there were even fewer people in the street, just a handful here and there. I felt like an extra on the film set, stealing too much attention in the absence of the main actors.

By the time I got home, I urgently wanted to get out of the blazing sun. I needed a cold drink and a quick meal, then I would wait for her under the shade of my palm tree. Today was not a day to be afraid.

'*Salaam*,' I said to the *shawarma* shop owner, a stocky Lebanese man.

'*Wa 'alaikumu salam*,' he replied.

'*Shawarma*, please.'

'Chicken or meat?'

'Since when do you think I eat chicken?'

'A troublemaker, eh?' he chided.

I grinned.

As I reached into my pocket to pay, I read the Islamic quotation pinned up behind him: 'Life is Temporary.' And in the mirror next to it, I saw the reflection of Abu Faisal, the beheader. He was coming into the shop.

His presence had an immediate effect. Men swiftly got to their feet and one after the other, they reached out to his famous right hand and kissed it with such passion, as if it were the Black Stone of the holy *Kabba*. Others showered his forehead and shoulders with more kisses. Someone shouted, '*Allah wa Akbar*.' 'May *Allah* bless you, our enforcer of justice.'

I stood looking at him. It felt as if the angel of death were knocking on my door. The thought made me shudder. I put my money on the counter to show I wanted to leave. So much for taking chances today.

Abu Faisal's eyes, like two soldiers hiding in a trench,

were small, rounded and narrow. How could he possibly look at the world with such small eyes?

I collected my food and made my way out through the pack of people. Outside, in the hot air, my stomach turned. I threw my sandwich into a rubbish bin and crossed over to the Yemeni shop.

I pushed myself through the few customers who were clustering around the old shopkeeper's counter, fanned the incense smoke from my face, and headed to the back of the shop. The amplifier nailed to the top shelf was softly playing *suras* from the Qur'an. I shoved the empty boxes on the floor aside, opened the fridge and rummaged to find a cold Pepsi.

The shopkeeper shouted, 'They all are cold, just take one and leave.' I ignored him and continued looking until my fingers stuck to a can. I picked it up, made my way to the counter and left half a riyal next to his till. As I strolled back to the shade of the tree opposite my uncle's old house, back to the black and white movie show, sweat rolled down my face.

I sat underneath the wide branches of the palm tree and guzzled the Pepsi, the cold liquid quickly hitting my throat.

I glanced around to my right. In the far distance, I could see a woman coming out of a house. I stopped drinking and focused my attention on her. Was this the girl? But wasn't that Zib Al-Ard's house she had just left? If he is fighting a war in Afghanistan, then how would it feel if his sister and I . . . Does Zib Al-Ard even have a sister? I wasn't sure, but I knew that his father had a second wife who lived a few yards down the road from Zib Al-Ard's house. I stood up and glared at the woman again. Maybe it was Zib Al-Ard's father's second wife who had dropped the note at my feet? It was possible.

Before he was converted to strict Islam by the blind imam, and when he was under the heavy influence of drink, Zib Al-Ard had talked about his father's second wife. He told me that one afternoon when his father was at work, he encountered her in their kitchen when she came over from her house to help his sick mother. She was only sixteen, the same age as him, and he said she wasn't wearing her *abaya* because she thought there were no men in the house. The moment they met, Zib Al-Ard said, they fell for one another and before long they had kissed. A few days later, they made love on the kitchen table. He lost his virginity to his father's second wife while his mother was sleeping in the next room.

The woman who came out from Zib Al-Ard's father's first house entered the second house. I sat back down on the pavement, but I didn't immediately discount the possibility that the second wife might be the girl.

A few more people passed by: a group of four women, two boys, a Yemeni man carrying a dagger under his belt, and an old man who came out from the villa opposite to chase away two pigeons who were mating on the tree overlooking his house. I counted the cars as they drove past. Number three was a Jeep with shaded windows. It drove so fast, shattering the peace, as if it were hurtling towards an emergency; someone was committing a sin somewhere in Al-Nuzla and they needed urgent punishment.

I was starting to nod off, my eyelids slowly succumbing to the soporific breeze that found me under the tree. I tried to force myself to stay awake. And it was when I turned my half-closed eyes to the left that I noticed a woman walking slowly towards me. But my mind was too tired to wonder whether it might be *her*. I turned my head away and lay on the cool pavement and drifted asleep.

The next thing I heard were busy footsteps close by. Sitting up on the pavement, I watched a scrap of paper falling in front of me. I looked up, but saw only a dark shadow hurrying down the street. I picked up the paper and jumped to my feet. I ran into the middle of the street trying to catch sight of her, but she had already disappeared. Nothing was moving. I looked over to my right and saw four women, all in full veil, moving silently.

I stood still beneath the scorching sun. Sweat ran along my forehead and dripped down my neck.

I looked at the yellow paper, already softening in my damp hand. I had forgotten that I was standing in the middle of the road. Faintly, as if it were a long way away, I heard the horn of a car. I was lost in my own dream and it took me an age to come out of it. Someone was yelling at me. It was Muhammad Ali Al-Hyrania – the nerd. His head was craned out the window, and his father stared at me from behind the wheel with both his hands on the horn.

'Get off the street,' the nerd screamed. I stepped aside to let them pass and walked back to my spot under the palm tree. I looked around to ensure I wasn't being watched, then I hungrily devoured the note:

Habibi,

I am taking a great risk in doing this. I walked past this tree every day since last Tuesday, more than once, hoping to find you. But for the past four days, the tree has been alone. I am not sure what you are thinking, but if I have to, I will come to this spot every day for the rest of my life to convince you that you are my special one.

In the name of Allah, I must tell you that it has been over a year since I fell for you, and my eyes have been faithful to you ever since. You have become the only companion in my lonely days and nights, summer or spring. When I saw your smile from a distance for the first time, I was like a thirsty person in a desert seeing a mirage. But when I came closer to your face, that mirage was in fact an oasis and for the first time in my living memory, I felt a surge of selfishness and wished that I alone could disembark at your oasis and take forever lasting rest.

Salam from the heart of a girl in Al-Nuzla.

I looked at the ground next to me as if she were sitting there in her black *abaya* reading her note out loud. I stretched out my full length on the pavement, embracing the note, feeling its warmth, its words sinking inside me.

On my way back to my room I dared to sing a song from the refugee camp. It was about a woman who danced against a frankincense gum tree; the singer trailed her for the rest of his life, his nose guiding him to her gorgeously scented being.

AT FOUR O'CLOCK the next morning, the telephone's ringing woke me up from my sleep. I staggered over to the receiver.

'Hello? Naser? Naser?'

'Is that Jasim?' I asked, rubbing my eyes.

'Who else would call you at this time of the morning? I miss you, my dear. I wish you were here. Paris is full of rain and I am walking in the dark thinking only of you.'

He kept talking about how much he missed me, and how sorry he was about Rashid. But I was too tired to say a thing. I ran the palm of my hand over my face as if it were water, trying to wake myself up.

'Naser, are you there?'

'Jasim, please, this is not a good time to talk.'

'OK, you are tired, go to bed, my dear. I can't wait to see you.'

I slammed the phone down and threw it off the table.

The night was hot. I was sweating all over. Before returning to bed, I took a cool shower. I came out of the shower with drops of water still glistening over my chest, wishing I could dry myself by lying against the warm back of a woman.

Instead I curled my wet body around the bed sheets and slept, holding her note.

I woke up around 8 a.m. When I stood in front of my bathroom mirror, I expected worse after such a restless night, but instead my features were sparkling, and there was no sleep in my eyes.

She had been looking at me for over a year and I hadn't been aware of it. If I had known, I would have made sure I looked my best every time I stepped outside, just in case she and I crossed paths.

I wondered what she liked about me. Was it my almond-shaped eyes, or high cheekbones? I knew I was well built because I had received so many compliments in Jasim's café and the muscles in my arms and chest were well defined from five years of washing cars. Then, and for the first time, I allowed myself to dwell on the words of men in the café. 'Naser, I would give everything for your slender and well proportioned body.'

Later that day, before I left my room, I took another shower, put on a new tracksuit and a white T-shirt, and sprayed myself with some of the perfume that I had taken from Jasim's. But my old doubts resurfaced. How could I be taken in by a few romantic words? Anyone in Jeddah could have written what she did. How many of us were sitting around with besieged feelings; and wasn't it the case that caged emotions make poets out of all of us, even the illiterate?

Pacing up and down my room, I remembered my past anger at not having had the chance to linger in the street and wait for an unveiled girl to pass and give me a seductive smile; my longing to capture the contours of a girl's lips in a simple kiss; the sleepless nights where I waited for just one touch of a finger, for her breasts to press against my chest, for her body to twist around mine, her heartbeat drumming against me.

*

The scorching sun pressed a heavy silence onto the street. Something was happening far away, in front of the nine-storey building. I could see a man standing on the hood of what looked like a big family car. I stopped and looked into the distance, my hand over my eyes to block the bright sun. The man was loading luggage on top of the car. Another lucky family leaving Al-Nuzla for a holiday, I thought.

I was crossing the street when I heard someone call my name. I turned my head and saw Hilal, my Sudanese friend, limping heavily, with a walking stick to support him. He was wearing his long white turban around his head.

'*Salam*, Naser. How are you, my friend?' he said.

'*Alhamdulillah*,' I replied.

'You are looking and smelling very nice, my friend, where are you going? To meet a girl?' He broke into hysterical laughter.

I smiled and shouted over his laughter, 'Dear Hilal, isn't life heavy enough without you wrapping seven metres of cloth around your head?'

His laughter abruptly stopped. He spat out his big *toombak* and some of his yellow saliva lingered on his chin, which he wiped with the sleeve of his *jallabiyah*. He leaned forward and said, 'Naser, I just came to tell you some good news. But if you are going to make jokes about my turban then maybe I should say goodbye.'

'No, don't go. What good news?'

'Very good news in fact,' he said, spitting again.

'Come on, tell me then.'

With a glint in his eyes, he said, 'I am going to Sudan with a visa to bring my wife here.'

I embraced him and kissed his cheeks and told him how happy I was for him.

'Yes,' he said, 'all thanks to *Allah* and to my *kafeel*. He is a very good man. As well as giving me his sponsorship to obtain the visa, he is paying for her ticket as well.'

His *kafeel* was an old Saudi man, called Jawad Ibn Khalid, who had lived in poverty before oil was discovered in the Kingdom but managed to accumulate a huge amount of wealth after he founded a construction company. He was a very kind and generous Saudi man. Nothing like my *kafeel*.

For a while, Hilal couldn't stop talking about the generosity of Jawad Ibn Khalid.

Just when he was about to leave, he told me of other news.

'You know Haroon?' he asked me.

'There are many Haroons in Al-Nuzla,' I replied. 'Which one do you mean?'

'The smiling servant of your *kafeel*.'

'What about him?'

'He fled to Germany.'

'What? Haroon?' I wondered how it was possible for an Eritrean with a UN passport to go to Europe. I had the same passport and had tried to use it to flee Jeddah when I worked in Jasim's café, but I was refused by all the European embassies. They all told me the same thing: that I was ineligible because I was in a safe country now and there was no reason for them to give me asylum. They also rejected my request for a tourist's visa, because they told me that when people with my passport were given a visa, they ripped up their passports in the toilet of the plane and never came back.

Hilal continued, 'A smuggler got him a fake passport and a visa. He said he'd met him in the Eritrean café. Do you know where it is?'

'Yes, but I have never been. I have always been too scared to find out what is happening in Eritrea.'

Hilal sighed, patting my shoulders. 'I understand. I understand, Naser.'

There was a brief silenc.

Then, I asked, 'Anyway, Hilal, do you know how much Haroon paid?'

'I am not sure, but he said it was a lot. No one knew that he had such a big plan hidden behind that eternal smile. What a man. Anyway, I will come to say goodbye before I go to Port Sudan,' Hilal said. He spat again on the ground, we shook hands, and he disappeared down a side street.

I decided to sit facing the street, with my back against the tree and my eyes panning from one side to the other, waiting for the girl to appear. But I couldn't sit still. Would she come at all today? If she did, would she come closer perhaps?

The heat surrounded my face. Bright rays of light bounced off the wing mirror of one of the parked cars. I walked over to the car and bent to take a look at my face in the mirror. Sweat dripped down my nose. I looked around for something – anything – to help me fan my face. All I had was my yellow note.

But instead of bringing a refreshing breeze, the note just brought me more questions. Maybe I should have written to her to tell her how excited I was? But what would I say? I had never written to a girl before. What was the right thing to say to them? Maybe I should compliment her looks?

I tried to picture what she might look like under her *abaya*. To begin with, I tried to imagine what she might look like if she were Saudi. But since I had never seen a Saudi woman's face either on the street, the newspapers, books or the TV – the only women on TV were old and veiled – I quickly stopped the thought. What if she were Egyptian? I remembered some Egyptian actresses I had seen in films and my favourite actress, with her big, beautiful, expressive eyes and her alluring smile, came to my mind.

There were people of countless nationalities living in Jeddah, many migrants coming to work here, so it was pointless trying to guess. Her looks would depend on whether she was Arab, African or Asian.

Suddenly the silence was shattered by the sound of police sirens.

The civil police cars followed by a convoy carrying my *kafeel*, the Blessed Bader Ibn Abd-Allah, drove along the road. I recognised the four grey Mercedes from his palace. The sight of him, even after all these years since that day in his living room when I was fifteen, still made my stomach turn.

I remembered how after he had finished with me that day in his house his servant Haroon hurried me out. I couldn't go to the religious police; not after what had happened to one of the *kafeel's* wife's servants, a Filipino woman who had lived a few blocks down from us.

She had been deported back to the Philippines with her two young children when she reported sexual abuse to the religious police. That had been a year before and I had seen her and her children being dragged out of her house by three religious policemen. She screamed that she was the victim of a rape committed by the Blessed Bader Ibn Abd-Allah. But a policeman smacked her on the face, yelling, 'We don't want whores like you coming to this blessed country.'

'Classic,' whispered our Saudi neighbour who lived on the second floor, and who was standing next to me. 'I am

86

sure the *kafeel* fabricated a lie against her to the religious police to hide his ugly crime and now she is the one being sent back home.'

'I thought the Sharia law should bring justice in this country?' I protested.

He sighed and said, 'The law, son, is only applied to the poor and to foreigners, not to the rich or the royal family.'

I managed to last for half an hour before I had to go to the Yemeni shop for a cold drink. It would only take me a second and I would sprint back.

As I returned with my Pepsi, I couldn't wait to quench my thirst, even though I was almost back at the shaded spot under the palm tree. I slowed down and flipped the ring pull.

I looked back and saw a woman rushing towards me. It was her, I was sure of it. She almost collided with me as she ran in front. She flicked a note in my direction before running back the way she came. I dropped my can, picked up the paper and ran after her. She didn't look back as she ran alongside the parked cars, her shadow dancing on their frames. She stopped, opened a door and disappeared inside a building.

I looked up and had to step further back to see where we were. I was standing in front of the famous nine-storey building. I crossed the road and took a better look. I looked at the folded note in my hand. It was on the same yellow paper as her last note, but this one felt bigger.

I pinned her letter on my wardrobe and gazed at it from my bed. It was written in beautiful calligraphy – every letter gave life to the next and the words all clung to the page like the flowers in the hanging gardens of Babylon.

I moved closer and blew lightly on the note, hoping that I might unchain the words and make them tell me the secret of the girl who wrote them – how did she look when she bowed her head and inscribed each one of them? I closed my eyes and imagined how her fingers moved with her pen from one side of the page to the other, from one line to the next; and how her waist, carried by her strong hips, must have danced with her words.

I stood up and read the note again:

Habibi,

It has taken me a long time to cram the infinite thoughts I have gathered about you over the past months into this small letter. So please understand if some words appear naked of meaning to you.

When I first saw you, I felt the planting of a seed in the middle of my heart. Since then, every time I have had a glimpse of you in the street, it is as though little drops of rain have watered that seed. And now, the seed has grown into a flower and its bud has opened.

I am proposing my love to you. Will you accept it?

Maybe you are the type of man who wishes hell on a woman who steps outside her house on her own, let alone roams the street seeking the man of her dreams with a love proposal in her hands. Maybe you don't believe in love and only accept an arranged companionship between a man and a woman.

It feels like a wide and treacherous sea of uncertainties separates us. But I am ready to take a voyage on this stormy ocean if, at the end of the journey, we might meet on the same island.

Please don't write back to me. It is too dangerous for me to bend down in the street. People might get suspicious and the risk is not worth it.

Salam from the heart.

The beauty of her words made me think there was a chance that she might be the girl I'd been waiting for. All these years I had been complaining that I was living in a country ruled by fear, by men who sought to take the joy out of life. But here was this girl who came to me with a proposal of love. Why was I hesitating? What was I scared of? Isn't life short? With a life as empty as mine, what did I have to lose?

That same night, I couldn't eat or sleep. With my eyes closed, I ran the tips of my fingers across the words in her beautiful note, over and over again.

IT WAS NOON. The afternoon prayer had just started and I could hear the blind imam's loud voice. I wanted to storm out, but I couldn't because the religious police roamed the street at prayer time to look for men who weren't at the mosque. So I stayed indoors until the imam finished his prayer. I paced up and down my room begging him to hurry up, to read shorter verses from the Qur'an. When he started the *takbeer* for the fourth and last set of the early afternoon prayer, I slid the key into the door lock, and turned the knob. When he said the *tasleem*, ending the prayer, I burst through the door and headed for my palm tree.

The street was suddenly full of men returning home from the mosques. But soon the busyness passed, and the street was reclaimed by silence once more.

I saw a veiled woman approaching.

I got up.

She slowed down.

I wanted to walk towards her, but that would be too risky. So I waited.

She beckoned me towards her with her hand and turned around.

I walked in her direction.

She turned left almost immediately. I hurried after her. As I followed her on the turn, we arrived at the shop famous for the over-sensitive Indian tailor. He had the habit of shouting and spitting every time he was challenged about his claim that he was as good a designer as those who lived in Milan.

The girl was going straight ahead. She turned a corner into the street that would lead us back to Al-Nuzla Street. A short distance from Al-Nuzla, she turned and cast a quick glance in my direction. She dropped a note and walked slowly on. I raced to pick it up. I continued to follow her without stopping to read it. She must have sensed that I was almost breathing on her neck, because she quickly looked back and pointed with her gloved hand at the note. She wanted me to read the note.

Habibi,

> *Read this quickly and follow me from a distance. When you walk behind me, look down and take a look at my shoes. I bought them especially for us. I asked my Egyptian friend to get them for me from Cairo when I saw them in her fashion catalogue. They are unique shoes and no one in Al-Nuzla has them. They will set me apart from other women in Al-Nuzla – when I am in the street, you will be able to recognise me.*

> *You followed me, so this means you have agreed to my proposal. Our journey begins now.*

> *I can't search for you in Al-Nuzla Street any more. The street before the dead end at Ba'da Al-Nuzla is a less risky place for me to drop my notes. I will come back with another note and look for you there. But I don't know when, because I don't own my days. I will drop the notes next to the rubbish bin as if they were litter, but only if there are no people around. Please pick them up quickly.*

> *I also wanted to say that I liked it a lot when you wore your fancy trousers and striped shirt.*

> *Salam from the heart.*

I looked up and saw her turning right back into Al-Nuzla Street. I followed her and looked down at her feet. As she walked in front of me, her shoes came and went under her black *abaya*. They were of a deep pink colour made of soft leather, and I could see that the leather sat comfortably around her feet, as it bent easily with every step she took. From behind her, the only thing I could see well were the medium-sized heels peeping out from under her robe. All of a sudden, the black and white set of Al-Nuzla Street was coloured. It was as if a pair of pink flamingos had arrived from a faraway tropical island.

PART FOUR

PINK SHOES

I COULD SCARCELY wait for the next day to go to Ba'da Al-Nuzla and wait for the mysterious girl. It was exactly a week since I had received her very first note.

From an old box underneath my bed, I took out my special trousers and shirt. I hadn't worn them for a long time – I had bought them to wear at Hilal's party over a year ago, to celebrate his return from Sudan after his wedding – and a musty odour wafted out as I unfolded them. I washed them in the shower and hung them out the window to dry.

I looked at the note once again. It seemed as if the ink of every word ran, the words sped towards me like a wave, washing the sleep out of my eyes.

As the call for the early morning prayer went out, I suddenly remembered that she couldn't specify the time of her appearance. She might be there at any time of the day. I got up and took the bottle of perfume from my desk. I held up my shirt and sprayed puffs of fragrance all over it, almost drenching it with perfume. I drank some of it too, making sure that if I had the chance to speak to her while she dropped her note, my words would smell as if they were imported from Paris.

Just after the end of the prayer, I left my flat dressed in my freshly washed trousers and immaculately ironed striped shirt.

I walked with my face looking up at the tallest building

in the area, *her* building. As I strolled past it, my gaze moved across each of the nine floors, wondering where her window was and in which room she was standing, perhaps in front of her mirror fixing her hair and matching her skirt with her blouse, or her earrings to the colour of her lipstick. I imagined her walking down the stairs and all the pedestrians turning their heads from the first moment she stepped onto the street, unveiled.

After walking down Al-Nuzla Street for about fifteen minutes, past the big mosque and Abu Faisal's house, I turned left into a small side street. On the corner, a short Filipino man stood next to his taxi.

I quickened my pace. I was now entering a different neighbourhood. I left the asphalt streets behind and my shoes kicked up the small stones on the dusty road. The street was full of one-storey houses, with some having the privilege of a waist-high wall separating the house from the street. I entered an even smaller street filled with red dust.

The street turned narrow and I knew I was approaching a dead end. I stood and looked around. I walked past a pile of garbage riddled with flies, the smell of which was barely disguised by the strong incense that seeped from a house close by. This is it, I thought to myself. This is Ba'da Al-Nuzla, and this is the street before the dead end.

In Ba'da Al-Nuzla I transformed into a lover in waiting: my head high, my jaw tensed, hands in pockets, and my shoulders straight.

I could hear someone preparing breakfast in a house nearby: the smell of morning coffee and scrambled eggs was delicious. I inhaled deeply as I leaned against a street lamp and waited.

The sun was rising over Jeddah and its rays left harsh yellow patches on the fading paint of the walls. Before long, I started to sweat. I unbuttoned my shirt to my navel. 'Only for a while,' I told myself. I took out the note and fanned myself gently with it.

For years, I had followed the teachings that men should avert their eyes from any part of female passers-by, and that they must not let a second look follow the first.

But now that the girl had shown me her shoes, I was walking everywhere with my head bowed in search of her pink feet. I had already started noticing that I could work out the shape of a woman's legs despite the loose *abaya* they wore. Those who walked with their feet parted much wider than their shoulders' width were either pregnant or had big thighs. A woman whose walk had a rigid, laborious and mechanical movement pointed to a lady with big shins or maybe ankles or thighs, or a combination of all of these. Narrowly parted feet was a sign of a woman with short legs. Hurried footsteps often indicated a woman with long, slender legs. Observing women with thin legs was exciting because their energy propelled their feet into a fast sprint. Watching them race up and down Al-Nuzla was like watching cars on a highway.

'Look at the feet,' I whispered in excitement when I saw the Pink Shoes turning right to the street with the dead end in Ba'da Al-Nuzla. But her subsequent movements confused my new theory. One minute, she came towards me with heavy feet. 'She must have large shins,' I told myself. Before I had the time to digest what I thought about this, the movement changed. Her feet were now widely parted. 'No, she can't be pregnant, can she?' The distance between her feet narrowed, but I was sure this wasn't because she had short legs. But then I noticed she was walking between two potholes and she needed to walk through the tight space. And then her feet gathered momentum, almost sprinting. But this is not because she has thin legs, I thought, it is only because she has finally seen me.

She quickly ran past, and I picked up the note that she dropped at my feet. I hoped she would stop for a second, even just to say hello. But I understood she must have been nervous. 'After all,' I told myself, 'thinking of the danger in dropping me her notes, what she is doing takes a lot of guts and bravery. I should be happy with this instead of being greedy for more.'

Habibi,

It would have been courteous of me of course to start my note with questions about your day, your health, whether you have been fine and whether life is treating you well overall. But since getting your answers is impossible in the current circumstances, I won't bother you with such formalities. Instead, you will have to tune in to some sporadic news, like the early evening bulletin.

If I could, I would have given you my phone number. But my father heard stories from his friends about some girls making phone calls to boys when the men of the household are out. So he disconnected our phone altogether. I want you to read my note as if I were speaking the words to you over the phone or saying them to you face to face.

Darling, I will come back here with a note in two

days' time. Later this evening, I am going to Mecca with
my parents for two days to do umra and visit the house
of a friend of my father.

Salam from the heart.

Two days later, she came to Ba'da Al-Nuzla just before the
early afternoon prayer. She turned into the road where I
was standing. The only way to really find out the shape of
her legs, I thought, would be for me to bring a spade and
flatten the street.

In her note, written in such a beautiful hand that I was
certain she must have studied calligraphy in Baghdad, she
told me that it was her best friend who had noticed me first.

We were coming back from college when she saw you
sitting under the tree. She nudged me and told me to
look. Since then it has been hard to stop looking.

Habibi, I have collected so many sightings of you:
walking, dancing in the street with your friends, playing
football, and watering your tree. I have a photo album
in my mind's eye.

And by the way, since tomorrow is Friday, I wish
you a good holiday and I hope the blind imam will
not ruin your day with his sermon.

When I watered my palm tree later that afternoon, I
hummed a song and her words were dancing in my head
like whirling dervishes.

The next day, I awoke at the break of dawn and stayed all
morning lying on my bed. I was amazed at how time can

pass so quickly when all a man does is think about a woman.

My room smelt as if it had had a visit from a woman. The scent of her hands on the notes was slowly being released to fill my bedroom.

I was still thinking about her notes and her elegant Pink Shoes, when I heard the *azan* for the Friday afternoon prayer.

The pattering of footsteps on the street was echoing inside my room. I opened the curtains and peeped out of my window on the first floor. It seemed as if all Al-Nuzla men were out on the street walking in the direction of the mosque. The men spilled over from the pavement and into the road. Most were talking to each other, but there were some who walked silently, looking straight ahead. The sun reflected harshly against the white *thobes*. Most women were inside their houses, preparing lunch while the men were out. They normally prayed at home, as they are not obliged to pray in a mosque.

When the crowd entered the mosque and the street started emptying slightly, I saw in the distance the blind imam being led by a tall man with a long black beard. This must be the Basil that Al-Yamani had mentioned, that night at the Pleasure Palace.

I stopped going to the mosque when I was fourteen. We were all gathered for the blind imam's Friday sermon. He stood on top of the *minbar*, dressed in a sparkling white *thobe* and *gutra*, and he began by praising *Allah* and His messenger. Then he announced that today's sermon was about 'vulgar pastimes'. His voice started rising.

'Oh *ya* sons, oh *ya Allah*'s slaves, for how long will you keep forgetting Him, the almighty? Until when will you ignore His blessings and continue to abuse His mercy? Why do you insist on sinning, day after day, hour after hour, second after second? While your sins mount, forming mountains of the highest altitude on *Allah*'s earth; while your heart blackens with your daily misdemeanours, leaving no room for Him to be upheld; while your eyes have been blinded with your pursuits of vulgar pastimes, blinding you from the straight path, from *Allah*, and from His messenger's message on this earth; and while you have done all of this with such contempt for the Creator, let me remind you of this *ya* Muhammad's *umma*: fire, fire, fire. Oh *ya Allah*'s slaves, your bodies will be torn apart, your hearts ripped from your chest, your bones turned into dust by the flame. Because He is the Distresser. He is the Avenger, the Harmer, and the Powerful. Beware of His mighty punishments, when He will turn the earth upside down and empty sinners into the inferno one after the other. He, the Almighty, will never forget those who abused His message on this earth. He will pursue you with his fire, fire, fire, from the moment you die to the Judgment Day and thereafter.'

He shifted in his *thobe*, threw one tip of his *gutra* over his shoulder and took a deep breath.

He went on: 'Oh, *ya Allah*'s slaves, listen carefully to this story. A bad Muslim man died suddenly. His grieving family buried him according to the Islamic rituals, but that wasn't the end of him. The graveyard was close to the family home, and every night they heard their son's screams, howling, listing his past mistakes. "Oh, *ya Allah*," he would yell, "forgive me. Oh *ya Allah*, I was mistaken, I should have followed the right path. Oh *ya Allah*, I shouldn't have sinned. I shouldn't have drunk alcohol or smoked cigarettes. Oh *ya Allah* I should have answered Your calls an i **pray**ed for You, the Greatest."

But such cries are like the tears of the crocodile, remorse in retrospect does not befit the Almighty. And thus an Angel responsible for grave punishment descended from *Allah*'s kingdom with an order to pass *Allah*'s judgment upon this foolish man. With every word this immoral man uttered, the Blessed Angel plunged his steep, pointed spear into the chest of the apostate. Over and over again he thrust his blessed weapon into the heart of this sinful man with the power granted to him by *Allah*.'

By now the imam was weeping with religious fervour. Some of the men listening began to cry as well.

I suddenly remembered his hate sermons against Jews, Shia and Sufi Muslims, Hindus and Christians. I recalled his hundreds of speeches that he repeatedly gave to drum into our heads that women are weak human beings and inferior to men.

I had a strong headache coming on. I felt like my head was about to explode. I didn't want to be there any more. I could no longer sit and close my eyes and pretend that I wasn't hearing what he was saying. I could no longer block out his voice obliterating my ears, poisoning my heart. I didn't want to hate anybody. I didn't want the imam to make me fear *Allah* more than loving Him. I remembered what our Eritrean imam in the refugee camp used to say: '*Allah* is compassionate and merciful. Always remember that *Allah* is love.' And I no longer wanted to betray my strong mother – the most beautiful person in the world who sacrificed her life for her children – by being in the same place as this man, a man who spread hate and lies against her just because she was a woman.

I just got up and left.

When my uncle came back from the mosque, he took off his belt and hit me for leaving in the middle of the imam's prayer. According to him, the blind imam could do no wrong. The harder he hit me, the more I remembered my mother and Semira and I knew that the pain of his lashes would fade away as I thought of their love. I wasn't going back to the mosque.

Years later, when I rented my own flat, I decided to keep myself to my room whenever I wasn't working and until I could return to my country, so that I didn't have to hear his or other men's poisonous remarks. I didn't have a TV, so I couldn't listen to what they said, but I owned a stereo with a big and powerful bass. When the blind imam read his Friday sermons, I closed my windows and played music as loud as I could to drown out the mosque's amplifiers. And when I walked down the street, or did my job, I bowed my head as if I didn't live there. If there was a place and time where I wanted to be deaf and blind, this was it.

That Friday afternoon, I blocked out the imam's voice thundering through the powerful tannoys into my room and as I caressed the girl's notes, I thought about what I would say to her if the opportunity came my way and I was given a few minutes with her.

The Pink Shoes were all I could see of her that made her stand out in Al-Nuzla. And every time I saw them, I noticed a new detail. They were pointy shoes, with the tips slightly curling upwards. There was a light pattern of small glittering silver-coloured pearls embroidered on the sides. When she walked, sometimes I could see the soles, which were black. In the beginning, they were shiny when her friend had just bought them in the shop, but the streets of Ba'da Al-Nuzla had made them rough and dirty very quickly. But my fear that the tips and the sides of her shoes would get black and dark, as they stepped time after time in the dirty dust of Al-Nuzla, never materialised. Her shoes continued to sparkle as if they were meant to last for ever.

Her Pink Shoes continued to contrast with her black *abaya*, the reddish dust of Ba'da Al-Nuzla, and the white houses in the street. Without them, I would have lost her in a world of dark shadows.

SATURDAY MORNING I was supposed to go back to work, but I couldn't abandon so soon what started as a fantasy but now held the promise of love. I had to be in Ba'da Al-Nuzla to meet the girl. So I rang my boss saying that I couldn't start work yet because I wasn't feeling well and needed more time to recover.

My boss flew into a rage, saying, 'You have to come. Don't pretend you are ill.'

I quickly lost my temper. Maybe it was because I felt that he was taking advantage of me. After all, I had always worked hard and long hours for him throughout the years and without any complaints. 'Naser, you have no family to go to,' he would say, 'I have two children. Please work longer and *Allah* will reward you, *inshaAllah*.' I would do the work until late just to help him. The previous two years I had even cut my holiday short because I got so bored by myself at home. 'Do you remember?' I screamed. 'I came back from my holiday early and you didn't even pay me extra.'

He fell quiet.

'Muhammad, please just give me one week more. Please?'

He didn't say anything.

I was ready to tell him I would resign and that he could look for another loyal worker like me when he said, 'OK, but we will talk about pay when you come back.'

'Oh, thank you, Muhammad. May *Allah* bless your work.'

★

That afternoon, the girl cheered me up with a funny note.

I saw her coming and I followed her Pink Shoes with my eyes. I enjoyed watching her approach, the way she navigated the jagged ground beneath her, like a performer walking a tightrope.

She dropped the note right next to the rubbish as if it were a piece of litter, just as she always did. I ran to pick up the treasure.

She told me a story that she had heard at college. A few weeks before the summer break, the head teacher visited every class in the college with the same news: the previous day, a boy wearing sunglasses who had been standing across the road from the college had been arrested by the religious police. The boy was accused of wearing sunglasses bought from America. The religious police had informed the head teacher that the boy had confessed that the glasses had special lenses that enabled him to see under the *abayas* and uniforms of the students. The religious police convinced the head teacher that such a thing was possible because, 'The evil Americans are capable of doing anything.'

> *Habibi, it made me realise how great it would be if these*
> *magic glasses really did exist. You could wear them and*
> *I could walk back and forth in front of you.*

I laughed all the way home.

ON SUNDAY MORNING, I went to Haraj Market to buy new trousers. I wanted to show the girl with the Pink Shoes that I was making a special effort too. Haraj was the biggest market in Jeddah. It was a place where you could find almost anything you wanted.

It was at the end of the market, past Haraj Textiles selling printed cotton and linen fabric, that I found a nice pair of black trousers, made of light Italian wool with deep side pockets and straight legs for only twenty riyals.

As I walked back to the bus stop, I bumped into Ismael, a motorbike mechanic. He owned a shop close to Al-Nuzla that sold spare parts for motorbikes.

We chatted for a few minutes. He told me that he was working on Yahya's motorbike.

'I didn't know it was broken,' I said to him.

'No, it is not. He wanted a new seat fitted. He said he wanted to make it as comfortable as possible for his boy.'

We started laughing.

'Take your time,' I told him, 'he won't be back until mid-September.'

He shook his head, saying, 'I know. But he wanted a special hand-made leather one. It is hard work. I don't want to upset that rhino, do I?'

As soon as I arrived home from the Haraj, I realised I was running late. I changed into my new trousers and walked down to Al-Nuzla Street. The trousers itched my legs, but they made me feel like a man going on a date with his girl. I felt energised.

When I reached the big mosque and looked across the street, I saw a flash of pink. When the sunlight landed on her shoes, I saw the colour flood back into Al-Nuzla, turning everything a shade of rose.

I slowed down and walked at her pace. I saw she had seen me as well. I kept watching her shoes. By now I pretty much guessed what type of legs she had from the way she walked but I didn't dare to dwell on that too much.

I closed my eyes and imagined we were strolling alongside the sea, a lovers' walk on the pavement of the Corniche, hand in hand.

When we reached the corner where I usually turned left to get to Ba'da Al-Nuzla, I stopped, but the girl continued marching straight ahead, drawing me along with her.

She was striding now, slowly, as if prolonging the moment. We walked in parallel to each other – she on one pavement and me on the opposite side – all the way to the bottom of Al-Nuzla Street and back.

That day she didn't drop a note, but the experience of walking on the same street as her, side by side and at the same slow pace, was so lovingly intense that it gave me even more to think back about once I came home.

The following afternoon, it was the last day of July and a week since she dropped her first note in Ba'da Al-Nuzla. She had a new note for me:

> *Yesterday, when we walked alongside one another, you on one side of the road, and I on the other, I wished for a sudden earthquake so that the wide street that*

separated us would fall into the open ground and then when the religious police would find us arm in arm, we could say, 'This is what Allah wanted when he shook his kingdom.' But then, I swore that slowly I will take myself into my habibi's arms without such a miracle. This I vow to you.

Her words were too beautiful to be true. They could only be written by a woman, I persuaded myself. For me, it was an act of belief to think that a woman existed under that *abaya*. For all I knew, she could have been a man wearing a veil pretending to be a woman. I couldn't be sure. Words were the only thing that I had from her to convince me she actually was a girl.

At times, this type of love drove me mad. When I crouched on my bed with her notes, and when I began to imagine the voice behind the notes, the colour of the feet in the Pink Shoes, the shape of her breasts, her hips, the smell of her skin and everything that made her feel and look like a woman, the desire to touch her would get hold of me. The urge to see a strand of her hair would consume my entire day and night. But all I could do to ease the frustrations ripping my inside was to read her notes over and over again. 'Because these words could only be written by a woman.'

Jasim arrived back from his trip to Paris on the first day of the new month.

I went to see him that evening. He looked slimmer, but stronger. He almost lifted me off the ground when he hugged me.

As soon as we went to his room and sat down on his bed, he said, 'I was so concerned about you. You must have been so bored.'

There was no chance I would have told him that in fact I was having the most exciting time of my life, it was too dangerous. So I said firmly, 'I have been reading a lot.'

'Good. Good,' he said, putting a foot on top of his luggage.

'Why haven't you emptied your bag yet?' I asked him.

'You are eager for your present,' he said.

'No. It is just that you normally unpack so quickly.'

'Well, my dear, I am travelling again in five days' time,' he said, sighing.

'Why?'

He stood up and picked a pack of cigarettes from the top of the TV and came back to sit on the bed. He lit one and threw the pack at me. The writing on the pack was in a foreign language. I assumed it was French.

'Do you want to know where I am going?' he asked me.

He leaned forward and took a flight ticket from his briefcase. He put it on my lap. 'Here, take a look.'

'You are going to Rome?' I asked him.

'Yes, and then we are going to London, and to Madrid, and to Washington, DC.'

'Who is "we"?' I asked him.

'Are you jealous now?' He laughed and added, 'Don't worry, I am going with my *kafeel* and his entourage. This time we are going for a month. We are back on the first day of September. But knowing this *kafeel* I wouldn't be surprised if we stayed longer. Remember two years ago when he fell in love with a lap dancer in Geneva? He made us stay with him for three months until he fell out of love with her.'

He put out his cigarette and holding my hand, he said, 'I will miss you if it happens again. To be honest I am tired and I don't want to go, but you know I can hardly refuse him. He likes my company and he helps me keep my business open. But I am lucky to have an assistant who I can trust to look well after my beloved café. And after all, the prince makes sure his entourage lives like royalty.'

Mr Quiet had told me before that when Jasim first came to Saudi Arabia he used to have a different *kafeel,* a Saudi man who owned two restaurants in north Jeddah. But then Jasim befriended Rashid. 'Rashid is the personal assistant to one of the most influential people in Jeddah,' explained Mr Quiet, 'and it was Rashid who introduced Jasim to his new *kafeel.*'

But, Mr Quiet said, no one knows the name of his *kafeel* or anything about him except that he is a powerful man. 'I assume,' Mr Quiet added, 'his *kafeel* would not want his name to be made public in a café like this.'

I tried to find out more about this *kafeel* from Jasim. 'So when are you going to tell me who your *kafeel* is?' I asked.

He brought his face closer. 'Some things can't be told, my dear. How many times do I have to say that to you?'

As I stood up to leave, he gave me my present. It was Tayeb Salih's *Season of Migration to the North.*

I had heard about this book from Hilal. Apparently it was a controversial book and prominent amongst the forbidden literature in the Kingdom because of its sexual content.

'*Ya Allah*, this is amazing. How can I thank you?'

Jasim held my hand and said, 'Why don't you stay the night? I have a lot to tell you.'

'I can't. I have things to do.'

'Just stay tonight. I am feeling lonely.'

'I can't,' I said.

He let go of my hand. 'OK, OK, just go.'

★

Her next note took me totally by surprise, and brought me even closer to her.

It was late morning, 4th August. I was waiting around in Ba'da Al-Nuzla for the Pink Shoes to appear and I was flicking through the newspaper. As was always the case in *Okaz*, most of the stories were devoted to King Fahd Ibn Abdul Aziz and other members of the royal family. There were pictures of the King opening a new hospital and visiting landmarks in different parts of the country. Anything new that was opened was named after him. My Saudi friend, Hani, once told me how bad it really was. 'I am serious,' Hani said, 'this King is so self-obsessed. Did you not hear the news last night?'

'What?' I asked.

'The football league will be named after the King and the cup league will be called after his deputy, Abdul-Allah Ibn Abdul Aziz.' He shook his head. 'I'm worried that one day the King will insist all of us are renamed after him as well.'

I strode back and forth on Ba'da Al-Nuzla, reading *Okaz*. When I had finished, I laid it on the ground and sat on it. Opposite, on the rooftop, I saw a boy staring at me so I stared back. Several minutes passed and he was still standing on the edge of the rooftop peering down on me. When I heard footsteps, I turned my head and saw the girl with the Pink Shoes coming round the corner. I looked up at the boy and then at the marching Pink Shoes before my eyes returned to the boy. 'Please go,' I mumbled to the boy as I stood up. And I wanted to shout to the girl not to drop her note. But she had already scampered past and dropped a new note next to the rubbish bin. I looked up at the rooftop and the boy started stepping back. He unfolded a prayer rug and started praying.

I quickly picked up the note and fled home. At home, I read her words aloud and excitedly.

A few years ago, we had a TV, video player and antennae. But then my father had a crisis of conscience and asked the blind imam if it was halal or haram to have these things. The imam ruled that it was haram, and told him about the punishment for those who watch TV and listen to music. So my father came back home, shaking from his trip to the mosque and destroyed everything. He even came to my room and took down all my pictures, and tore up all my photos because they are haram. So I don't have any photos of me to drop to you with my notes, but habibi, if I am good at one thing it is painting, and I confess this to you: I have made a small drawing of you that looks exactly like a real photo of your face. I tucked it inside my bra between my breasts. I promise you that it will always be attached to my chest like a permanent beauty spot, until it is replaced by the real you.

When I read that she had made a sketch of me and where she kept it, I could barely breathe. It was as if my whole being was transplanted to that image of me which lay in that secret place between her breasts. I would be the first to smell her morning breath, the first to shower in her sweat, and the first to watch her eyelashes fall like glittering Kashmiri curtains at the end of another day in this world: a sad world where daydreams triumph over reality, the articulate are turned into mutes and their voices replaced by signs; a place where a lover must become a fugitive and hide against the skin of a woman whom he might never meet.

SATURDAY MORNING, I woke up early. I opened my window and the day flooded into my room, bringing fresh air and birdsong. As I stretched my arms, the sun painted bright spots on my skin and aroused in me all the desires and hopes of the previous night.

At about 7 a.m., I went to work. I was planning to stay until late morning, then I would go to Ba'da Al-Nuzla, collect her note, and return.

My boss agreed reluctantly. 'Just for today, ah, I will allow you to do this. I am happier now that you are back. You look like you are capable of washing all the cars in Al-Nuzla.'

At 10 a.m., I came back home, ripped off my work overalls, took a quick shower and changed into my trousers and shirt and went to Ba'da Al-Nuzla. By half-past ten, I was there, and as I stood next to the rubbish bin, I saw a woman entering the street. I looked down at her shoes, but they were black.

All the girl's previous visits to Ba'da Al-Nuzla had been between eleven and noon. But midday arrived without her, only with more heat. All the women who walked in the street turned out to be bearers of false hope. By around 12.30 I felt exhausted under the burning sun. I needed to go and buy water but the nearest shop was about ten minutes' walk. What if she came looking for me when I was at the shop?

I knew I had to go back to work, but I wasn't going anywhere until she came.

The streets of Jeddah were hazy and hot. Only her most recent note that I held in my hand kept me standing there. I wiped the perspiration from my face and as I stretched my legs I heard the *azan* for midday prayer. I tried to drag myself out of my lethargic state. I had ten minutes before the start of the second *azan* – summoning worshippers to line up behind the imam for the beginning of the prayers – ten minutes before the religious police would start patrolling the street to arrest lapsed men who don't go to the mosque. The last thing I needed was to be caught, flogged and my name registered in their books as an apostate. Even though I had been in Saudi for ten years, I was still a foreigner and I didn't want to risk deportation.

With the little energy I could muster, I trudged back home. I got to my door just as the *muezzin* started announcing the second *azan*. As I shut the door behind me, the blind imam began the prayer.

I shuffled to the kitchen and gulped down an entire glass of water, followed by two more. The phone was ringing continuously. It could only be my boss, I thought. I ignored it.

I knew that she was unlikely to be there during prayer time, so I set my alarm for fifteen minutes past one.

I made sure I was better prepared for the afternoon. I took three bananas and filled one of my drink bottles with cold water before I left the house for the dead-end street. I also wore my black baseball cap to keep the sun out of my eyes.

I arrived in the street in good spirits, but as the afternoon progressed and my shadow grew, I started losing my strength again. The time for the next prayer, *Salat Al Asar*, was approaching and there still wasn't any sign of her. I dropped down to the floor next to the garbage bin. Just then, the *muezzin* started his call. I pulled myself up from the floor and ran home, my feet almost tripping over each other.

Maybe there had been a change of plan. Maybe it was easier for her to come later on in the day because of some family matter. Or maybe it was getting too hot for her to walk all the way to Ba'da Al-Nuzla in the morning and so she had decided to make her trip during the cooler evenings.

Half an hour later, I was back for the third time that day in Ba'da Al-Nuzla.

But nothing happened. The smell from the bins was disgusting. Gradually, the daylight was disappearing with the departing sun. There were fewer women in the street now, and the black and white movie was coming to an end. I hoped the girl with the Pink Shoes might be one of the few who, for one reason or another, managed to stay out later without upsetting the men in their families. So I continued to hang around for a bit longer.

Night set in. A street lamp was broken and its light was flashing on and off. But I decided to keep waiting. 'Just for a bit,' I told myself.

Then suddenly I heard a soft and feminine voice yelling at me. 'Is that her?' I asked myself. I looked around. There was no one. Then I heard the voice once again: 'Look up. Here, up.' It was the boy with the prayer rug standing on the rooftop. 'You again?' he asked. I turned on my heel and ran straight back home.

Back home, and with shaking and tired hands, I washed my trousers and shirt and hung them out of the window; just as I had the previous night. 'You must keep presentable, because tomorrow she will be there.'

The following morning, as I made my way to Ba'da Al-Nuzla, I couldn't care less about the boy or my work. I was more worried about being betrayed by the girl than by the boy with the prayer rug, or whether I might get sacked from my job. All I hoped was that I would see the Pink Shoes again.

But the girl didn't show up that day either.

I had walked up and down, watching the feet of every woman that walked past in the street, so that by the end of the day the whites of my eyes were saturated with the unrelenting black of their *abayas* and their shoes.

That night, as darkness fell, I didn't go home. I went down lanes that had no street lights and kicked at the dark with my legs as though it were something I might be able to scare off. But it didn't work. The night came on, as it always did, and I was left wondering whether the Pink Shoes had ever existed.

Then I heard the boy's voice again. 'Excuse me,' the voice said. This time I didn't run but turned around to look at him. He was now standing next to me. The boy was small and slim, and his small hands barely fitted around his rolled-up prayer mat. His large black round eyes looked up at me, ready to fire a question.

Not wanting to talk, I looked away. My eyes scanned the street hoping to see her shoes even in the darkness.

But the boy kept nudging me and pulling my shirt down to get my attention.

'What do you want?' I shouted, without looking at him. 'Go on for *Allah*'s sake, say what you want and leave me alone.'

'Are you in love?' he asked me.

I looked at him again, trying to act normal.

'Why do you ask that?'

'Because,' he said, 'my father told me that in our village in Chad, lovers walk day and night aimlessly under the stars, moon and sun. Their bodies look like they belong to those who are dying because they don't eat; and their eyes are all over the place, because their hearts are always shifting.'

I didn't reply to the boy. I just staggered through the dusty streets of Ba'da Al-Nuzla back to my room.

Next morning, I still didn't go to work. Instead, I headed to Ba'da Al-Nuzla and waited there from early morning to late in the evening. At times, I would walk up and down the dusty street, or sit on the burning sand, or stand leaning against the smouldering walls and suffer the sun's reflective heat, and other times I would just crouch in the corner, wearily looking at every woman who passed down the street. But there were no Pink Shoes.

I felt stupid. Maybe this was all a game to her? Maybe she wanted revenge against men and wanted to make an example out of me, watch me fall on my knees and beg for her reappearance? Or maybe she wanted to demonstrate to her friends that she could bring a man to the brink of madness with just a few romantic notes? *Ya Allah*, maybe, now that she had got me where she wanted me – sitting next to a stinking rubbish bin all day long – she had decided to throw away her stupid shoes and was laughing under her veil.

The hot sleepless nights had taken so much energy out of me that by Friday morning, after another four fruitless days, I thought back to what the boy had asked. Was I in love? How could I love someone whom I had never seen or heard? I was just one of a thousand Al-Nuzla boys, hungry to talk to a girl and yearning to be loved by her.

No, I can't be in love, I thought. All I have seen of her that makes her stand out from the rest are those Pink Shoes. I had read that men fall for intricate details of a woman's body: a delicate mouth, or seductive eyelashes, and it is even said that the way women roll their hips can force a man's heart into declaring instant love. But shoes? I must be the first man in history to fall in love with a woman solely because of her shoes. I needed to step back from this make-believe world and forget about her. 'No, I am not in love,' I told myself. 'I just dreamed of loving a woman for so long that I am falling in love with the idea of love.'

I tried to convince myself to stop waiting and to stop thinking about her. 'I must go back to work tomorrow morning, and beg my boss for forgiveness,' I told myself. 'I must forget about her. It's over.'

BUT ON SATURDAY morning I woke up smiling. I had had a beautiful dream and it had given me my strength back. Some dreams you can easily let go of, but others get hold of you so tightly that even as reality uproots them, you can find another spot to replant them and start all over again.

I had an idea.

I will go where she lives, I thought. I will go to the nine-storey building and wait for her. I would write her a note myself. There must be a way to get a message to her safely. 'That's right,' I told myself enthusiastically, 'it is my turn now to tell her that she has cast a spell on me ever since she told me I was the only flower in the garden of her heart for all these weeks and months.'

And that day, another journey started, as I went in search of the girl. 'This time, I will not fail,' I said to myself as I rinsed my dirty clothes.

Just then my boss phoned me. He said he had been ringing me for the last few days and shouted, 'What kind of a foreign worker are you? Do you know how many people across the sea would give their lives to come to this country to work? I have men coming to me every day begging me for a job and you treat me like this.'

I said nothing. I just listened to him venting his anger; my mind was elsewhere. I was already beginning to compose a letter to her, struggling over whether to scorn her for her disappearance or dedicate the entire letter to how much I missed her words and shoes.

'Naser? Naser?' he kept yelling. Just before he slammed down the phone, he shouted, 'I am tolerating you because of the loyalty you have shown me over the years but if you don't show up tomorrow, you are fired.'

I hurried to my desk, took some paper from the back of my diary and wrote my first love letter. It wasn't easy, but I wanted to write something that a poet might be proud of. Like the poems that made our poet in the camp great, and maybe even like the poetry that helped Antara Ibn Shaddād – the pre-Islamic poet and the son of a noble Arab father and an Abyssinian female slave – win the heart of the beautiful Abla. It took me various attempts to write something on paper that I was finally happy with. Antara would have been proud of me and wish me luck, I thought gleefully. I folded the letter until I could fit it in the palm of my hand, and got ready for a lover's walk to the place where she lived.

IT WAS SUNNY; a beautiful start to the day. Al-Nuzla was bubbling with life. People filled the street, and a chorus of voices swept across it. On my way towards the nine-storey building, a small child raced past me carrying a watermelon.

I arrived at the building, my folded note in my hand, intent on staying there until she appeared.

I stood opposite her building and looked up. The roof was covered with large antennae. Every floor contained two flats, each with a balcony. Air conditioners were attached to the outer wall, in the same place on each storey, forming a vertical line of black boxes. The water dripping from them had made blotchy streaks on the bricks.

All the people entering or leaving the building were dressed in full Saudi clothes. And none of the women were wearing Pink Shoes. I lamented that in all those times I saw her in Ba'da Al-Nuzla, I had focused only on the shoes and not on her other attributes. Why didn't I take a mental measurement of her height? And why didn't I notice something else about the way she walked, the width of her shoulders or a particular scent – anything that could have helped me find her again?

At exactly one o'clock, I heard the announcement for the early afternoon prayer beaming over the tannoys from the large mosque. I didn't move an inch. Even though the second *azan* had started and the blind imam was already praying, I was still standing there. The only fear I had was that I was maybe chasing an illusion, that there was no girl any more, only a mirage of love in a loveless place.

I turned my head when I heard the heavy sound of an engine pulling up. It was the large, threatening black Jeep of the religious police. I turned away to look at the building. There was another car parking up outside the building.

The black Jeep stopped right in front of me, blocking my view. The shaded windows scrolled down and a man shouted. I heard what he was saying, but I didn't bother to answer. I craned to see two women getting out of the other car. Just before they went inside, one of them turned her head towards me. She faced me for a few long seconds, before she quickly turned away.

Could that have been her? I thought. Should I try to pass her my note?

'What are you doing here?' shouted the religious policeman from inside the Jeep. I realised the note in my hand was incriminating evidence. I crumpled it and shoved it inside my mouth. I chewed it, mixing it with lots of saliva so the ink would start running, and turned my head away from the Jeep and spat it out. The sweet words I had written for *habibati* had dissolved in my mouth.

The religious policeman jumped out of the car and walked towards me. I took a deep breath. He was holding his stick. It was made from a thin, flexible wood so that it didn't break when used.

'Why aren't you in the mosque?' he asked.

He wasn't interested in the remnants of the note. I felt relief, but still I was tongue-tied. I looked at him.

He poked me hard between the ribs with his stick. 'I am talking to you,' he said. 'Why aren't you in the mosque?'

I kept quiet.

'Oh *ya Allah*, we ask you forgiveness,' he yelled to the

sky. Then he glared at me. 'Tell me what is more important than praying, ah? It is the only thing that differentiates us from animals. If you don't pray you are an apostate.'

I didn't say anything. I kept my eyes trained on the entrance to the building.

The policeman slapped me on the head. 'On your knees,' he barked.

Without talking, I did as he asked, but my mind was elsewhere. As he lashed me with his stick across my back, all I was thinking about was her, my lips quivering with a different sort of prayer: that she might open the curtain at her window, or make a sign to tell me that she was there, that she existed.

They dragged me to the Jeep and drove me away. We stopped outside the big mosque and the policeman who had flogged me took me to the door and threw me inside, hissing, 'The prayer is already underway, go and pray, animal.'

I tripped on the thick carpet with its *Kabba* drawings. Worshippers in straight rows were standing facing Mecca. As they knelt down in unison, I picked myself up and ran to the other end of the mosque and out through the opposite door.

It rarely rained in Jeddah during the summer, but that evening I heard the rain coming down in streams. I opened my window and felt warm, humid air pump into my room. I wanted to scream over the rhythmic noise of the continuous rain splashing in the street.

It was one o'clock in the morning and I couldn't sleep. But it wasn't just the pain in my back from the beating that was keeping me awake. I just couldn't stop thinking about her.

I sat on my bed and wrote a new note. The words from my first note were still fresh in my memory as if by chewing them I had ingrained them in my head. I folded the note, put on my clothes and made my way to her building in the middle of the night.

I jogged along the empty street, through the rain. When I reached the pavement opposite her building, I stood and read my words out loud to her, even though the rain was drowning out my voice:

Habibati,

> *Can you leave your sleep and hear me? Can you come outside to your balcony, veil yourself in the darkness, and listen to my words?*

> *Ya princess of the princesses, can't you hide under the wind to come closer and fly around me? Can't you find an autumn leaf to carry you far into the dark sky where we might meet? Can't you take your shower outside under the rain this evening?*

> *My princess of the moon, I wish I was a gypsy singer, I would circle the earth with my 'oud and collect the most beautiful lyrics to sing to you.*

> *Sometimes, I imagine I am a crippled man sitting at your feet, looking up at your face, watching your lips pronounce my name, and your eyelashes swing to my words.*

> *How I wish all of us in this country were blind, so that we were all equally hidden from each other. I would then find you by your scent, and when our faces met, I would kiss you quietly but so passionately.*

> *I saw you in my dream, habibati. I saw you entering a park. All the flowers were drunk with my sadness and their buds fell to the wretched ground.*

SHE FINALLY REAPPEARED the next day. It was Sunday afternoon. The rain of the previous day had evaporated. It was blazing hot and Al-Nuzla was desolate. I was standing on the pavement opposite the nine-storey building. A woman came out of the building. I looked at her shoes. I stood paralysed. They were pink.

She looked left and right and waved with her gloved hand for me to come towards her. As I crossed the road, she hurried down the street and suddenly let a note drop.

Habibi,

Please forgive me for not having come out earlier. Remember, I warned you that I don't own my time. So I'm sorry but this might happen again. This time it was an unforeseen event — I had to deal with something personal. I would love to share it with you, but it would need more than a note to tell you everything, my darling.

Anyway, everything is fine for now and I am so happy to be here, walking on the same street as you.

I saw you from my window standing outside in the suffocating heat. I never thought you would take so much punishment for me. I watched when the religious policeman unleashed his wrath on you. Your eyes, habibi, didn't flinch one bit as his stick landed on your back. And when it rained unexpectedly last night and I looked through my window because I couldn't sleep, I saw you standing tall. I could see your lips moving. I longed for

the wind to carry your words to me. I wanted to stretch
out my hand to touch your face, but instead I took out
my drawing of your face and kissed you softly on your
lips.

Darling, I am still scared to kneel in the street to
pick up your notes. I feel ever more nervous of even drop-
ping them for you. A few days ago, a friend told me that
a girl she knows was caught by the religious police, just
down the road from here, dropping a note to a boy.

But I have an idea. Let's meet at the Yemeni shop
tomorrow at half-past one, after prayers. I will be going
there with my mother and everything you say to the shop-
keeper will bounce off the walls and dance towards my
waiting ears.

Salam from the heart.

I spent the rest of that day and night practising what I wanted
to say in the Yemeni shop. I was determined to come up
with something that would shake the ground of Jeddah. But
I could think of nothing to say. Phrases that I had written
for her inside my head evaporated when I tried to say them
out loud. I stayed awake all night trying to find the words
I wanted to speak to her.

I walked into the shop. The owner was busy stocking the
shelf behind the counter with cigarette boxes. I looked up
at the clock at the back of the shop: 13:25. As usual the
incense swirled in the air, and the amplifier was softly playing
suras from the Qur'an. The shopkeeper turned his head and
looked at me with a smirk on his face.

I strolled to the back of the shop and started looking
around. I picked up a beautiful incense burner made from

earthy brown clay. I looked underneath and read that it was from Marib in Yemen, the land of the Queen of Sheba. The shopkeeper snarled at me, 'You know that is too expensive for you. Put it back and hurry up and get your Pepsi.'

I stood holding my can in front of the counter. I looked at the clock. 13:35. She wasn't here yet. I walked back to the fridge and changed my drink. 'What's wrong with the other one?' the shopkeeper asked.

I didn't respond. I put the can on top of the counter and looked around in silence. A Mecca mural hung next to the cigarette shelf. The next shelf displayed a stack of yellow and white tins of Nido powder milk. On the other side, some colourful Yemeni clothing hung from the wall.

'Come on,' he said, 'this is not a museum. Pay and leave.'

Just then I heard footsteps coming inside the shop. I turned my head. There were two women, and one of them was wearing the Pink Shoes.

'Come on,' the shopkeeper said, 'I haven't got all day for you.'

I couldn't say a word.

I looked at the shopkeeper and then almost immediately I glanced back at the immaculate Pink Shoes which looked so out of place next to the dirty boxes on the shop floor. She was behind the corner of the shelves, out of sight from the shopkeeper. With one of her gloved hands she grabbed her *abaya* and pulled it up to show her right ankle. For the first time, I saw an inch of skin, her skin. I closed my eyes and gulped. There was a small scar on her ankle. I had doubted her so many times and wondered if I was chasing nothing but a ghost. But yet this woman existed. I saw the proof in the dark, shiny and smooth skin of her ankle. My dream of falling in love was alive. I almost wanted to jump up and down, shouting my happiness. The scar seemed like a small tattoo, it was short and curved, like a jewel of black stones clinched to her skin. I wondered if I ever would hold her feet one day and kiss that scar slowly and lovingly to erase the pain it might have caused her.

Suddenly I began to talk. 'How are you?' I slurred at the shopkeeper.

'What? Speak up, boy,' he yelled.

'I said it is a nice . . . in the name . . .'

'Wait,' he said as he turned off the radio. 'What did you say?'

I straightened my back and said confidently, 'I just want to say something that I have wanted to tell you for a long time.'

'Since when do you speak? I didn't think you had a tongue in your stupid head,' he said.

'That little scar on your ankle has just given me the inspiration to talk.'

'What ankle? Mister . . .'

'My dear, there is a time for everything. Let me say that it is with so much happiness that I introduce myself to you. My name is Naser, and I am from Eritrea.'

'I didn't ask and I don't want to know,' the shop owner said.

'I am twenty years old and I have been living in this country for ten years.'

'Yes, I know that. I have had the pleasure of serving you all these years,' he said.

'And even though I don't know your name, I will call you Fiore, if you don't mind, which means flower in Tigrinya, taken from the Italian.'

'My name is Safwan Saad Shakir, *ya* boy,' the shopkeeper

said, leaning over the counter and grabbing my shoulders through my shirt, 'as you would know if you ever bothered to talk to me. Now get out before I introduce you to my fist.'

He shoved me hard. I stumbled and fell against a shelf. I lunged back to the counter and added, 'I have so much to tell you, so much to share with you, and all I want to do is talk and listen to your voice.'

'Well, I am delighted with that,' he said. 'Why don't I come out and break your back, that way you can sit here for ever and tell me your life story.'

He pushed me out of the shop, saying, 'Next time, come to buy your Pepsi. If you want to talk go somewhere else.'

Habibi,

I felt incredible yesterday in the Yemeni shop. How I loved the name you gave me.

What a beautiful name Naser is too; and I loved your voice when I heard you speaking. When I saw you lifting up your chin slightly, your eyes closed for a moment, when I saw a small drop of sweat travelling down from your forehead without you wiping it, I knew then that I had been right all along.

My darling, as you know, September, pregnant with autumn, will soon be upon us. And autumn will bring with it Jeddah's notoriously sudden and strong winds, which might blow my notes to the wrong feet. But I want to hear more from you, and I want us to write to each other at length rather than these small notes.

The blind imam of the Al-Nuzla mosque is also the religious teacher at our college. It is because he is blind that he is allowed to teach us. College will open

again when September comes and as I am called a 'leader
of leaders' in our college, I am tasked by the headmaster
to guide the imam inside. Habibi, if you could be his
guide to the college from his house, and carry his bag,
we could use him as our love-letter courier. The pro-
cedure would be simple. You would bring him to the door,
ring the intercom, and say you are with the imam. Then
I would come over and wait behind the gate. I would
open the door. But you wouldn't see me, as I need to
stay behind the door. Then guide the imam through the
open door and pass me his bag with your letter and I
would take him from there. When you come to get the
imam again after his lecture, you would find my letter
for you hidden in his bag.

For the first time, though, if you manage it, just
write a small note to let me know that you have succeeded
in recruiting the imam as our love-letter courier.

Your Fiore

Later that day, I phoned Hilal to tell him I wanted to resign
from my job and that I would appreciate it if he could tell
my boss since I was scared to face his anger. It meant I had
to spend my savings, which I still had from my work at
Jasim's café. But I wanted to dedicate myself entirely to this
exciting journey. Hilal tried to persuade me to change my
mind. 'Leaving the job? How are you going to live?' he asked
me repeatedly. I just answered that I needed some time to
myself and that I had enough savings to pay for a few months'
rent.

'OK, do what you want,' he said, and put down the
phone.

PART FIVE

BASIL

I HAD LONG been a convert to her ideas. Even though her plan meant I would miss her notes for a while, it made sense to keep the distance between us while I tried to recruit the blind imam as our love-letter courier. I had so much to say to Fiore.

I knew what I had to do if I were to try and get close to the imam at the grand mosque. So I immediately set to work. Although it was years since I had left school, I remembered most of the things I needed to know because each year we had covered religious studies in greater depth.

I woke up before dawn and started preparing. I had dug out my old school uniform, which was correct Islamic dress. I put on my old *thobe*, which my uncle had bought for me when I turned fifteen. The *thobe* was short on me now but that was just what was needed. It was seen as proper by the *mutawwa'in* to wear a *thobe* high above the ankle; it showed that its wearer was following in the footsteps of Prophet Muhammad, peace be upon him.

I heard the *azan* for the first prayer of the day. I kissed my mother's picture and shook my head, remembering how I had sworn never to set a foot in the blind imam's mosque, and here I was, about to break my oath. I smiled at the power of love. And with that I left for the mosque.

The street was filled with men on their way to prayers. As I joined the sea of white *thobes*, I instinctively began looking over my shoulders fearing that I would be spotted by one of my friends. They would never accept me having become a *mutawwa*. But I calmed my anxieties. We were only at the beginning of the month, and they were not due to return from their holidays for a couple of weeks yet. 'I will deal with them when they come back,' I told myself, continuing on my way to the mosque.

The mosque had recently been repainted in glistening white. I removed my shoes and stepped into the main hall which could accommodate hundreds of worshippers. The carpet was rich green with the black image of the holy *Kabba* woven into it. The walls were also white and there was no sign nor any writing on them. I walked closer to the *mihrab*, which pointed towards Mecca, and the place from which the imam led the daily prayers. There were people praying all over the hall, and all were at different stages: some were bowing, others kneeling and some had their foreheads bowed to the floor.

The blind imam was guided to the front of the congregation. He put his stick next to the wooden stairs of the *minbar*.

I closed my eyes and assured myself, 'Everything will be fine.'

After the prayer had finished and when most men had already gone home, a small group formed around the blind imam. His guide was sitting to his right.

'What is the name of the imam's guide?' I asked the worshipper sitting next to me, even though I already knew the answer.

'Basil,' he said. 'What a pious man.'

I remembered what Al-Yamani had told me and Yahya about him that night at the Pleasure Palace: 'He always looks for bad boys to recruit to gain as many rewards in heaven as possible.' But I also remembered that his past hadn't been so clean, and that he had a soft spot for fresh and pretty boys. We will see if his time with the imam has put an end to that, I thought as I watched him.

That morning it was difficult to get his attention because he was involved in a long conversation with the imam, so I stood up and went home.

It was when I arrived for early prayers the next day that I had more luck.

As soon as the imam finished and moved to the side of the mosque where the group gathered, I got up and prepared to say a special prayer. I tried to think of *Allah* as the Punisher, just like the imam does, and when I pronounced, '*Allah wa Akbar*', I started crying. After I finished my prayer I turned to look at the circle around the blind imam and I saw that Basil had noticed me. He smiled.

When I joined the circle, some boys congratulated me for breaking down before *Allah* saying, 'What a faith, *mashaAllah*.'

I saw Basil leaning towards the imam and whispering in his ear. '*Allah wa Akbar, Allah wa Akbar*,' the blind imam exclaimed seconds later. 'Make this boy who was crying in front of *Allah* sit next to me.' I was led to him.

Even without a microphone, his voice was just as powerful. He had broad shoulders and his beard was long and interwoven with white hair. He draped one end of his head-dress across his shoulder. As I sat down, he put his hand on my head and felt his way to my face. He collected some of my tears with his left hand and said, 'Those tears, my sons, are not tears, they are musk. He who breaks before *Allah* must be His most obedient slave. I heard the weeping of this child and I could feel his submissiveness to *Allah*, what an honour.'

He asked Basil to give him his bag. I was later told by one of the boys in the mosque that the imam's bag was full of booklets. He couldn't read them; but he just liked to carry them around to be able to point to them in sermons. He had lost his sight through a serious illness more than twenty-five years ago, when he was just twenty years old. By then he was already a learned man.

I looked closely at the bag as Basil passed it to the blind imam. It was old and made out of black leather. The imam took out two small books and gave them to me. One was about rewards in heaven and the other one was about punishment in hell.

Later, when the imam was talking to other students, I approached Basil and told him, 'I have just converted to the right path after being a bad Muslim for many years. I need all the help I can get from you, brother, to make up for years wasted in sinning.'

I held his hand, as if to shake it, but left it there. His fingers trembled slightly. Smiling softly, he said, 'I will help you, inshaAllah. May Allah bless us all.'

But, as I discovered when I started going to the mosque, Basil already had a protégé. His name was Abdu. I found out that there were others vying for Basil's attention too, because he was the bridge to the blind imam, the source to more rewards. Basil obviously enjoyed this role.

To have the honour of guiding the imam just once, Basil told us, was the equivalent to rewards gathered during months of walking to and from the mosque.

It seemed like an impossible task. But I vowed: 'I will do anything and everything to achieve the plan, Fiore.'

AS IT TURNED out I didn't have to work hard on Basil. He made a mistake and I took full advantage.

It was Friday, 25th August. It had been ten days since I first started visiting the mosque – my sole aim to recruit the blind imam as a love-letter courier. My daily routine was simple. I woke up before dawn, re-read Fiore's notes, changed into my Islamic dress, and went to the mosque. I secluded myself in the mosque, reading and praying for hours at a time. With every prayer that passed, Basil took more and more interest in me. 'Brother Naser,' he said one afternoon, 'you are on the right track with us. I am growing to like you.'

Friday meant another Friday sermon. I dreaded the sight of the blind imam being led by Basil to the *minbar*. But then I saw the imam's black leather bag dangling from Basil's hand and Fiore came into my mind. I closed my eyes and smiled. When I opened them, the imam was standing on top of the *minbar*. He was wearing a gold-edged cloak over his *thobe* and red *gutra*. I bowed my head, closed my eyes again and tried to think about what I would say to Fiore in my first proper letter to her.

Later that afternoon, we were sitting in a circle in the heart of the grand mosque. There were about ten of us. I was sitting to the left of Basil.

Basil's black beard almost touched the top of his belly. He smiled after each sentence and his white and perfectly lined teeth were, as one of the boys told me, 'A showcase for the purity of his heart'.

In front of us were books and anecdotes compiled by Arab mujahideens in Afghanistan.

Because the imam wasn't around now – he was resting at home before an Islamic lesson he was due to give later that day – Basil was addressing the group. The circle was getting bigger as more people joined us. At one point Abdu arrived breathless. I had never had a long conversation with him, as he preferred to focus all his attention on Basil.

Abdu managed to squeeze into the circle and sat to the right of Basil. He was sweating. Basil shook his head. As he sat, Abdu yelled, 'Forgive me, *ya* sheikh, but our summer school's exam started later than we thought. The examiner fell sick just before the exam and had to be replaced.'

'You are the future of Islam in this country and the whole Muslim world will one day look to you for guidance and yet you have no regard for this meeting,' Basil replied. 'How, I ask, can you, His slaves, be ready to become carriers of the Islamic flag, if all you care about is this useless life? Didn't I tell you what the Prophet Muhammad . . .' when he mentioned the messenger's name we all shouted in harmony, 'May peace be upon him.' Nodding his head, he continued, 'You are so weak, *ya* brothers, that sometimes at night I can't sleep when I think about you, worrying about you. Brothers, always remember that *Allah* and His message come first before anything else in this life.'

'We will, *inshaAllah*,' we all replied.

Sheikh Basil then turned to me and whispered, 'These boys have a lot to learn. You see, brother, what I am trying to teach here in Al-Nuzla?'

'Yes, *ya* sheikh,' I whispered back, looking deep into his eyes, '*Allah* will, *inshaAllah*, reward you for your patience, hard work and foresight. In the name of *Allah* in the little time I have been here I have learned so much from you. You order me and I will do whatever pleases you, *ya* blessed sheikh.'

As he smiled, I saw a twinkle in his eyes. Then: 'You see,' he screamed his delight at the rest of the boys in the circle. 'This boy brings with him natural wisdom, obedience and knowledge. He is in this mosque day and night. He doesn't go to summer school, or go on holidays, or play football. He is dedicated to his cause. And he will be rewarded, *inshaAllah*.'

Most in the group mumbled with delight, but others – especially Abdu – stared at me. I smiled when I caught his gaze, but he looked away almost immediately.

People started muttering. Basil clapped his hands and said, 'Quiet. Quiet.'

'I have a big plan,' he announced, flashing his teeth before holding still for a dramatic pause. He panned around the circle taking us all in with his eyes. With his smile, it was as if he was trying to remind us that every word he uttered was a finished article ready for public show. 'My plan,' Basil continued before pausing yet again, 'is big but we have to start small. That is, we must recruit more boys at a great speed. Because without them, we will not be able to achieve the big plan. But we must not forget to start small. Because the big plan . . .'

'Sorry to interrupt you, *ya* sheikh,' said the boy known as the Afghan veteran even though he was just sixteen. I had learned that this boy had gone to Afghanistan with his father when he was fourteen, but when his father died a year and a half later, he missed his mother and was allowed to return home. The Afghan veteran continued, 'I would prefer *ya* sheikh Basil that you let us know exactly what your plan is instead of going round in circles like the rotor of a helicopter.' He always talked like this; he claimed that when he was in Afghanistan he had shot down a Russian helicopter with a rocket-propelled grenade.

Usually, whenever he mentioned the helicopter, he would get congratulations and adulation from the group. But not that time. I could see that some were about to yell '*Allah* is great,' but when they noticed Basil's face turning red with rage, they decided otherwise. Basil stared at the Afghan veteran for a few seconds and said, 'Patience, *ya* Afghan veteran. I will not reveal the entire plan now, only in due course, *inshaAllah*.'

Late that evening, after the last prayer of the day, we were sitting in a circle as usual. Basil asked me to wait behind for him. He wanted to talk to me privately.

'Shall I wait too?' Abdu, who had overheard us, asked Basil.

'No, may *Allah* bless you,' replied Basil to Abdu. 'You go home and remember *Allah* before you fall asleep.'

Abdu nodded his head and left without saying anything to me.

I felt sorry for Abdu, but I knew that I was getting closer to my goal.

I waited against the wall at the entrance. Some of the group were still sitting in the mosque, reading. There was a breeze outside and I imagined that I was leaving the mosque to go to Fiore's house. We would go for a long walk and there would no longer be any need for a love-letter courier. I was deep in my daydreams when Basil suddenly said, 'OK, let's go, Naser.'

I didn't know where we were off to but I hesitated to

ask him since we had been taught not to question the sheikh's judgment.

As soon as we walked past the Al-Qadisyah secondary school and the Saudi Telecommunication building, I worked out that we were heading to his neighbourhood.

As we walked under the flyover, he looked around and stopped.

He stretched out his hand and I gave him mine.

'There is a quiet park around here,' he said.

In the park, we sat on the bench next to the only light post that was working. The illumination was dim.

We sat with a space between us. We didn't say anything to each other, and I didn't ask him why he'd brought me to that place.

Then Basil moved a bit closer and rested his hand on my leg. 'Oh, brother Naser,' he said, 'from the first time I saw you, I felt you were a good listener.'

'May *Allah* bless you,' I said.

'I feel like I can tell you many things.'

'Thank you.'

'You know, brother Naser, it has been four years now since I became a *mutawwa, Alhamdulillah.*'

'*MashaAllah,*' I replied, 'what four years they must have been, spending your days and nights earning rewards.'

'Yes, indeed.'

He fell quiet.

He moved closer to me. At that moment, we heard the soft cracking of glass. We both looked down. His right foot rested on top of some broken syringes.

He said nothing for a while, and his voice only returned when he heard the sounds of motorbikes screaming past the park. He got up as if he wanted to jump over the fence and join them. But instead he started mumbling, 'Please, forgive me, *ya Allah*. Oh *ya Allah*, forgive me.'

Standing in front of me with his back towards me, he asked me, 'How old do you think I am?'

'I don't know,' I replied. That was one thing the boys in the mosque hadn't been able to tell me because they didn't know.

'I am twenty-four,' he replied.

'*MashaAllah*,' I said.

'Yes, I am twenty-four and not married yet.'

I didn't know what to say, so I kept quiet and stayed seated on the bench.

He rebuffed me for my silence. 'Brother, I said you were a good listener, but that doesn't mean you have to be mute. Don't you know how to keep a conversation going?'

'What do you want me to say?'

'You can start by asking me why I'm not married.'

'Why?' I asked him.

'Saudi women are expensive, brother Naser. You know, some greedy fathers ask for almost a hundred thousand riyals dowry. Even a good father asks for fifty thousand.'

'Yes, I heard that.'

He shook his head. 'Where do these parents think we are going to get this amount of money? I will never be able to afford to marry.' He bowed his head slightly and spat.

'Why don't you marry a Muslim woman from another country?'

'Anyway, let's keep quiet now,' he said.

He was still standing in front of me, still looking at the gate of the park. He then knelt down and picked up a discarded empty can and started fiddling with it. He threw it away after a while and put his hands in his pocket. He stepped backwards and sat down again. Our thighs touched. He put his hand on my lap, but moved away, uttering, 'Oh *ya Allah* forgive me. Please, *ya Allah*.'

I could see he was squeezing his hands, crossing and uncrossing his legs. He got up and paced up and down in front of me. He then walked further to the left where there were no lights and disappeared in the darkness.

There was silence for a while. Then I heard a soft moan.

'My Fiore,' I mumbled, 'you will soon read my letters.'

Later that night, I received a phone call in the middle of the night. It was a woman speaking a foreign language. The only word I understood was Berlin, which she kept repeating. 'Berlin . . . Berlin.' I told her that I couldn't understand what she wanted and was about to slam down the phone when I heard laughter in the background. I had lived with that laughter for years. It was high-pitched and interrupted with short squeaks. 'Jasim, is that you?' I shouted through the phone. 'Jasim?'

'Yes, my dear.'

'What's going on?' I asked.

'Are you jealous?' he asked. 'That was Rebecca. I just met her this evening.' He laughed. He paused, and added, 'I miss you, my dear. I wish I could come back now, but the *kafeel* is insisting that I stay here with him.'

There was a long silence. Then suddenly a loud scream in the background. 'Naser, I have to go. The *kafeel* is drunk. *Salam*, my dear.'

THE NEXT DAY, Basil's eyes were shining.

Later that evening, as usual, he led the circle. After hours of talking about religious matters, he rose to his feet, saying, 'OK, Naser, come with me. We are going somewhere important. The rest of you, read the Qur'an before you go home.'

'Sheikh Basil, you promised to give me a lift home today,' Abdu said.

Basil sighed and said, 'OK, let's go, hurry up.'

We followed Basil to his Mazda. Abdu casually walked to the front passenger seat. 'No, you are not sitting there,' Basil said to Abdu. 'Naser is sitting in the front seat from now on.'

Abdu didn't move. He was still standing by the front door when I approached, his hand holding to the car's door handle. He stared at me for a while, before he let go. He shoved me with his shoulder as he moved to the back.

Before I got inside the car I looked up at the tall nine-storey building which towered over the other houses in Al-Nuzla Street. I thought about Fiore's crumpled notes; how I missed picking them up and how my hands shook when I opened them, how I missed seeing her walk along the street in her Pink Shoes. I felt in my shirt's pocket and touched the note I carried with me.

Habibi,
It is hard watching you in the street and not being able to act on the urge to come and touch you. I am no

longer sure who is the lucky one: you — blind to my face
— or I, who have seen you for so long now that my
desire to be with you rips me apart.

I got inside the car and shut the door and we drove off.

Basil slipped in a tape of the Qur'an read by the grand imam of Mecca.

'What a beautiful voice,' he said. 'He is the luckiest man on this earth to be blessed with such a voice and to be the imam of Mecca. You know what that means? It means he is the imam of all the mosques in the whole world.' He circled his index finger in the air as he said that. '*MashaAllah. MashaAllah.*'

'Sheikh Basil, I would say that your voice when you read the Qur'an is better than any other I have heard. It merits to be recorded and distributed all around the world,' Abdu said.

Basil's face lit up. He looked in his rearview mirror in Abdu's direction and said, 'May *Allah* bless you.'

Not to be outdone, I needed to think of something nice to say to Basil. After a moment, I exclaimed: 'In fact *ya* sheikh, I have been to Mecca on countless occasions, and I prayed behind its imam, and let me say this, once he retires, there will be no better person than you to be the imam of the Holiest place on earth.'

He swerved his car aside and stopped. I was worried that I had said something bad. I looked in shock when he stretched both of his arms towards me and kissed my forehead with his hands tightly holding my face.

Basil parked his car on a wide street between Al-Nuzla and Mecca Street. It was where Al-Nuzla police department was based next to a big scrapyard where the police kept cars damaged in accidents. 'Here we are,' Basil said to Abdu, and told him to get out of the car. I turned my head to the back seat and for a moment I thought I saw Abdu's proud shoulders sink into his chest.

'Come on, move it, Abdu. I am in a hurry,' Basil yelled.

The moment Abdu was out of the car, Basil accelerated so fast that my shoulders pressed against my seat.

The park was darker than the last time Basil and I were there. The only working light post was now flickering on and off.

I looked at Basil, his face disappearing every time the light flicked off. When it flicked back on, he was still there gazing at me. I felt a deep disgust and I looked away.

He took my hand and he held it. This time, he didn't ask forgiveness. Instead, he squeezed tighter.

'Naser?' There was a soft gleam in his eyes, something I had seen before in many of the men's eyes at the café.

'Yes,' I replied.

The light went out again and took his face with it, but his voice remained: 'I am going to tell you something.'

The light came back on. 'You know, it is now four years since I have become *mutawwa*.'

'Yes,' I said again.

'You know what that means for a former bad boy like me?'

'Four years of virtue,' I replied.

The light flickered over his face. 'Four years since I last have been with my boys.'

I remembered what Al-Yamani had said about Basil. 'The blind imam,' he said, 'found Basil at a moment of extreme weakness, having just escaped death on his motorbike. It was easy for the imam to convert him like that. But deep down, Basil is a street boy, he always was and always will be.'

I looked at Basil and said, 'You will be rewarded, *inshaAllah*. I heard that you have sent ten young boys to Afghanistan.'

'*InshaAllah*,' he said in a hurry. The customary glimpse at the sky and bowing of the head were absent. I suddenly felt his hands under my *thobe*. And when the light returned his face was almost touching mine. He tilted his head slightly to the side, and his eyes looked to my lips. He moved his head forward.

I grabbed his neck with my two hands, and hissed, 'Do what you are thinking of doing and I can assure you, in the name of *Allah* the merciful, I will break your beautiful white teeth.' I was surprised at the cruel threats coming from my mouth, but I seized my opportunity. 'And tomorrow, I want you to make me the imam's guide in front of the group. I want to collect rewards as well. If you don't, I will tell the blessed imam what you tried to do tonight.'

I pushed him away. The light went out again. I found my way out of the park without looking back.

At home, as I went over the incident with Basil once again, I still couldn't believe what I had done. The pursuit of love, it seemed, was opening up another side to me I didn't know. But this was a battle to pursue love, and in battle blood is spilled, I told myself with a heavy heart, feeling that worse was still to come because I was in no doubt that Basil would seek revenge somehow. Basil was a street boy and in Jeddah, street boys have a long memory.

The next day, just after the Sunday morning prayer while we were sitting in a circle, Basil stood behind me and putting his hand on my shoulders announced in front of the group, 'Naser, from now on you will be the imam's guide.'

I looked at the floor in a daze. I couldn't believe it. Finally, my Fiore, we will get to write to each other.

I looked up at Basil to thank him but he wasn't smiling.

PART SIX

THE LOVE-LETTER COURIER

AT EXACTLY HALF-PAST six on the morning of Saturday, 2nd September, I left my house on my way to guide the blind imam to the girls' college. The humidity that had been sitting over Jeddah the entire summer was finally receding. It was a sign that autumn was coming, my favourite season of the year in Saudi – the cool air always refreshed my soul.

There were lots of students in new uniforms heading back to school. I left my house and immediately bumped into the nerd. He stood stock still and looked me up and down with his unwavering eyes. I stared back, stretching my eyes wide open with my fingers to match his gaze. 'So you are a *mutawwa* now?' he asked me in his high-pitched voice.

'Yep,' I replied, '*Alhamdulillah*.'

'Since when?'

'Look, nerd . . .'

As soon as I said that, he shouted, 'You see, you can't be a good *mutawwa*. They would never call others bad names.'

'It is a slip of the tongue, may *Allah* forgive me.'

'You are not a *mutawwa*,' he insisted.

'Why not, is *Allah* yours only?'

Just then I saw the Pink Shoes in the distance. I left the nerd for what he was and turned my back on him. She was walking a few yards behind a man, who must have been her father, and whom she had referred to in one of her notes. Then with bated breath, I realised I could actually try to guess what she looked like from his features. He looked an attractive man. He was of medium height, dark-skinned, with a round face, deep brown eyes, full lips, and a tightly trimmed black beard. His elegant face inspired awe in me, like that of the famous Egyptian actor Ahmed Zaki. Saudis' complexions varied dramatically. There were very light-skinned Saudis, as well as brown and dark-skinned ones. He could easily be a Saudi, I thought to myself. But he could also be from any country in the Gulf, or maybe even from Africa?

I wondered whether she had inherited any of his features.

He walked with his left hand resting on his round belly, holding the hem of his headscarf in place with his fingers. His head was high, and he didn't make eye contact with anyone along his path. Perhaps he was walking her to college.

I hurried towards them. As I approached, I looked over his shoulder at Fiore. I knew it couldn't be long before I would finally write to her.

By a quarter to seven, I was outside the imam's house. Before I went inside, I said a prayer, 'Please *ya Allah* forgive me for taking advantage of the sheikh's blindness, but I hope that I will only be balancing his sermons of hate with my search for love.'

The imam's door was open. I entered after knocking three times, as Basil said I should do. 'I am on my way, Naser,' he yelled from the women's side of the house. 'OK, may *Allah* prolong your life,' I called back. I took off my shoes and made my way to the living room. It was a small room with modest furniture. His living room had traditional Arabic *majlis* seating, with cushions and mats on top of a thick blue carpet. To the left of the room, there was a long shelf full of Islamic books. Next to the shelf there was a door which led to the rest of the house, to the imam's study, his bedroom and the women's section. The old black leather bag was lying on one of the mats. I looked towards the door to check that it was safe. I sat next to the bag and opened it. I peeped inside to see where I could easily hide my future letters to Fiore – that morning I just had with me a small note. It was a test really, to see if our plan worked, and to say that I had successfully recruited the imam and that now we could send each other as many pages as we liked. There were four small Islamic booklets, a bottle of musk, some pens and a small address book.

I tucked my note to Fiore between the booklets, making sure it wasn't visible when you just opened the bag. I stood up and went to sit down on a cushion opposite the bag. I crossed my legs, and fixed my eyes on the bag hoping nothing would go wrong.

The imam came in, walking slowly but steadily as if he was a seeing person. I noticed his feet stuck in brown sandals. He had neatly trimmed nails, but his skin looked dry. I stood up and kissed his forehead. I picked up the bag, swung it over my shoulder and took him by the arm to lead him to the door.

We left his house in Al-Nuzla Street and turned right into Market Street, which was busy with many shops and traders. After about ten minutes, I could see the girls' college: a tall white building fenced by high walls. I turned to the imam and said, 'We are almost there.'

At the gate, as I helped the imam pass through, I said in a loud voice: 'Dear imam, your servant Naser will pick you up again ten minutes before the day ends, so I don't need to see the girls coming out of the gate.' I shouted to make sure that Fiore, on the other side of the door, would hear me and know that I had finally managed to open a new path of communication with her.

'Speak more quietly, may *Allah* curse the Satan,' the imam hissed. 'I am blind, not deaf.'

LATER THAT AFTERNOON, I returned to the college to pick up the imam and guide him home. I arrived at the building, as I had been instructed, ten minutes before the end of the school day, so that I wouldn't be around when the girls left.

I buzzed at the heavy iron gate and announced over the intercom: 'My name is Naser, I am here to bring the imam home.'

I waited by the gate and it opened a few minutes later. Fiore. I knew she was the girl chosen to bring the imam to the gate. I stood still, hoping to hear her voice, hoping that she would wish the imam goodbye or warn him to be careful, or pray a short prayer. But the only sound I heard was the imam as he struggled to pass through the small exit door. He handed me his stick first and then his black bag. I hooked his arm through mine and tucked the black bag under my other arm, close to my chest.

On the way back to his house, all he did was talk. I listened without really hearing anything. My mind was else-where: did she find my note? Would she have read it by now already, and did she have the chance to write back? I brought the bag close to my face, as if somehow I would find out by inhaling the smell of the old leather.

As I helped the imam through the door of his house, he asked me to put his bag in the living room. 'You order me, *ya* sheikh and I will do it,' I replied.

Once in the living room, I opened the bag and took out the books. There, in between his booklets, a white envelope was hidden. I almost ripped the cover off a booklet as I snatched the envelope from its hiding place. I dropped it into my pocket and was about to run when I remembered to replace the imam's pamphlets and close the bag.

With the envelope safely tucked in my pocket I called out to the imam, who was safely in his study: 'I will see you later, *inshaAllah*.'

'May *Allah* bless you, son. Walk slowly and make sure you pray with every step you take,' he demanded.

'I will, *inshaAllah*.'

As soon as I had closed the door, I sprinted back home.

I got home in no time, ripped off my *thobe* and sat bare chested on my bed. Two whole pages from Fiore. When I read the first paragraph, I looked up at the ceiling. My hand moved across my open mouth in disbelief.

Like me she had Eritrean blood; she was the daughter of a second-generation Eritrean man, the man I had seen her with that morning. How strange, I thought, that I never guessed he was Eritrean. But now, thinking back, I realised it was entirely possible, as Eritreans had mixed for centuries with the people from the other side of the Red Sea.

Her father called himself Saudi even though the government never recognised him and never granted him Saudi citizenship. Even so, he was relatively well off because of his job as a personal assistant to a wealthy Saudi businessman of Southern Yemeni descent, who owned many properties and large shops in Jeddah. Her mother was the daughter of an Egyptian man. But unlike her father's family, her mother's side had been granted Saudi citizenship.

I quickly glanced over the rest of the letter and flipped the pages back and forth in my hands.

Fiore said it would be too dangerous to tell me her real name in writing in case any of the notes got lost, but she loved my new name for her – she wanted me to call her that. Fiore. She was nineteen, she said, and the number was underlined in pencil. Then she went on to tell me the story of how her mother and father met and were married.

The marriage happened after my father and my mother's father met in a café. They started talking and seemed to like each other from the very first word they spoke to each other.

Just days after they first met, the two men had many deep conversations. It would start off with talking about the weather, but soon they realised that they actually had a lot in common: they thought alike and finished each other's sentences.

So one day they both agreed that it was about time that they cemented their relationship. 'Have you got a daughter?' my father asked the Egyptian Saudi. 'Yes,' the older man replied. 'So,' my father said, 'I would like to ask for her hand and make her my wife.'

'I would be honoured,' replied my mother's father.

On the hottest day Jeddah had seen for a decade, the two men stood in front of a sheikh. The sheikh told my mother's father, 'I pronounce this man the husband of your daughter. For a long and happy marriage, inshaAllah.'

But that decision didn't go down well in my mother's father's family. 'Make him divorce her,' the elder of the family ordered my mother's father.

'Never,' he replied. 'Give me one good reason.'

The elder stood up and said, 'Well, I am in a generous mood today, so I will give you two reasons: he is not an Arab, and he is black.'

'But there is no difference between an Arab man and a non-Arab,' came the reply.

'That was in the old times. Now there is. If you don't divorce your daughter from this Eritrean man, you will be kicked out of our family.'

My mother's father shrugged his shoulders. He didn't care.

My father was also disowned by his Eritrean family for not taking an Eritrean wife.

I was born a year after my mother and father were married.

I am sad that I don't have a family from either side of my parents, but at least I have a strong relationship with my mother. She is my best friend and means so much to me.

She then wrote about what happened after her parents' marriage. Apparently, she was the only child because her father couldn't visit her mother's bed at night any more. When her mother asked him why, her husband thundered, 'Because of this,' waving a doctor's certificate declaring that he had 'an acute medical condition'.

But, according to Fiore, her mother believed that her husband's inability to pull his fat legs over to her bed had nothing to do with any medical condition, but everything to do with his lifestyle: too much fatty food, smoking *shisha*, and spending all his time with his wealthy friends in cafés around Jeddah drinking one sweetened coffee after another.

★

The next morning, in the imam's living room, I hid my reply to Fiore between the pamphlets in his bag. We walked out of the house and turned right into Market Street. Today he didn't talk much, which was good as my mind was with the letter in the bag, wondering how she would react to it.

Fiore,

> *Beginnings are always the hardest. And it is easy for my mind to succumb to the impossibility of composing even one sentence for you. But I am resting the stricken poet inside me and obey your order, my Fiore, to introduce myself without a moment of delay.*

> *My name is Naser, but you know this already. I am from Eritrea and I don't know my father's name. But in my United Nations Travel Document, my full name is Naser Suraj. Suraj was the name my uncle chose when he came to take me and my brother to Jeddah from the refugee camp in Sudan.*

> *When we first arrived at the camp, I was told to find the man with the red cross on his shirt, to register our names in the camp list as new arrivals. It was only two days earlier that I said goodbye to my mother in Eritrea. My little brother Ibrahim, who was three years old at the time, was strapped to my back.*

> *Inside a tent, I stood in front of the man who would register us. He greeted me smiling. I told him my first name and when he asked for my father's name, I replied, 'Raheema.' He peered at me through his glasses and asked if Raheema was a woman's name. 'Yes, but it is my father's name too because she is also my father.'*

> *He laid down his pen and held my hand, urging me not to be scared because there would be no bombs dropped on the camp. And he tried again to make me*

tell him my father's name. 'Raheema. There is no father in my life. There is only our mother and like I said, she is our father, mother, and our best friend.' But he insisted that he could only put a man's name down, and that my mother couldn't have had me without a man. I said I had only seen that particular man once and it was when he came to visit my mother one night. That man was my father, I told the officer at the refugee camp, but I only knew him as 'The Perfume Man'.

When my uncle arrived he insisted I take his own father's name, Suraj. Even though my mother's name was not on the forms, I was pleased because Suraj was her family name too.

After a quiet pause, habibati, I return to the present to wish you all the great things that love can bring.

Your Naser

I KNEW IT would happen some time, but I was surprised it had taken so long. The next morning, I was on my way home after I had delivered the imam to the college, and I bumped into Gamal.

'Naser? Is that you?' he asked.

'Yes, Gamal, it is me,' I replied, confidently. He was one of the men who frequented Jasim's café and he owned a restaurant just off Market Street.

He was wearing a white apron, marked with spots of red and yellow spice. His most famous dish was tripe and liver with ginger, lime, plenty of turmeric, chilli powder, and fresh garlic.

'You should say, *Assalamu alaikum*,' I said, taking in the fresh scent coming from his hands and apron. He was holding four fresh red chillies, and a lime.

He came closer and took another good look at me.

'Your *thobe*,' he said, 'it is short. You are a *mutawwa*. I can't believe what I am seeing. What happened?' he asked.

I shrugged my shoulders.

'Go,' he said, cutting the conversation short. 'Don't let me see your face again.'

Later that afternoon, I collected Fiore's letter out of the bag of the love-letter courier. But I couldn't go home to read it, because after I led the imam to his house, he wanted me to stay longer to take him to the mosque later. 'I have an important speech to deliver,' he said.

I knew what was disturbing him. The previous day, he had a visit from a sheikh working in Jeddah's largest court. The official had told the imam: 'Women, *ya* blessed imam, are becoming disobedient. They are finding ways to entice our boys into their web of evil. I am worried about our young men. A few days ago, may *Allah* forgive me for saying this in front of you my blessed brothers, a woman from Al-Nuzla unveiled her face in the middle of the street, a face full of powder and paint, to Hamid and winked at him. But *Allah* was with us, because this cursed creature didn't know that Hamid is one of our religious policemen. Even though it is *sunnah* to have a long beard, his won't grow, but it is a blessing from *Allah*. Please, *ya* imam, remind our young-sters how to avoid the enticement of women, tell them that a loose woman is the path to hell.'

'Now, stay with me but keep quiet as I prepare for the sermon,' the imam ordered, sitting on the floor mats.

I looked at him. He was deep in his contemplation. I knew he was soon to make a lecture warning boys to be careful of immoral women. But it was too late for this boy. If only he knew that a proud lover was sitting next to him in his very living room. The thought made me smile.

As I guided the imam to the mosque from his house, he was panting. It was as if I was delivering a raging bull to a ring. I looked up at Fiore's building. I still didn't know which floor she lived on, but I hoped she lived as high as possible from the ground floor, because the imam's speech was going to burst through all the houses. I remembered what Jasim once told me about this imam's speeches, 'You can hide from rain by running under a tree, and if there is a storm you can barricade yourself inside the house and you will be safe, but this imam's voice is so powerful that not even those inside their houses are safe from his lectures.'

I sat in the front row. I looked to my right and caught Basil staring at me. He clenched his jaw and looked away.

The imam started his speech: 'Oh *ya* Muslim brothers. My heart weeps today. My soul is hurt, my ears are ringing with unbelievable pain. How, I ask myself, did the Prophet's *umma* reach such destitution of soul and mind; how, I ask myself, can people whom *Allah* led to the right path, descend to this unforgivable level of sinning? You are asleep and your daughters and wives are walking around the streets unveiling their faces seeking out your boys, seeking to spread their ills on our future generation, seeking to entice our men into despicable evil. Where are you, oh men of Islam, who once ruled with iron fist from east to west? Where are you, oh men of Islam, who used to be the eyes, ears, heart and soul of your households?'

As I was listening to the imam's lecture, I felt Basil's eyes many times on me. Whenever I turned my head to face him, he smiled at me mockingly, shaking his head at the same time.

ON TUESDAY AFTERNOON I received Fiore's reaction to the imam's speech of the previous day. I had managed to sneak a look at her letter in the imam's house lavatory, but only could read it properly once I reached home in the evening.

I started to read, knowing that only a hundred metres away from my house, Fiore was in her room, probably doing her homework. How I wished I could order a magical messenger to infiltrate her building, creep up the staircase, tiptoe through the men's section, slide under the door to the women's section and into her room, slowly crawl up to her desk and take her voice and run with it as fast as it could, faster than all the men in this city, and bring it to me.

> *Habibi,*
>
> *I heard the imam's speech yesterday. It's funny he says that the problems in our society stem from women having too much freedom. If I had any freedom, I would come right now to your room and tell you these words in person instead of this rigmarole of writing at night and having to wait a day before they get to you.*
>
> *Did the imam forget that Khadijah bint Khuwaylid, the trader and businesswoman, was Muhammad's employer before he became a Prophet? Didn't she take him under her wing when he was only twenty-two years old and teach him the skills of the business trade? How*

can he say that the reason women can't work is because they are inept? Doesn't he remember that Khadijah was one of the most successful business people in those old days, days in which her tribe buried babies alive if they weren't boys? Wasn't she successful in a time when the ruthless bandits filled the path of the trade route from Mecca to Syria, when the traders had to go through swathes of deserts, and when the unforgiving terrain was difficult to negotiate even for the toughest of men? How can he forget that Prophet Muhammad himself always talked about Khadijah's financial support? As well as being the first convert, she had the wealth that was used to finance the Islamic expansion in those days. Her money helped Prophet Muhammad to free slaves, assist his male companions when they went bankrupt, and it was her wealth that the Prophet used to help with his followers' migration from Mecca to Medina. How can he have forgotten all of this?

And how can he say that the reason women can't be rulers is because we are emotionally weak and because we bleed? If he could see, he might climb the minaret of his mosque and look across the Red Sea towards those African countries where many queens have ruled some of the most illustrious kingdoms that ever existed. If someone read him history books from these countries he would learn about Sheba, Cleopatra, Nefertiti, and he would hear that the ancient Nubian kingdom was controlled by queens for many more years than his life time.

Habibi, please forgive me for my angry tone, but I hope you will understand my frustration. Even Khadijah, may Allah bless her soul, who lived over a thousand years ago, had more rights than us girls living in the twentieth century.

Anyway, now back to you. So you told me you are a woman's son. From now on, when I think of you, when I call your name in my room, I will say: Naser Raheema. I can proudly say: 'This cub is from that lioness.'

Will you tell me more about your mother and your life with her? What kind of a woman was she? And about your father, the mysterious Perfume Man?

Tomorrow, when you come to pick up the imam's bag, can you place your hand that little bit further over his cane; mine will be waiting for you. I want to touch you, so that when we retreat to our separate worlds, we will have something of each other to cling on to.

Kisses from the heart of an angry soul,
Your Fiore

ON WEDNESDAY AFTERNOON, the gate opened and I approached the small exit. I saw a gloved hand pushing the imam's cane in my direction. I stretched out my right arm to receive it and our hands touched.

I froze.

She pressed her fingers down on the back of my hand, just for a second. I closed my eyes. She squeezed my hand, and then caressed it with the tips of her fingers one at a time. The glove felt warm and velvety, and made the skin that she touched glow. I felt the pores of my skin opening as if they wanted to capture that warmth. I pressed my lips tightly together to repress my excitement.

My other hand loosened its grip of the bag and it fell. She let go of my wrist and the glove disappeared. The sheikh stumbled out of the exit. I was busy examining my right hand. 'Naser, are you all right?' the imam asked. I was retracing her fingers' movements, and replaying her touch in my mind. 'Naser? Answer me. Where are you?' I looked at him, he groped with his hands till he found my face. 'Ah, there you are.'

I knelt down and picked up the bag and held his arm with my left hand. 'Are you all right?' he asked me.

I thought for a moment, then I said, 'Yes, *ya* sheikh, I am but I hurt my right hand earlier today when you were teaching. I know it is not allowed to lead you with my left hand, but can I do it just this once? I am in real pain.'

'What happened, son?' he asked.

I brought the back of my hand closer to my face, and silently kissed the spot where her fingers had touched me.

'Naser?' he said, raising his voice. 'I am asking you a question.'

'Yes, *ya* imam. Please forgive me,' I said, still looking at my hand, as if her finger marks were still there. 'I was boiling water and I accidentally spilled it on my right hand.'

'*SubhanAllah*, pass it to me and let me read the Qur'an over it, it will heal, *inshaAllah*.'

'No, no.'

'What are you saying? Are you refusing to let me read the Qur'an over your hand?'

'No, it is not that. But . . .'

'No buts or ifs, just pass me your hand, Qur'an is the best medicine.'

I stretched my hand towards his mouth, his mouth was already slightly opened ready to spit on my hand after he'd recited the *sura*. I pulled it back. 'No, *ya* blessed sheikh, it is not that I don't want you to read the Qur'an over my hand. It is just that, actually . . .'

'Actually what?' he demanded.

'Here, *ya* imam. Read,' I said and shut my eyes.

IN MY NEXT letter to Fiore, I told her about my mother and what happened on her wedding day. I also told her that Ibrahim and I were the children of an occasional love affair between my mother and the Perfume Man.

My mother was once almost married to a man called Hagouse Idris, two years before she met my father. But the marriage lasted only an hour.

My mother and her husband consummated their marriage on the night of their wedding, in line with the tradition in our village to the north-west of Asmara, while guests were waiting outside their hut. When the midnight hour arrived, the husband's best man went inside. He lit an oil lamp and placed it next to the bed. On the pillow he put a square of white cloth.

When he came out, he announced that everything was ready and it was now time for the bride and groom to go inside. All the guests stopped dancing and singing and blew out the other oil lamps in the compound. They stood silent outside the hut waiting for the main news of the night: the piece of cloth soaked with my mother's virgin blood. The guests heard the first moan, and the best man edged closer to the hut's door in readiness to receive the cloth.

But inside the hut, the husband had finished making love to his wife but there was no blood. He held the piece of white cloth and he sat there motionless. 'Why didn't you tell me?' he asked my mother. He didn't yell, she told me, he just asked her gently.

She responded, 'And why do I have to? Did you tell me what you have been up to before our marriage?'

She held his hand. He pushed her away, saying, 'But I am . . .'

My mother didn't let him finish his sentence. 'You are what? A man? And that because you are a man, you can do anything and everything you want. My dear husband, of course I have had other lovers. And I know for a fact that you have slept with other women. The only difference is that you are not condemned because of it.'

He pulled up his trousers. My mother stared at him.

'My dear husband,' she said, 'listen to me, please. I know a lot of women who sleep with men before their marriage, and then go to some doctor in Asmara to have an operation and regain their virginity. But I chose not to do that, because my past is mine, just like I would never ask you to erase yours.'

'I was warned about you,' he said to my mother, as he searched for his tie. 'I should have listened.'

My mother bowed her head and clutched her hands to her chest in desperation. 'But you have been with women too, was that traditional?'

'I should have listened to the other men. But my heart blinded my sense. I refused to believe what they told me. What will I tell . . .'

She looked up. 'Tell who?' She threw the bedcovers away from her. 'This is between you and me,' she said. 'I believe our hearts are like the ocean. They are deep enough to bury count-less secrets, hide the past, and still have the capacity to give. Let's forget about the past and love each other.'

'But what will I tell our guests? They are waiting outside. How will I face them?'

At that moment, my mother jumped to her feet, put her clothes on and took the oil lamp and the white cloth from her husband's hand and stormed out.

'What are you doing?' he shouted. 'Where are you going?'

She pushed the best man aside, still waiting outside the door, and headed towards the guests. 'Here is the cloth,' she said, waving it at them. 'And yes, my dear guests, it is still white.'

Moments later my mother's husband stormed out from the hut and from the village, for ever. Her family also walked out of her life. But Semira, my mother's childhood friend who lived on Lovers' Hill, was so overwhelmed by what my mother did that she swore to stand by her.

A year after the failed wedding, and when she was living with Semira and the other girls on Lovers' Hill, my mother fell in love with a man called the Perfume Man. But he was an Ethiopian man who vowed to lead the life of a traveller. He sold perfume, imported from around the world by sea, in different corners of Abyssinia. Even though they loved each other dearly, he left her a few months after she was pregnant with me. My mother could never really forget him. And when he returned to our village when I was six years old, his visit lasted only for one night, the night in which Ibrahim was conceived.

A week had passed since her college had started, without my realizing it. It was difficult to imagine that I was writing to a woman in Jeddah with all my secrets and dreams, telling her what made me feel happy and sad. I had never been happier. I woke up with the dawn, singing like the birds outside my room; in bed at night, I covered myself with her letters as if they were the gates to her world.

It was all bliss, but it wouldn't last long. I knew that it was only a matter of time before Yahya, Hani and Jasim returned. Then there was Basil. Every time I saw his face and smile, I remembered the park and the threats I had used against him.

THE FOLLOWING MONDAY, I had been asleep for a while when suddenly there was a loud knocking on my door. I sat up. Who could it be?

But then I heard a familiar voice calling. 'Naser? *Ya* Naser?' It was Yahya yelling at the top of his voice. I could hear he was high on drugs. I punched my pillow. I thought he and Hani were due back later. I had no idea how to deal with them. And if Yahya found out I had become a *mutawwa*, he wouldn't let me rest a moment in peace. I remembered what he had said when Zib Al-Ard turned *mutawwa*. He swore that he would hunt out whoever did this to his friend.

I crept towards the door.

I heard Hani's voice too. 'Yahya, it's one in the morning. Maybe he is sleeping. Let's go.'

'Let me try one more time,' said Yahya.

He thumped on the door, shouting, '*Ya* Naser? Naser?'

A moment of quiet, then there was a loud bang on the door once again. I heard Hani shouting at Yahya, 'Why do you always have to be so violent?'

'Shut up, Gandhi,' Yahya shouted.

I couldn't help grinning. I'd missed the boys. I wanted to open the door, but I couldn't. I tiptoed back to bed and tried to go back to sleep.

I had a sleepless night. I didn't know what I would do if my friends saw me in the street with the imam. Hani wasn't really the problem. He worked during the day in his father's import and export business, and he only came to Al-Nuzla occasionally. He was also more understanding and would leave me alone if I asked for it. But Yahya wasn't like that at all. He lived off his father's inheritance. We all used to joke that Yahya's full-time job was chasing boys, and he put in plenty of overtime. I was bound to meet him on the road before long and I needed to think up an excuse to stop him bothering me.

Tuesday morning, and I still had no idea how to avoid Yahya.

The afternoon arrived. I picked up the imam and as I was walking the sheikh back from the college, I heard some people having a loud argument. I looked around and saw it was Yahya on his motorbike.

I quickly turned my head away. I looked out of the corner of my eye to see Yahya speed away down the road to Al-Nuzla. There was a boy sitting on the new leather seat of his motorbike. Ismael the mechanic had finished the job in time, it seemed. I kept my head down and walked faster. 'Slow down, son,' the sheikh urged.

'Sorry, *ya* blessed imam,' I said. I could only pray that I would be able to avoid Yahya.

But the encounter with Yahya happened soon after. He caught me the following morning. It was the last day of the school week and I was escorting the imam back home. It happened very fast. When I heard the sound of a motorbike behind me, I immediately recognised the spluttering noise. I turned around. Yahya was driving towards us, his eyes fixed on me. He parked his bike and came towards me and the imam. He grabbed hold of my free arm to stop me.

'Naser?'

I shrugged him off and kept going.

'Naser? It is you, oh *ya Allah*! What's wrong with you? What are these clothes for?' he shouted.

'Who is this?' the imam asked me.

I didn't respond.

Yahya grabbed my hand and this time he pulled me towards him away from the imam. The imam lost his balance and almost fell over. I turned with the force of his pull and my face almost hit his. 'What's wrong with you?' he hissed.

'It is He *Allah* who guides people to the right path,' the imam rebutted. 'Who are you, may you be punished by *Allah*?'

'I am talking to my friend,' Yahya answered. 'Stay out of this.'

'May *Allah* curse you; do you realise who I am?'

Yahya faced the imam and shouted at his face, 'Yes, I know who you are. You are the one going around changing all my friends.' He turned to me and shouted, 'Didn't you say you would never change? Didn't you say you would never go to the blind imam's mosque? Because he is –'

I swung the imam's bag and hit Yahya so hard in the face with it that he staggered back across the pavement and into a street seller sitting next to four huge burlap sacks full of dates from Medina.

I immediately turned to the imam and said, 'He is lying. He is just jealous that I am your guide. But I hit him really hard. He is on the floor.'

'I know, son, I heard it. May *Allah* bless you.'

I looked back, and Yahya was being restrained by the date seller and his friends. When we reached the end of the road I could still hear the obscenities he was screaming at me.

YAHYA HAD SPREAD the word. That weekend the entire gang stalked me. Already on Wednesday evening, Yahya had come with some of his friends and stood across the road from the mosque, like demonstrators ready to protest. He came with Hani, and two other boys whom I didn't recognise.

But it was Yahya who was the most persistent. He followed my every move, tracking me on his bike, his boy sitting on the back seat, wrapping his arms around Yahya's waist. He shadowed me when I led the imam to other mosques in the neighbourhood, in which he delivered his speeches; when I took him to see his friends and to visit his doctor; and to a meeting with someone working for the Ministry of Higher Education.

I knew he was waiting for the right moment to trash me.

On Saturday afternoon, I was in a tailor's with the imam; he had just gone into the back room to have his measurements taken. Yahya stormed into the shop. He dragged me aside, ignoring the sales assistant, and threw me down on top of a pile of fabric. He brought his face right up to mine and threatened me, 'If you don't leave the imam soon, I will break every bone in you. I don't want to lose any more friends to that imam. You hear me?'

He shoved me in the chest and left the shop, waving his huge arms at people and shouting, 'What are you looking at? If you want some of this, tell me.'

*

The next day, Yahya and Hani came to my flat late at night. They tried to talk me out of being a *mutawwa*. But I stood firm to Yahya's threats saying that I had chosen the right path and there was no going back. 'You can do whatever you want,' I said to him.

Suddenly Yahya jumped at me and started to punch me in the chest on the doorway of my flat. I just received his fists without fighting back.

I had never seen his eyes filled with so much hurt and anger. The more he hit me, the more I realised that he was doing so because he thought he was losing another friend to the imam like he had lost Faisal and Zib Al-Ard. I felt his grief more than the power of his fist. I was sorry not to be able to share with him and Hani why I was leading the imam, sorry I couldn't explain to them my happiness at finding Fiore. I wanted to stop Yahya's beating and tell him the truth. 'Look,' I wanted to say to him, 'I am not going anywhere. I am not going to die in Afghanistan. I am alive. In fact, I have never felt more alive than now. Because I am in love with a woman.' But I didn't say anything. I received his thrashing in silence. I couldn't tell him about Fiore. I was living a dream and I knew that had I told Yahya and Hani, it would have been too much for them to hold the secret of a love story between a boy and a girl in Al-Nuzla.

I lay on the floor holding my stomach. Yahya leaned over me. I thought he was going to deliver the punch in my face that would have avenged him for my betrayal. But instead he said, 'Our friendship is over. Don't you dare to call me or talk to me if you see me on the street, you hear me?'

He slammed his clenched fist into my stomach.

'Enough,' Hani yelled at Yahya. 'He chose the imam over us. He can go to hell. Let's go.'

DAYS PASSED AND I continued to communicate with Fiore via the love-letter courier. Even though being associated with him cost me the last two friends I had left in Jeddah, he was invaluable to me. Without him, I wouldn't have been able to write to my Fiore and read her beautiful, sensual writings. I was having the best time of my life. I was deeply in love.

Friday afternoon the college was closed and so there was no letter from Fiore. After the Friday prayer, I led the imam to his house and he asked me to stay for lunch. 'An important guest is coming to visit me,' he said, 'and I want you to be here.'

I had to agree even though all I wanted was to be alone in my room with Fiore's letters. By the time we arrived from the mosque, the imam's house already smelt of *kabsa* rice.

A few minutes later, the doorbell rang. It was Basil with a man I had never seen before.

Basil shook my hand enthusiastically, exclaiming, 'How are you, Naser?'

I was wondering why he was so happy and what he was up to when he let go of me and introduced me to the man standing next to him. 'This is Sheikh Khaleel Ibn Talal,' he said, 'he is a chief in the religious police department of Jeddah, may *Allah* bless him.'

I felt cold sweat creeping up my back.

The police chief looked at me without flinching. I stretched out my hand and he slowly raised his. We shook hands and as I kissed his forehead to show my respect, I said with a quiet voice, 'It is my pleasure to meet you.'

He was bearded, light-skinned, tall and slim and walked with a slight stoop. He was around the same age as the imam. He was wearing a red and white chequered *gutra* and his *thobe* fell slightly above his ankles.

Inside the living room, we sat in a semicircle. The chief religious policeman sat between the imam and Basil. I sat to the left of the imam, almost directly facing Basil.

I tried to understand what was going on. Although I knew the imam was on very good terms with Jeddah's religious police department, a visit at the imam's home like this was highly unusual. Did this have anything to do with me?

Every time I looked up, Basil would peel his eyes away from the imam and the chief religious policeman to stare at me with a grin on his face.

Suddenly there was a loud clap. It was the imam's wife. Lunch was ready.

The imam didn't like a woman's voice to be heard in public, and he would often preach that it was *haram* for a woman to speak in the presence of a man who is not her *mahram*. So when the food was ready, the imam's wife stood behind the closed door leading to the rest of the house, and clapped her hands instead.

'Naser, please get the food,' the imam ordered.

Before opening the door that led from the living room to the corridor and from there to the women's section, I clapped my hands and announced, 'I am here to take the food.' I heard her quick steps hurrying away, so I knew the corridor was empty. I opened the door and picked up the big plate full of fried meat spread over a bed of rice cooked with raisins, cloves and cardamom. There were also four glasses of fresh mango juice.

Back in the living room, I put the tray on top of the cloth on the floor, around which we sat to eat.

We all said, '*Bismillah*', and dug in our hands almost simultaneously.

For a while we were all quietly eating, using our fingers to form balls of rice mixed with meat and throwing them into our mouths.

I wondered whether Basil had finally found out the truth about me and he was now ready to turn me in to the religious police. I ate fast to press away my worries about him and almost choked on a piece of meat inside the rice ball I had made. I coughed loudly to clear my throat. I reached for my glass of mango juice and emptied it in three large gulps.

'Is that you, Naser?' the imam asked.

I gasped for air. 'Yes,' I replied.

'Eat slowly,' the imam ordered me. 'Don't you know that eating slowly is a sign of being a good Muslim? Don't you know that *Allah* entrusted us with our bodies?'

'Yes, my blessed imam,' I said, looking at his big belly which inflated with every massive rice ball he shoved into his mouth. 'May *Allah* bless you for your advice.'

We continued to eat in silence.

After a while, the senior religious policeman spoke, 'We want to thank you, *ya* imam, for recommending Basil to be part of our team in Al-Nuzla.'

I put down the ball of rice I had just pressed together and stopped eating. Since I knew Basil, he hadn't stopped talking about his dreams of becoming one of the leading imams in Saudi Arabia. Becoming a religious policeman had never been part of his big plan to reach heaven.

'In fact,' said the imam, 'I wanted him to stay working at the mosque with me and help me guide young boys to the right path. But he volunteered himself, may *Allah* bless him.'

This must be it, I thought. Basil must have found out something. I wanted to look at him to see if he was still grinning at me. But I bowed my head and continued listening.

The senior religious policeman added, 'Basil, *ya* imam, will have a very hard but an important and blessed task. Al-Nuzla Street is becoming infested with moral corruption. In fact just last week, *ya* imam, a case was brought to my attention. A woman and a boy were caught, may *Allah* forgive me for saying this in front of you my blessed brothers, committing the ultimate sin. She is married and when confronted with the evidence in court of her adultery, instead of repenting, she said, "Because my husband never gives me love, I have to find it elsewhere." And this married woman will be stoned to death, *inshaAllah*. But can you believe it, *ya* imam, that when we told the boy that since he was single he will only be lashed, he begged us to stone him as well. A stupid man. A colleague of mine rebuked him saying, "If you want to be a martyr why don't you go to Afghanistan and fight the infidels instead of trying to sacrifice yourself for a cursed woman." But we will treble his lashings until he forgets her and the fear of *Allah* is sown in his black heart.'

'Curse on them,' said Basil loudly.

I looked up. The imam started to praise Basil. I remembered the park. I wanted to tell them that Basil was a street boy and I wanted to confront him and let the others know what had happened. But now that he was a religious policeman an accusation of this kind against a man entrusted with bringing morality to the streets wouldn't work. I glanced in his direction. He was smiling broadly as he fixed his *gutra*.

What do I do now? I asked myself. How can I put a normal face over my fear and hold back my sweat? How I wished then I could sprint to Fiore to share with her the danger I felt was closing in on us. But the next thing I heard was Basil's voice. 'Naser? Aren't you going to congratulate me and ask *Allah* to bless my work?'

He lowered his head waiting for the kiss of congratulation. I stood up with great difficulty. Holding his face with my hands, I kissed his forehead. 'May *Allah* bless your work and make you successful in catching decadent people in our streets,' I said in a weak voice.

His Amen and theirs reverberated across the room.

AS I WALKED home from the imam's house that Friday, I felt like the most wanted man in Saudi Arabia, a man who has the bounty of a place in heaven for anyone who catches him red-handed expressing love. It felt as if the imam knew everything about my activities and that he was playing a fool but sooner or later he was going to catch me and watch me get punished.

As I walked, I looked over my shoulder, trying to see if Basil was following me, if there was a religious policeman behind a tree, or another suddenly springing up from the corner. Even the white buildings, lined up like soldiers, felt as if they were in disguise, fitted with silent cameras rolling as I passed alongside them capturing my every move and hearing if my heart was beating to show them that I was in love.

Suddenly, I hated life. All I want is to be with this woman, I thought, as I quickened my pace to my flat still looking behind me to see if Basil was following me.

Without realising, I was talking to myself like a madman, sharing with the street everything that was going on inside me. I sped along. The angry thoughts hurried with me. The world turned dark, colourless and full of men and women walking side by side without looking at each other, without touching each other, without whispering, and without even breathing. It was a gloomy world where everyone feared something, a world where laughter was a sin, where kissing a woman was like a theft, where looking at a woman's face and admiring her was the equivalent to a serious crime that deserved punishment in hell.

I wanted to leave Al-Nuzla and the pain that had been building up all those years behind me. I remembered how much I missed my mother and how my brother and uncle left without even saying goodbye; I remembered what my *kafeel* had done to me and what had happened in the back room of Jasim's café. I couldn't go home. It was too lonely. I took the bus all the way to the Corniche.

When I got there, I saw the Saudi singer holding his *'oud*, but he wasn't singing. I walked behind him and down to my secret rock. His head was bowed, as if he had finally been broken and the weight of the memory of his lover had become unbearable, as if the sermons in the millions of mosques of Jeddah had finally convinced him that he would be condemned on both earth and in the afterlife, that men like him who wasted their time on the memory of a woman were destined for nothing better than a place in hell where the worst of criminals belong. That there was no heaven for lovers, as he used to sing, and that he and his lover would never ever meet again.

THAT SAME NIGHT, back late from the Corniche, I sat on my bed and kept thinking about Basil. Why did he want to become a religious policeman all of a sudden? I had no answer. After Basil had left with the chief religious policeman I asked the iman about Basil's decision to join the religious police, but all he said was that Basil was a blessed man and that he must have thought he could do more to help restore morality and obedience to our streets.

I tried to be convinced by the imam's explanation. I thought back to what Al-Yamani had told me and Yahya about Basil's hunger to earn more rewards in order to counter his sins accumulated over years of living as a street boy doing anything and everything imaginable. But the truth was that this explanation didn't entirely persuade me. 'If he is only after awards why doesn't he follow his own preaching, go to Afghanistan and seek martyrdom?'

I thought back to my time in the mosque, and went over every minute I had spent there, wondering if I had left a clue for Basil somewhere or made any slip that would have given him reason to suspect my motive for vying for the imam's hand. But I couldn't be sure that I had in no way aroused his suspicion.

Nothing was clear to me.

Suddenly a strange thought came into my head. What if Fiore had told him about us?

My head started aching badly. Maybe she was playing a game? Maybe she was a fully paid member of the religious police and was out to get lapsed men who were prone to fall for women's advances? How was I supposed to know?

Although I couldn't dismiss that possibility, inside me I was convinced Fiore had nothing to do with this, and like me, she was a victim of the pursuit of love in Jeddah. Without reason perhaps, but I had so much faith in her.

I did wonder though what would happen if Basil caught us corresponding through the imam.

Since both of us are single, I thought, according to the law, we would be lashed in Punishment Square. It made me think back to the deep lines of fire on my shoulders after the religious policeman lashed me that day when I stood outside Fiore's building with a note in my hand. He lashed me more times than I could count, each time on the exact same spot where the previous one landed. I feared I would end up in two halves.

And I'm a foreigner, I thought, my heart beating a step faster. If they find out I used the imam as a courier of love letters, my punishment will be even harsher. Would they deport me? What might they do to me?

What about Fiore? I recalled what Mr Quiet had told me when the religious policemen strode past us in the shopping mall looking out for illicit love. 'If two unmarried lovers get caught,' he said, 'then the man will be flogged but will live a full life. He will say I am sorry, *ya Allah* forgive me, and that's his ticket to a happy and a normal life. But the woman, she will find out that once the pain of the lashes subsides, she will endure a greater pain. She will be shamed for ever. No man will touch her, no man will want to be her husband, and she will live like a dog with rabies, because if a bullet didn't kill her, then the pain of loneliness and rejection will.'

PART SEVEN

THE BLACK JEEP

I HAD WONDERED whether I should write Fiore a last letter to say that this all was too risky for both of us, and tell her about my suspicion of Basil. But it was too late. She had become my obsession and I couldn't imagine living without what she gave me, for even if it wasn't physical love, the idea that I was in love was enough. I decided that it was better to continue holding on to an idea, even if it was dangerous, in the hope that it would one day become more, rather than continue living in a loveless world.

'Isn't life temporary?' I reminded myself to gain strength.

Saturday morning, and I left my flat for the imam's house, with a new letter to Fiore in my pocket.

I saw her in the distance, in her Pink Shoes, walking behind her father. They were coming towards me. I walked slowly, so I could be with her on the same street for as long as possible. I saw a beam of pink light reflecting off a piece of broken glass that she pushed aside with her right foot. I imagined that Jeddah's sky was ablaze with fireworks, as though her shoes were the cannon from which this pink was fired up to brighten a normally sad sky with happiness.

I felt that she was whispering to me with her shoes, 'Good morning, *habibi*. I hope you slept well.' I felt it was like seeing her uncovered with a big smile on her morning face.

I remembered the drawing of my face that lived between

her breasts, caressing them with every step she took to her college. I hoped my picture would crawl up along her neck and give her a passionate kiss on her lips and then whisper back, 'And good morning to you too, *habibati*.'

I rejoiced, feeling happy that I had not lost my nerve.

I planned to breathe in the morning air greedily when I passed her, hoping to catch a whiff of the scent of her shampoo and body lotion.

I looked at her father and noticed he was walking as if he was a living king on Al-Nuzla Street. I studied his face, trying to find more clues about his daughter in his features.

I was wrapped up in my thoughts when I saw the familiar Jeep pulling up behind Fiore. It was enormous, taking up almost the entire width of the street.

It drove alongside Fiore, its thick dirty tyres nearly touching the pavement on which the blessed Pink Shoes were walking. Fiore turned her head towards the Jeep, but as she did, her ankle twitched and the side of her shoe touched the dust. Her shoes spoke to me of her fear. 'Please, Fiore, hold your nerve too,' I prayed. I kept walking, my eyes fixed alternately on her and the Jeep, but the Jeep passed Fiore and beeped its horn. Fiore's father looked at the Jeep and bowed his head, touching his chest with his right hand in respect. A hand stuck out of the Jeep to wave back. When Fiore and her father had passed me, I heard my name:

'Naser?'

I pretended I didn't hear, looked ahead, away from the Jeep, and kept walking.

'Naser?'

Basil's voice was too loud to ignore, and I turned my head to face the new religious policeman of Al-Nuzla.

'Come over here,' he said.

I did as he asked. In the distance, I could see the Pink

Shoes disappearing. That was the right thing to do. We had to be as careful as possible. There was no room for errors, and hasty and frequent back-glances are certainly a big give-away for the religious police.

Basil leaned out of the Jeep window and smiled at me.

As I walked towards him I wondered again what could have motivated him to become a religious policeman. Revenge or genuine desire? Part of me couldn't help thinking that all he was doing was posturing, that he was trying to impress me, like he must have done when he was competing for pretty boys' hearts. It is possible, I thought as I examined his face, hidden by his thick beard. Being a religious policeman would give him the authority to force anything on me, even the very thing I had refused to give him in the park.

Deep inside me, I hoped that this was the case, that Basil was overcome by lust and nothing else. I could handle that, I thought as I approached his Jeep.

But his words didn't instil much hope in me. 'Greet the imam,' he said, 'and tell him that Basil will never let him down. That he, with the help of *Allah*, will crack down on anyone who dares tarnish our blessed way of life and deviates from the right path.'

In my letter to Fiore that morning, I didn't mention anything about Basil or his becoming a religious policeman. Perhaps it was my fear that I might lose her at any moment that made me want to tell her now about my deep-seated desires. I wrote choosing the most beautiful and precious words, weighing each sentence ten times before I committed it to paper.

For the first time, I realised I had started to think about her sexually. This was a person I couldn't see, hear or touch, and yet I knew she existed because of the inch of skin she had shown me in the Yemeni shop, her letters and the Pink Shoes. And the longing her sudden presence in my life had instilled in me was making me adore her with the same fastidiousness a pious man might feel towards his invisible God.

Fiore,

I hope that you will take kindly to my foolish manners but today I have decided to talk to you not about earthly matters but instead focus my energy to admit to you my desire. The moment for this might be inappropriate and the forwardness of what I will say may make you regret knowing me, and even give you reason to reject me as a man of ill manners. A man who started to twist pure love into a medium for desire. But I have decided that if I am to be as faithful to you as lovers must be to one another then I must convey to you all the feelings inside me.

It has been so often the case that wherever I am, be it walking down the street, waiting for the imam at his house, in the mosque or outside the college, all I think about is you.

On occasions, I travel with my mind far into the distance, to a place where you are waiting for me in the middle of the desert. So I come rushing towards you. At first you appear covered. But as I come closer to you, the black cover turns out to be nothing but your dark skin under the searing sun of the desert. You are alone. Like a plant in the desert, keeping yourself alive, self-sustaining. Your feet stand firmly on the yellow sand like roots with a thousand years of history, and your chest and neck look up to the sky with the pride of an Abyssinian queen.

When I reach you, I am breathless, like a man who has been wandering this earth with only one aim: to find the woman of the legend, the lover about whom men talked, and whom women feared, for thousands of years. The myth that men passed on from generation to generation with the same lust shaking their bodies as when they first heard it from their fathers.

When I found you, your magic was that you were able to fill the sky with countless stars and turn the desert into a bed of flowers upon which we lay naked, our bodies meeting for the first time. As we kissed, you confessed to me the truth. 'I might be mentioned in a legend,' you said, 'but I am new to the land of lovers because I have been all alone for my whole life waiting for you to come.'

'We are both novices then,' I reply. 'Virgins like one another. But we have a lifetime to teach each other how lovers make love, beginning from now, habibati.'

THE FOLLOWING MONDAY afternoon, I collected the imam from the college as usual, knowing a new letter from Fiore would be inside his bag. The police Jeep approached and parked just in front of us. I stopped abruptly. 'What's the matter?' asked the imam. I let go of his hand and pulled the black bag tighter under my arm. 'Naser, tell me, why are we stopping?'

Two religious policemen got out of the car and headed towards us. One of them was Basil. He shouted, '*Ya* imam, *ya* Allah's lover. *Assalamu alaikum.*' Both hugged the imam and then Basil turned to me. But this time he didn't smile as he usually did.

'*MashaAllah*, welcome to *Allah's* eyes and ears on this temporary earth,' the imam wailed, beaming. He rarely smiled, and I never heard him laugh. 'Because,' he said in one of his sermons, 'too much laughter weakens the heart, a heart that must be always strong to love *Allah* with all its might.'

'How are you, *ya* Allah's slaves?' the imam asked them. 'I hear satisfaction in your voices.'

The other religious policeman was taller than Basil, with big hands and broad shoulders. He was young and handsome. He was also beardless, a sign that he was the undercover policeman I had heard about in the imam's house. Basil addressed him as Hamid.

'*Alhamdulillah*,' replied Basil. 'We need to talk to you.'

He took the imam's hand and as he guided him to the Jeep, the imam ordered me to wait for him where I was.

'Don't you need your bag?' Basil asked the imam.

I took a step backwards. I looked out of the corner of my eye to see if I could pick out a way to flee, ideally a lane that was too narrow for the Jeep. I noticed the alleyway around the corner from the bakery. It was only half asphalted. I hid the black bag behind my back, holding it tightly with both hands.

'In fact,' added Basil, 'we can give you a lift after we talk in the office.'

The imam paused and ran his fingers through his beard, then tilting his head sideways, he nodded and said to Basil, 'Can you take my bag from Naser?'

Basil extended his hand towards me. I stared at it then looked up at him but didn't react. My hands were still behind my back holding on to the bag.

'Does he have the bag, *ya* imam?' Basil asked, without blinking. I pulled out my right hand from behind me and shook his hand firmly.

Basil smiled.

'*Yallah*,' the imam ordered Basil. 'Let's go.'

I had to give the bag to Basil. He stepped into the police Jeep and took Fiore's letter with him.

THAT DAY *ALLAH* was on my side, and gave his blessings to mine and Fiore's love story. No sooner had the Jeep driven off, and before I even had time to kick the wall in frustration, it stopped and reversed to where I was standing.

The imam climbed out saying that he had forgotten that he was expecting a visitor from the Ministry of Higher Education. He wanted me to guide him home.

I never kissed his forehead as warmly as I did that time, and I thought I even felt tears in my eyes.

Habibi,

I call my father a mutawwa who sits in cafés. You would think anyone who dares to call himself a mutawwa would go to the mosque and pray day and night. But my father is no devout worshipper. When a real mutawwa is praying and his mouth is busy remembering Allah, my father's lips are stuck to his shisha pipe.

A few days ago, I knocked on the men's door at home.

'What do you want?' he shouted at me. 'I am busy.'

'Doing what exactly?' I replied. He came out thundering. That's the way to get him out of that room and away from his shisha.

'How dare you speak to me like that? What kind of a woman are you?' Then he called my mother, 'You see, all of this is your fault. She is becoming disobedient.'

But soon, he calmed down. 'What do you want?' he asked me as he sat on my bed.

'I would like to at least have my eyes free in the street. It is not haram for a woman to reveal her eyes. Look, I can read it for you from this book.'

'No, you've asked me this before. I told you I went to the blind imam but he said if I let you do that I would —'

'Go to hell?' I said mockingly.

'Don't be rude and show respect for me and the imam, ya dog.'

'I am sorry, Father,' I said. 'I swear to Allah, it is allowed for me to show my eyes, even my face. Look, I am not even a Saudi.'

My mother pinched me for saying this. My father sat on my bed and lowered his head. He stood up and left the room. My mother followed him. After a while, he came back and sat next to me.

It had been a deliberate strategy to mention the thing about not being a Saudi. That's when he becomes nicer. He held my hand and said, 'I am a second-generation Eritrean and they still won't consider me a Saudi. Look, I don't need a citizenship document to make me feel Saudi. I am one. And don't listen to the girls at your college, when they call you a foreigner. You are a Saudi.'

I asked him the same question again, 'Can I show my eyes, please Father?'

He quickly answered saying, 'No, you might think you are not a Saudi, but hell doesn't differentiate.'

He went back to his room and his shisha.

Yesterday, after my argument with my father, my mother tried to make me feel better by saying that women with eyes as beautiful as mine do better to be veiled. I went into my room and locked the door.

I thought about you.

I took a blank piece of paper and a box of coloured pencils out of my drawer and put them on the bed. I took your drawing from inside my bra and put it on the bed too.

Then I stripped off my clothes and stood naked in front of the long wall mirror. I examined my body, from toe to head. To draw a very honest self-portrait, I decided to take an exact reading of my body, with all its birthmarks, spots, unhealed wounds, finger scratches, beauty spots, curves, and the length and width of every bit of me. I even wanted to study my behind very carefully. But as I turned around, my hair blocked my sight, so I pulled it up and tied it together.

But when it was finished, I decided not to send it to you, because I remembered my vow to bring myself to you. I will keep the drawing and will only send it if I fail to deliver on my promise.

Tell me that things go better with you.

Your Fiore

The next morning, I went to the imam's house carrying a letter that told Fiore of my urge to see her and be close to her, my hope that one day I would see her take a shower, so I could watch the water dripping over her body like the Niagara Falls. I asked her if we could find a way to meet or at least somehow find a way to talk. I was ready to do anything to hear her voice.

At the imam's house I found Basil in the living room browsing the bookshelf. He was holding a long thin stick. I wanted to confront him and ask him what he was up to. But there was a lump in my throat and I didn't dare say anything.

I sat on the floor mat, watching him in silence.

He selected a book and started reading; it was as if I wasn't there.

I wanted to leave, run before it was too late, but I tried to concentrate on him and pick up any clues. But he didn't say anything else. He just closed the book and shouted to the imam in the other room that he was leaving and would see him later in the evening.

Basil was killing me slowly. When he smiled, it was as if every tooth was a bullet he was firing at me. Every time we met, he created new holes in my body. I was being drained of everything that made me live, and Basil was watching me vanish with that smile on his face.

When I was about to leave his house that afternoon, the imam asked me to stay again because he wanted me to take him to see his friend, a sheikh who lived on the way to old Jeddah, after he'd taken a nap. I had already taken the letter from Fiore out of his bag. I was still thinking about my encounter with Basil early that morning and I wanted to be in my room by myself with Fiore's letters. I had no choice but to obey.

When the imam lay on the mat and his soft snoring assured me he was fast asleep, I started reading her letter.

Habibi,

I feel so sad. Sadness, which has been knocking on my door for a long time, has finally burst inside and inhabited me last night. Normally, I would stay up most of the night re-reading your letters, but tonight I will be in my bed with my eyes closed, giving myself up to the

illness of sorrow and loneliness. I wish you were here
next to me. Anyway, I am sorry this is a short letter,
but my hands don't have the energy to write much more,
my darling.

    Salam from the heart.

I brought her letter close to my lips and kissed it, not knowing what else to do with all the sadness of Fiore in my hands. I had the urge to avenge *habibati*, to burn everything and everyone who stood between me and her. But I could do nothing. I felt useless and angry with myself. *Habibati* was hurting yet there was nothing I could do. What was the use of words written over half a page offering heartfelt support if all she needed was someone to be there next to her, to listen to her and to give her a hug.

Tuesday morning, my mind was preoccupied with Fiore's sadness. I went to the imam's house with a letter to try to console her. I slipped my letter inside the black leather bag and we set off to the college as normal.

As I helped the imam through the gate, I could see Fiore's gloved hand stretching to receive his cane. I wanted to touch her again, but she withdrew her hand quickly. I put the black bag under the imam's arm. But he banged himself accidentally against the door and the bag fell to the floor. 'Please, Naser, get the bag,' he ordered. I knelt, expecting her to take the opportunity and stoop too. She didn't. She stayed hidden.

I felt like crossing the gate to take her hand and run away with her. A voice inside my head kept encouraging me: 'The door is opened. It is not an electric gate. It is not wired or booby-trapped. It is not manned with armed soldiers ready with their bullets to empty them in your chest. What is it you are afraid of? It is just a gate and behind it is your sad Fiore. Hold her hand and run with her.'

But I looked at the imam. Even though his eyes stared at an undefined point in the distance, and I knew they were not of use to him, I still feared that he would know if I broke the rules. It could mean I would hold Fiore once and then never again. So all I did was put the bag on the other side of the door and scuttle home.

Two weeks had passed since her last note, and Fiore still hadn't sent me a letter. My last proper letter had been the one where I admitted my deep-seated desires, but I had passed her a few short love notes via the imam's bag, asking her to write back soon. Even though I couldn't be sure, I could only hope it was she who stood behind the black gate receiving the imam. When I opened the black bag I found nothing from her, but still my notes were gone.

I was in the dark as to what was going on. The gate at her college seemed to grow higher and wider every time I delivered the imam, and the men standing around in the street seemed to have got bigger and more aggressive. The Pink Shoes had disappeared from Al-Nuzla.

I was waking up in the mornings with a heavy heart. I began to feel angry with her. She doesn't care, I started to think. If she did she would have written to me at least once just to say she was OK. If she loved me she would know I would be worried about her.

Tuesday, 17th October, a month after Fiore had last written to me with her sad note, turned out to be my last day at the mosque.

There was a cool breeze blowing that evening; the leaves and litter shifted softly from one side of the pavement to the other.

When I arrived, I found the imam sitting cross-legged talking to the group. There were many new faces. The Afghan veteran had moved to Riyadh, and Abdu had left the mosque and gone back to his friends in the street. He said he had had enough of the imam, and he missed playing football, listening to music and watching TV, all of which the imam and Basil had ruled were *haram*.

I greeted the group, kissed the imam on his forehead and sat to his right.

Moments after I sat down, a man came rushing in. I had seen him before with the imam. He was an old disciple of the sheikh and worked at the Emergency Unit at King Fahd Hospital. He greeted all of us, knelt behind the imam, and started whispering into his ear. The imam got up. He put his hand on the man's shoulder and they both walked to the far corner of the mosque. The man was gesticulating as he talked to the imam and looking increasingly agitated.

Moments later, the blind imam was led back. The hospital worker excused himself and he disappeared at the same speed as he had arrived. The imam sat, crossed his legs and coughed. Everyone hushed. He told us that another life had just ended tragically. He swayed his head side to side, saying, 'Because, yet again, one of our precious children has chosen the path to hell instead of heaven. This boy had a car accident. His car crashed into the bottom of the bridge and it was smashed to pieces. But the fire brigade, may *Allah* bless their work, managed to get him out. And when they heard the car's tape playing a song, they shattered it to pieces. They tended to the boy whose soul was about to depart. One of the para-medics held the boy's hand and asked him to intone the *shahada.* "Son, you are dying, say, there is no *Allah* but *Allah* and I testify that Muhammad is the messenger of *Allah*." But no, the boy remained mute. The paramedic urged him again, "Say it. It is your passport to heaven." But his mouth refused to utter the blessed words, and he started singing the song that he was just listening to instead.'

He paused and lowered his head and continued, 'You know why he couldn't intone the *shahada*? Because it is *haram* to listen to music and it is forbidden to replace reading the Qur'an with listening to music. But *Allah* punished this boy for refusing to heed his call. And because of this, this boy's path is hell.' He thundered the words three more times: 'hell, hell, hell.'

Listening to the imam, I felt a low headache starting at the back of my head, just like the time I first left his mosque all those years ago, when I was fourteen. As the story went on, the pain got stronger, and the imam's words were pounding between my eyes. They repeated themselves in my head, over and over again. I wished I could put my hands over my ears to shut out the words of fear and revenge, of hell and Satan.

I closed my eyes. 'Why am I going through this?' I asked myself.

But then, and for the first time since she had stopped writing to me, I confronted myself with the truth that I didn't want to face. Maybe, I thought, she had found another boy and was now starting to exchange notes with him. Or, if that wasn't the reason, maybe she converted to the right path and was now repenting that she ever had anything to do with a bad Muslim like me. Or maybe she saw there was no way of continuing. Writing love letters via the love courier was as far as we could go. 'And for how long are we meant to go on writing like this?' I asked myself. 'It only makes us want to see each other, and there is no chance of that ever happening.'

I was back to the doubts and questions and the ifs and buts that had almost driven me crazy at the beginning of our love story. I didn't want to go through all that again. 'I should have known. What good could have come of this anyway?' I wondered, trying to force myself to accept that I might have lost her for ever. 'That's it, Naser. It is over.'

Slowly I stood up, in a sweat, and stepped out of the circle of boys, vowing never to step a foot in the mosque again.

What had happened to Fiore that had made her desert me? I didn't understand. I had become a *mutawwa* for her, and we had both risked everything to come together. And now she had gone as quickly as she had arrived. She had disappeared back into her concealed world. Jasim's friend Omar had been right, I was just a rich girl's plaything and now she had found someone else to torment.

I would try my best to forget her.

I STAYED AT home for nearly two weeks after leaving the mosque. It was in the seclusion of my room that I tried to grieve for Fiore. But I had very little to remind me of her. I hadn't seen her face, or even her eyes. I hadn't even felt her skin, or stroked her hair. Her body remained a mystery to me hidden behind her veil.

All I had seen was that inch of skin; the scar on her dark ankle. But above all, it was the Pink Shoes that kept flashing in my mind. They were what I kept watching for during our entire adventure.

I remembered her deep pink shoes as a rejected lover remembers his loved one's face. I remembered the small pattern of glittering pearls on the sides of her shoes, as if they were the earrings in her ears, the necklace around her neck, or the glittering belt around her dark hips. I remembered the pink colour as if it was the colour of her favourite lipstick, her bra and underwear. I remembered how the first time the black and white set of Al-Nuzla Street was interrupted by her shoes, she looked like a pink flamingo. For many of the days that followed all I wanted to do was shout to the men of Al-Nuzla that this woman with the Pink Shoes was my girl. With every step she tied my heart to her shoes that bit tighter. Without them my heart could not survive.

Maybe it was my fault that she deserted me. Maybe I should have gone further in my letters. I couldn't remember whether I ever told her how fond I was of her Pink Shoes. And I certainly couldn't recall ever suggesting that we both run away. Maybe she was waiting for me to take her by the arm and run with her from this black and white movie.

I wanted to ask her for another chance. I felt like standing outside her building to show her how much she meant to me. But Basil's constant patrolling of Al-Nuzla Street with his band of religious policemen put an end to that dream.

I must be condemned to live a lonely life, my only company being the memories of those I loved. Everything that was beautiful lay in my past: my mother, my brother, and now Fiore. I even grieved for the friendship I had lost with Yahya and Hani.

PART EIGHT

A SCENE FROM EGYPT

I FINALLY EMERGED from my room one night in early November. I went to the Corniche. I was still wearing the Islamic dress that I had been wearing to the mosque, the same short *thobe* with the deep side pockets in which I had hidden Fiore's letters.

The Corniche was full of young men. It was as if the Red Sea was the Mecca for lost lovers and they had all made their pilgrimage this night.

Everyone was staring out to sea, which was quietly listening to all who sought relief from loneliness.

As I stepped down to my secret rock, I saw the Saudi lover playing his *'oud*. I admired him for managing to look his best even though everything he used to demonstrate his love was decaying: his *'oud* sounded as if the strings had rusted and his deep voice was cracking. His words were disjointed and he was struggling to connect the lyrics together. His voice couldn't hide the breaking of his heart. His words brought tears to my eyes:

My love, my days are numbered now that my voice
    is deserting me.
I will never stare at the sea in silence.
If I can't sing to you what I feel inside my heart
    then life has no use for me.
Oh, *habibati*, the end is near.

A FEW DAYS later, I had taken off my *thobe* and *gutra* and gone back to wearing my usual shirt and trousers. I was starting to go back to my normal life. I asked Hilal if I could go back to my old job at the car-wash. 'That job is gone,' Hilal said, 'it is your fault you left it in the first place. There are so many foreigners coming into the country and they're all prepared to work for a pittance.'

But he promised he would help me look for a new job. Within the hour, he had called me back asking if I could cover for one of the Indian boys at another car-wash just fifteen minutes' walk from my old job. 'One of their men is sick,' Hilal said, 'but it might not be for long.'

Jasim had finally returned from his long trip with his *kafeel*.

That evening I went to meet him at his café. The café's tables, which lined the pavement and overlooked the small roundabout and the shoe shops across from it, were covered with new yellow plastic cloths. The terrace was packed, and the two men sitting at the table immediately to my left were playing dominoes.

The waiter smiled at me and gestured with his eyes to Fawwaz sitting at the other side of the small terrace. I understood that Fawwaz was still not married and that they were still lovers.

Jasim was sitting at a table outside, buried under the smoke of *shisha* leaving his mouth and those around him.

He hugged me and I hugged him back tightly. I just

wouldn't let go. I knew I wasn't my real self when I heard his whisper: 'Ya Allah, Naser, you never hugged me like this before. Never. Does that mean you finally . . .'

I pulled back and said, 'I am just very happy to see you.'

'Can I offer you dinner? I want to tell you about my holiday. I have lots of news.'

'Yes, I would like that,' I replied.

'Let's leave then,' he said.

'OK.'

He held my hand and squeezed it, but I pulled away.

I called Hani and Yahya to tell them that I had left the mosque. But they refused to talk to me and Yahya even threatened me should I ever call him again.

So I was surprised when one evening there was a knocking on my door and I opened it to find both of my friends standing there. 'I am so happy you are here,' I said.

'Let's go to the Pleasure Palace,' said Yahya. 'You have a lot of explaining to do.'

At the Pleasure Palace, they fired off hundreds of questions to find out why I had become the guide of the radical imam. But I just kept repeating that I wasn't the only one and certainly wouldn't be the last one to join the mutawwa'in and then leave.

'Just like that?' asked Yahya.

'Yes,' I replied. 'Look what happened to Abdu.'

'Who is Abdu?' asked Yahya.

I explained how he had wanted to be the imam's guide, but had then thought better of it and joined the football club instead. Hani nodded in agreement. 'In fact Al-Yamani keeps joining and leaving the mutawwa'in in Mecca Street.'

'Anyway,' Yahya said, 'I am happy to have you back to

normal again. But never let that imam change you again. You hear me?'

If you only knew why I did all this, I thought to myself.

We sniffed glue and Hani and Yahya started talking about our friends Faisal and Zib Al-Ard who were still fighting in Afghanistan. There had been no news of their death so we assumed they were still alive.

'I miss them,' Yahya said.

'I wish there had never been a war,' Hani said. 'Our friends would still be here with us.'

How many times I had wished there wasn't a war in my country. I would never have needed to leave my mother and Semira behind. Tears welled up in my eyes as I thought about how much I missed them.

Fiore was always there. Her smell had seeped out of her letters and conquered the walls of my room. I was colonised by her memory. I couldn't sleep. I couldn't eat. I feared I was going mad. I had to talk to someone to save my sanity. I thought of Hilal. I didn't think he would betray me. He was the only person I knew of who lived his life for one person only – his wife.

And when I finally told him about Fiore he looked at me for a while with his eyes and his mouth wide opened. Then he embraced me and warmly kissed me on my cheeks, saying, 'Now I believe in miracles. Love is a supernatural force, like the moon, the sun, or gravity and no man will be able to stop it, no matter how strong or brutal he is.'

★

But while I was trying to pull my life back together, Basil kept creeping up on me.

Three weeks after I had left the mosque, as I was outside the garage washing a car belonging to one of the local grocery shop keepers, I heard the sound of a familiar engine approaching. I stopped washing the car and looked up behind me. The Jeep parked just yards away with its engine still running.

I pretended to continue scrubbing the bumpers, my hands trembling badly. I looked behind me and saw the Jeep's front lights flashing on and off. I decided to ignore it and carry on with my job.

I kept glancing back to the Jeep, but nothing happened except the revs of the engine increasing slowly. I was wiping the same spot over and over again, when I heard the Jeep approach and finally halt behind me. There were a few seconds of silence and I had no idea what to do. I just stood there looking at the big car, not knowing what was going on behind its shaded windscreen.

Then Basil opened the door of his Jeep and ordered me to wipe his windscreen. 'We are in a hurry,' he said before slamming the door shut again. Without looking at the Jeep, I soaked my cloth in the soapy water and stretched out to wipe the shaded windscreen with it.

I was about to rinse the cloth when I saw the blackened window of the Jeep being scrolled down slowly. Basil leaned out and looked at me silently. He followed me with his eyes throughout the cleaning job. When I finished, he asked me, 'Why did you leave the mosque and the blessed imam, *ya* apostate?'

I didn't respond.

'No one disobeys the imam and gets away with it,' he said. He drove off without paying.

*

I was back to my old world without her watching over me. Wherever she might be: in the street, at her window, on the bus, or in her father's car, I had to accept she was no longer looking for me. If she still loved me, she could have followed me, if she wanted to, as I went about my daily activities: walking down Al-Nuzla; going into any one of the dozens of shops in the neighbourhood; drinking tea at the Blue Café, just after the roundabout and behind the big supermarket. She could have seen me when I was playing football with my friends up the road in Al-Nuzla in the big space in front of the factory; or sitting under my tree, where she dropped her first note. She would have seen me walking the streets with my head down, looking at all the women's feet, searching for her Pink Shoes, just in case.

My short job at the car-wash finished when the Indian worker got better, and I begged Hilal to find me another one. I just wanted to forget the summer and keep myself busy. He said he would keep an ear out.

One evening Hilal and I took the bus to the Corniche for a drink. As we sat drinking freshly squeezed juice in a café overlooking the Red Sea, he told me that he had been thinking about me and Fiore, and that he wished I had told him about her before she disappeared. 'Naser,' he said, 'had I known about this, I would have taken you both to a special place where you could have been alone, where you could be with her and talk to each other without fear of her father or the religious police.' After a pause, he added mysteriously, 'It is a secret spot at the other end of the Corniche. Anyway, let's walk now, I want to tell you about this place without anyone listening to our conversation.'

★

One evening, I was standing with Hani, across the road from my house. I was holding the Pepsi can so that Hani could pour more glue into it. He was dressed, as always, in a tracksuit and T-shirt; even though he was a Saudi, he hated *thobes*.

I sniffed the glue and then I took another look at the boy sitting on the hood of his car, Hani's cousin. His name was Fahd and he was visiting from Riyadh. I was examining his clothes: a green shirt, yellow-striped black trousers, white trainers and black sunglasses.

'What? Why are you smiling?' Hani asked me. He saw me looking. 'His clothes, right?' he asked, pointing to his cousin.

I nodded.

'I told you not to be a fashion rebel!' Hani screamed at Fahd. 'At least drop the shades. It's night-time, for *Allah's* sake.'

'I am not going to let a boy from Jeddah tell me what to wear,' retorted Fahd. 'I am from the capital, my friend.'

Hani bent double, laughing. He added, 'Are you telling me you Bedouins dress better than us in Jeddah? Naser, are you listening to this?'

I was, but for different reasons. I asked Fahd if in Riyadh he had ever come across a boy called Ibrahim who lived with his uncle Abdu-Nur.

But Hani interrupted saying, 'I am sorry, Naser. I already asked him. He doesn't know. The world sometimes is not as small as they say it is.'

'Never mind,' I said. 'Anyway, why don't we go to the Pleasure Palace? Who are we waiting for?'

'Yahya,' replied Hani.

'Where is he?' I asked.

'Guys, look. Look.' Hani almost wailed the words.

A few buildings away, we saw a woman entering a house. She came back out and went to a nearby van to collect some luggage and small boxes. The breeze blew her hair about. We looked at each other in disbelief. The only quivering hair that we were used to seeing around Al-Nuzla was that of men's long beards.

She was wearing tight jeans, and her high heels stabbed the street like knives.

We approached her, moving shoulder to shoulder.

'She is cutting me to pieces,' Hani said, whispering.

'You see, guys. Don't you regret that you're not dressed up?' Fahd took off his black sunglasses only to replace them with another pair, this time with gold designs round the edges. 'Better to be ready than sorry. Even if it is for a once in a lifetime opportunity. Now who is the fool?'

Hani was dreaming. 'I wish I was an endless street for that woman to walk up and down all day long.'

The woman noticed us. A man came out of the building and took the bags from her hands and hurried inside again. She walked towards us.

I looked at Fahd and sweat was falling down his face. He took my hand and squeezed it firmly.

'What are you doing?' I asked Fahd.

'She is coming towards us. Slowly. She is taking for ever to get here.'

'Can't you speak softer? Anyway, that's the way some women walk. One step at a time.'

'How would you know?' he snapped.

'I grew up surrounded by women.'

'Good afternoon, gentlemen,' the woman said to us. 'I'm Nahid. My husband and I are just moving in.' She pointed to the building behind her.

I recognised the accent. She was Egyptian.

'A woman is speaking to us? Oh *ya Allah!*' Hani cried, as he turned to her and fell down to his knees. 'Oh please don't ever wear the *abaya*.'

Fahd shook his head and barked at Hani, 'Look at you; I have never ever seen you pray. Not even once. Don't you know that only to *Allah* we bow and submit ourselves? Get up.'

She laughed and said, smiling, 'Maybe I'll see you soon, guys.' Fahd and Hani looked at each other and Hani said, 'Maybe you will see us but we won't see you. Next time, you will be covered.' They shook their heads.

She walked away. Our eyes rolled with her hips, as she walked back to the entrance of her new home. The door slammed shut, and we were denied another moment's sight of her hair, her jeans, her swaying hips, her long neck. We were back in the blind world of men.

I got into the front seat of Hani's car, with Fahd in the back. 'Hold this,' Hani said, giving me the Pepsi can, and he put on a tape of an Egyptian singer. 'Let's be silent. I want to dedicate this song to the Egyptian woman,' he said. 'I can still see her walk with her high heels, throwing her hips to the mercy of the wind.'

Fahd laughed and said, 'Just drive. You will die from frustration. Miracles stopped happening here.'

He was just about to pull out, when I glanced in the side mirror and noticed a pair of shoes. My hand shook and I dropped the Pepsi can.

I opened the door and looked again at the shoes. The Pink Shoes. I almost lost my balance as I left the seat.

'Naser, what's wrong?' asked Hani.

'I am fine,' I stuttered. 'Wait for me at the Pleasure Palace, I'll catch up with you there.'

'Oh come on. Where are you going now?' Hani asked me.

'I'll see you in a minute,' I said firmly.

They drove off. My eyes were still on the shoes. Was this really Fiore? The woman who had deserted me? Or was this some sort of trick? I looked up and her gloved hand was beckoning me. I hurried towards her. She turned back and went down a side street. We took a long walk down Helm Street. We passed the grocery shop, a restaurant, the Afghan bakery and the Pakistani electricity shop. She crossed the street to avoid a small café where men were congregating outside. She turned right into a narrow street, and as I followed her I let out a cry of recognition. We were back in Ba'da Al-Nuzla. She had taken a different route to the one I made in the days when I used to pick up her notes by the rubbish bin. But surely this had to be Fiore?

There were a few boys playing football. This was the place where the street turned narrower; we were reaching the dead end. She ducked into an old doorway, set back from the street. I caught up with her.

There was no one around. I had to speak.

'*Habibati?* It is you, right? How are you? Where have you been? Why didn't you explain? Just one note would have been enough for me.'

She stood motionless.

'Fiore, I missed you so much,' I whispered. 'All I want is a small touch, all you need to do is walk out of here and bump into me by mistake. We are human, we all make mistakes. I want to smell you and touch you. I want to hear your voice. I want to know that you're real.'

She stepped out of the doorway. Her silky *abaya* brushed my hand, electrifying the nerves of my whole body.

She turned her back and walked away fast, disappearing down the dark street. I stood watching her go. I couldn't move. There was a piece of crumpled paper at my feet.

I bent down and opened the note.

Then I buried my face in my hands and wept.

Habibi,

One day, a year ago, our Arabic literature teacher asked us to write the story of our life. She said it had to be five pages. I wrote: 'I am the daughter of a second-generation Eritrean man and a fifth-generation Egyptian woman.'

The teacher called me aside and said, 'My dear, you are the best student in this college. I was expecting more than this. I wanted five pages, not ten words. Is everything OK with you?'

I replied, 'I have no problems, but this is my life story. That's all I have to say.'

'What's wrong with you?' she asked.

'I will not write my life story until I have a life that I have made,' I answered.

The day I finally had the courage to approach you, I felt as if I was just starting to build my own life. But that was also the day everything began to fall apart. My father brought home a friend of his and I was introduced to him as his future wife. What happened after that is a long story. Ever since I wrote you my last letter via the imam, I have been battling against my father and this proposed marriage. I have starved myself these past few weeks and I have made myself a nuisance, I have said things that are not expected of a polite woman so that the proposed man and his family are scared of me. I have told them I have plenty of ambitions of my own, that I want to go to a university and work and make money for myself. My father is furious but I think I may have won the battle. I swear to you no man will lay his hands on me except you. I swore this a long time ago and I am not the type of woman who breaks her oath. And I want to be close to you. I have now reached the point of no return and I need you to take the next step with me. I am ready to face the consequences of love.

Are you?

PART NINE

THE CONSEQUENCES OF LOVE

Habibi, you will be wearing Saudi clothes, and we will meet in the central Jeddah shopping mall by the fountain on the ground floor, and from there, we will leave as husband and wife to go to your secret place. You know how a married couple is expected to behave, I hope. We must not make a mistake. Even a small slip and that's it. So a reminder: always walk a yard or so ahead of me, don't even think about touching me, be calm, confident, and hold a string of Islamic prayer beads. I'll be wearing my Pink Shoes. Sorry about the shaky handwriting.

I got off the bus at the last stop, just five minutes from the shopping mall.

It was early evening and there was a soft breeze. I could see the mall up ahead, imposing and dressed with long lines of blinking light bulbs. Cars were queuing up behind one another on both sides of the road. I slid between two white Mercedes. But the traffic on the far side had started to move and a Jeep was speeding towards me. I instinctively pulled back and bumped into a pedestrian behind me. 'It's OK, son,' said the man, repositioning the *ogal* I had knocked out of place.

On a second try, I made it across the road.

I passed Punishment Square. Although I tried to stop myself looking, my gaze wandered over to the shiny white tiles where the executions took place. I remembered the story once told to me by Majid, a Saudi classmate in school. Before the start of our first class, the boy had whispered that he wanted to tell us a story about Abu Faisal and the innocent man. In the lunch break, we all, including Faisal himself, gathered around him. The boy warned Faisal that the story reflected badly on his father. Faisal said it was OK, so the boy told his story. His brother and his friends had watched their Pakistani neighbour beheaded on the previous Friday for a murder he didn't commit. When Abu Faisal had cut off the man's head, and the guards had snatched the sword away from his hands, our friend told us that the blood dripping from the tip of the sword marked the words 'I am innocent' on the white floor tiles. At that point, our classmate's brother and all his friends were yelling: 'Look. He is innocent!' while the rest of the crowd screamed, '*Allah wa Akbar, Allah wa Akbar.*' Majid's brother and his friends had renamed their street 'I Am Innocent Street' because of what they had seen.

After Majid told the story, I found Faisal weeping in a corner. He cried because his father had killed an innocent man. He cried throughout the break and didn't stop even when the Arabic literature lesson started. Faisal was lucky it was the Arabic literature teacher who found him crying, because he was the nicest teacher in school. When we told him why the tears on Faisal's face wouldn't stop, he held his hand and said that it was good that Faisal was different from his father.

I pushed on and walked into the shopping mall. Everything glowed. The reflection of the lights on the gold in the jewellery shop windows became a stark yellow light in the corridor. Voices beamed out too, even though it was less crowded than outside the mall.

I walked to the centre of the mall, sat by the fountain and waited.

A woman walked towards me. I stood up immediately. But I sat down as soon as I realised she was following a man wearing a *thobe* without a headscarf. Boys holding hands strode past; they were laughing loudly, chewing gum, and looking confident.

Men and women were coming and going. A woman was standing to my left and another to my right. 'Which one is Fiore?' I asked myself.

The mall was filled with mirrors, and the number of black *abayas* was multiplying as more people came inside the shopping mall and their shapes were reflected back at me.

After a while, a woman came and sat down next to me. Sweat stood out on my forehead. I couldn't move. My hands were stuck to my prayer beads. I wanted to turn my head towards her but I hesitated. Was she supposed to make the first move? Or was I? I couldn't remember. Just then a man came out of the shop opposite to where I was sitting and came towards me hurling insults: 'What kind of a man are you sitting next to my wife? Don't you have any shame? Didn't they teach you to get up when a woman sits next to you? Move, and may *Allah* guide you to his straight path.'

I stood up and went to look in the window of a jewellery shop. I looked back to see if there was any space at the fountain. Nothing. As I turned back to look at the gold necklaces on the display busts, and the diamond earrings next to them, I caught a glimpse of two religious policemen reflected in the window. They walked with their hands behind their backs, their sticks tucked under their arms and their heads turning from side to side as if they were machines.

When I looked back I saw that there was now enough empty space in the seats by the fountain. I hurried to recover my place and sat facing the mall entrance. There were the Pink Shoes. Fiore was walking at ease, so slow that I started to think that the distance between us was growing with each step rather than lessening. My eyes took her in, from her shoes right up to her head. For the first time, I felt that she was my girl and I was her boy. 'Ya Allah,' I whispered as she sat to my right.

I couldn't turn and look at her. My wide eyes stared stubbornly at the space in front of me.

'Naser?'

No, I thought, you didn't hear that.

'Naser?'

I had lived in this country for ten years and I couldn't remember the last time a woman had spoken my name. Her voice was soft and low, with every sound so clear, so melodious.

'Habibi, please keep calm. It's me. Concentrate.'

Silence.

'Naser, habibi, stop shaking. I am here now. Where I want to be, where you want me to be. Next to you.'

She breathed in. I heard it. Then she exhaled. I felt her breath pass over my face. I drew the deepest breath I had ever taken and held on to it.

'Naser, wipe your face or you will attract attention and this will all be over before it has even begun.'

A tissue landed on my lap.

'Habibi, please, I beg you, hurry, I want to be with you for ever, not for a few seconds. Wipe away your sweat. Yallah.'

I picked up the tissue and for the first time I could smell her scent. 'Habibi.'

Again, 'Habibi.'

And again, impatiently, 'Habibi.'

I folded the tissue and put it in my pocket. I wiped my face with the sleeve of my thobe.

'Listen to me, Naser, if you calm down, we will be all right. Let's go, my love. But remember we have to play the couple.'

I didn't react. She quickly pinched me on my thigh. 'See, I am real, now get up and let's go. Where do we go to get the bus?'

I got up. She remained seated by the fountain. I sat back down.

'What are you doing?' she hissed.

'Waiting for you.'

'Sweetheart, you should know by now. The religious policemen are around, so I need to walk behind you. You think I like this? When we get to the Corniche, we can walk side by side. Now, go, go, I will follow you.'

As I pulled open the exit door another pair of religious policemen were coming through. I gave way to them.

I walked a few yards in front of her. I looked back twice, but each time she frantically waved her hand, making it clear that I shouldn't. We passed Punishment Square, and then walked between the sports shops. A crowd of young men were coming towards us. They were followed by an equally large number of women dressed in black. Fiore and I lost each other momentarily. I looked down for the Pink Shoes. They were there.

We reached the bus stop. I went and stood at the front of the line, she stayed at the back. The bus came minutes later. I got on at the men's section and she went in the women's entrance.

I sat as close to the back of the section as I could. We were separated by the full-length panel. I looked through the tiny window and saw four women standing. I wished I could have seen their shoes. I leaned back and took out the tissue she had given me and covered my face with it.

HOW COULD LIFE suddenly be this beautiful? Fiore was now just in front of me, leaving a trail of pink steps along Jeddah's Corniche. 'When a woman walks,' the Eritrean poet in the camp once said, 'the earth walks with her.' Only now did I understand what he meant. It was as if she had walked away with the earth, leaving me floating without gravity. I watched where she put her feet and trod on exactly the same stones that her shoes stepped on.

The Corniche was brimming with life. We walked down the pavement past the amusement park, which also had separate sections for men and women. There were people picnicking, kids running around, and at the edge of the pavement next to a big bench there was a group of men sitting in a circle playing cards. I took the steps down from the pavement to the sand. A young boy riding a pony was speeding towards me. I stepped aside. Fiore was only now making her way down the steps. Three camels hobbled past, bearing children as their passengers.

The light was getting dim when we arrived at my private rock. But we couldn't sit there. It would have aroused too much suspicion. Fiore stood still and took a quick look around before walking up the stairs and back to the pavement.

I stayed behind for a bit. I looked over the water and blew a kiss to my mother before I made my way up the stairs.

I looked in both directions and found the Pink Shoes. I went towards Fiore, who was sitting by herself. Suddenly I stopped. The place where the 'oud player usually sat was empty. I knelt by the bench and touched it to see if I could feel his warmth. I looked towards the sea and whispered, crying silently, 'My dear singer, I am now here with my love. I will miss you but I hope your heart will never stop beating, even if you are now under the sea on its colourful bed.'

SHE WAS THE first to say something.

'*Habibi*, I wish I could take you in my arms.' She paused. We sat for a moment in silence. Then: 'Tell me, my sweetheart, why did you fall in love with me? For me, at least, it was love at first sight, but it is strange that you could fall in love with me.'

I didn't answer. The reality had struck me, as if up to that point I was dreaming. I was sitting next to a woman. Even after she had asked me her question and she was silent, her soft voice was echoing around me, filling my ears with beautiful sounds.

I looked out to the sea. I could hear the waves making their rolling noise, almost like singing; then a loud roar, as the waves climbed one on top of the other. A blackbird landed on the tip of a light post in front of us. It sat with opened wings, like a plane ready for departure ready to fly into the sky and pierce through the clouds.

One of Fiore's Pink Shoes nudged my right foot. I took my sandal off, I shut my eyes, and I caressed her Pink Shoe with my foot, my toes kissing the leather.

'Naser?'

I didn't respond.

Again, she called me, '*Habibi?*'

This time, I answered, 'Yes, darling.'

'Please tell me why is it that you fell in love with me without seeing me?'

I looked at the sea ahead of me and imagined myself

saying: 'Fiore, I read about people falling in love, the kind of love at first sight you talk about. I assume people feel this when they see their lovers' faces, look into their eyes, have seen the shape of their bodies, and heard their sweet words: their hearts make the decision there and then that this is it, this is love. But my feeling for you was love *before* first sight. I've wondered, at times, why this was. How was I falling in love with someone whose face I hadn't seen, whose words I hadn't heard, and whom I hadn't walked alongside? How come, I asked myself, I allowed a simple handwritten note to take control of my mind? I have no idea if you, Fiore, have the beauty I have read about in smuggled romantic novels, the type of gorgeousness that makes the heart bleed before you can find the right words to express its desire. I can't tell if your body, concealed underneath your *abaya*, is of the kind that would make even the greatest painters spend an eternity trying to capture its curves. And I didn't even hear you speak at first, there were no sounds to sink deep inside me. True, I sometimes thought you were just an illusion, the work of a hungry heart that forced me to fall in love with an imaginary person. But whenever I felt these doubts, I would take a look at your notes; your beautiful letters gave me courage.'

But I didn't say it. I wasn't sure whether it was the right thing to start talking about what was under her *abaya* just yet. So instead, I said to her: 'Fiore, my love for you is a love built on faith. The type of faith a believer shows to his Creator, the type of faith Prophets demanded that we show to our God. After all, when Prophet Muhammad came with the Qur'an, we had only his words to believe him, and we did. You dropped note after note and I read word after word, that is how it is. Words, my darling, are powerful. I answered your call and chose to become your lover.'

I turned to look at her. All I could see next to me was the outline of a woman, a dark shadow next to me on the bench. When I listened carefully I could hear her breathing.

We both remained silent for a while.

'Fiore?'

'Yes, *habibi*.'

She repeated the words once more: 'Yes, *habibi*.'

'All this time, I have done what you asked me to do. I have followed you like a faithful disciple. I have given you the most precious thing that I have, now that I am all alone in this world. I have entrusted you with my heart.'

'*Habibi*, I swear I will do whatever you ask of me, unconditionally,' she said.

'I want to see your face.'

'Here?'

'No. It is too busy here. I have heard of a place where we can look at each other for as long as we want without anyone interrupting us.'

'Where is it? It must be across the sea,' she mocked.

I wanted to take her to the place that Hilal had told me about. It was one of those very well hidden secret places that Jeddah was full of: like the Pleasure Palace, it was out of the reach and sight of the religious police, and all things *haram* could take place there without punishment. It was on the furthest possible spot on Jeddah's long Corniche, almost outside the city. It wasn't really a place where locals would go.

'No, it is in this city,' I said to Fiore. 'Can you leave your house for an entire afternoon?'

Later that night, I went to Hilal. I told him that I needed to take Fiore on a date to the secret place on the Corniche.

He agreed to help me, but made me swear not to tell any of my friends, as he was sure the place would be closed down if all of a sudden locals started going there.

Hilal couldn't drive because of his bad leg, but he said he would get in touch with a trusted friend – a vendor who worked near the Corniche. 'He always drives me there,' Hilal said. 'I could have found him a better job but he insisted on street selling because he wanted to be his own boss and work by the Red Sea.'

THE NEXT DAY the vendor was waiting by his handcart. I greeted him. He put his cart aside and asked me to follow him to his taxi. The car was covered with dust. He used his *gutra* to wipe the window and asked us to get in. I sat in the front seat, and Fiore got in the back.

We drove for a long time down an old, bumpy road that hugged the coastline. It was hard to believe we were still in Jeddah. To the left was the Red Sea and to the right, apart from the occasional birds flying over the desert, there were only dry bushes. Little dunes had built up in the potholes, swept in by the wind.

The driver veered on to an even rougher road. The car started jumping up and down, throwing up dust. We hit a hole and the car's underside made a shrieking noise. The driver stopped and got out of the car, mumbling a prayer to *Allah*. I closed my eyes, drew a deep breath and opened them again. The dust around the car had settled. I looked in the rearview mirror and knew that Fiore was staring at me but all I could see was the shape of a long nose through her veil.

We stayed like this for a long time. The driver eventually got back in and drove on, aligning the car's wheels to avoid the holes as big as moon craters. We might as well have been on the moon since hardly anyone living in Jeddah could go to where we were heading now.

The driver fought with his jammed gear. The car slowed down, but only for a moment. It started speeding up again.

We passed a two-storey villa. A Land Rover was parked outside and a foreign white woman appeared on the balcony. She was wearing a bikini and had a towel around her waist. Ahead of us there were two little white girls and a boy playing football. The driver beeped his horn, lowered his window and stuck out his hand in a thank-you gesture, with his eyes staring straight ahead. I turned my head and looked at Fiore. She was still looking straight ahead.

I looked to my left and saw a young woman, who had been lying flat on a towel, being helped up by a black man wearing skimpy trunks. She leaned forward to dust off the sand from her thighs and calves then they both ran together, down towards the sea.

The car slowed. The driver beeped his horn again. Three girls with sunglasses and swimming suits were strolling by. He stopped the car and looked across at me and grinned. We had arrived.

Ahead of us, there was a long broken wooden fence, stretching from the edge of the sea to a small wooden building in the distance. 'I will come back later in the evening,' he said.

I nodded and turned to Fiore. She had already jumped out of the car and was now running towards the broken fence, past the sign that read, STRICTLY WESTERNERS ONLY. I ran after her.

She stopped and grabbed the end of her long *abaya*, pulled it up above her knees, and sprinted towards the water's edge where the waves touched the white sand. She stumbled, then fell forward, kneeling in the water.

I stopped to watch.

She was still kneeling, looking out to sea. She got up, took off her shoes and put them neatly behind her, out of the way of the lapping waves.

Down the coast, I could see a white man in swim shorts diving into the water. His companion, a woman in a yellow bikini, clapped her hands and leapt after him, into the belly of the sea.

Fiore had her back to me when she removed her head cover. I held my breath. Her hair was tied up with a silver pin, which she took out while shaking her head. Her thick, black curly hair rolled down over her back. I staggered towards her.

She stood up, and let her *abaya* slide over her shoulders and drop at her feet in the sand.

I stopped walking. My heart was beating so fast.

'*Ya Allah*, *ya* great Creator,' I mumbled to myself. She was wearing a pink linen dress with short sleeves which fell just below her knees. The dress hugged her slim upper body tightly, and although it fell loosely down her back, it still showed the outline of her curved hips. It was the sweetest dress I had ever seen, and I imagined it had the most beautiful body underneath.

She turned around to face me.

'*YA ALLAH, YA* great Creator. *Ya Allah, ya* great Creator.'

There were still a few metres between us. Fiore was sinking deeper into the water and I was sucked in by the sand. Her long hair was flying in the wind in huge dark tangles.

'Fiore,' I whispered.

She gently touched my face and felt my dry lips. With her index finger she wiped my tears and used them to wet my mouth.

'*Habibi*, here I am, at last, for you. Don't let your tears veil me from your eyes. Stop crying. It is your turn to look at me now.'

First, I had to fend off everything that stood between me and her: the blinding sunlight, the wet sand and the wind whipping up her hair and hiding her face.

I spread her veil on the sand and we sat on it together. I turned so that my shadow shielded her from the sun. Then, carefully, I lifted her hair from her face, lock by lock, so that finally I could see her properly.

I was opening my eyes to the beauty of the world for the first time.

She didn't wear any make-up because she said she wanted me to see her natural without any added layers. 'No veil and no make-up,' she said, with a nervous laugh. Her skin was dark but lighter than mine. I lost myself in her brown eyes.

One of them was slightly smaller than the other, making her gaze feminine and fierce at the same time. Her nose arched elegantly over her face. Her mouth was slightly open, weighed down by her full lower lip, but she didn't say anything.

I wanted to bring a smile to her face. I pretended that I was drunk with her beauty and made myself like a fool and swayed my head sideways before gently placing it on her lap. I looked up. And there it was: a wide, generous, beautiful smile.

The front of her dress was closed with a long series of buttons, in the same pink fabric as her dress. The first three stood open, revealing the soft skin spanning her collarbone. I moved my hand over the buttons, and opened three more of them, revealing her white cotton bra. My hand touched her skin whenever I opened a button. I counted a hundred finger steps from her navel to the tip of her chin. I placed my head on her chest, and with my hand kept the dress from falling sideways. Her hair was hanging over her shoulders next to my face, and her arms were around mine. She knotted her legs around my thighs.

'Fiore?'

'Yes, *habibi*.'

'You know that drawing of me you told me about that you wear inside your bra?'

'Yes.'

'I think it is time I replaced it.'

As she breathed in, her chest rose towards the sky and her breasts, like a swell in the sea, softly caressed my face before they sank back down. She breathed deeper and again her breasts heaved against me, my head like a small boat, rising and falling on the tide of her chest. I had taken the place of the scrappy drawing, and my head now lay between her deep curves.

We stayed like that for hours.

Before the sun set, before the sea changed colour, before the Westerners left in their Land Rovers, before the vendor returned to pick us up and take us back to Al-Nuzla, she stood up and asked me to come with her.

I inhaled the hypnotising scent of jasmine she left behind her. She was kicking up the sand with her feet. We reached a steep sand dune overlooking the sea. She started to climb. I toiled behind her. She reached the top of the sand dune and faced the sea.

The wind blew. Each curl of her thick black hair twisted upward towards the sky like a thousand belly dancers in a slow groove.

She then turned around. As we both sank deeper and deeper into the crumbling sand, as our hands touched, her smile sparkled. And when the wind lifted up the sand and sprayed it over our heads like rain, and we lifted our arms in the air, our words echoed in each other's mouths: 'I love you, I love you, and I love you.'

It was time for the vendor to take us back to Al-Nuzla. Fiore was about to put on her *abaya*, but I urged her to wait. 'Please wait for a bit. The vendor is not here yet.'

We were still standing on the edge of the sea. We looked into each other's eyes without blinking. I told her that I hoped no day would pass without my head and her breasts meeting. We ripped the little drawing apart. And that's when she said, 'Naser, I have a plan.'

★

'*Habibi*, when I saw you walk in Al-Nuzla Street for only the second time, I was on my way to visit my friend in Al-Nuzla Al-Sharqyhya. You were wearing blue jeans and a white T-shirt. I admit I turned my head and followed you with my eyes. But it wasn't broad shoulders that brought a smile to my lips. It was your features. I was instantly attracted to your tender characteristics.' She paused. We were holding hands, facing the sea.

'Tell me, what is your plan, Fiore?'

'I want to take you home with me, I want you in my room and I want us to have all the privacy lovers need. Here's the plan. I want you to dress as a woman and arrive at the nine-storey building as if you were my best friend from school coming to study with me. You'll need an *abaya*, long gloves and a face veil, just leave the rest to me.'

'*Ya Allah*, you are crazy. What about your father?'

'We will meet in the women's section. After all, it was his idea to put the wall up between our section and his. And you don't need to worry about my mother. She will understand. She hasn't lost her belief in love.'

As she put on her veil, I looked away to the sea with my back to her. She wrapped her hands around me and put her head on my back. 'Naser, don't be sad,' she said, 'you will see me again soon. OK?'

I turned around and even though it felt strange to kiss a woman in *abaya*, I kissed her lips through her veil. 'OK. The vendor will be here any minute now.'

That same evening, I went to the shops near the roundabout in Al-Nuzla Street and bought a black robe, a long scarf, face veil, black gloves, knee socks and low black shoes.

I was just leaving the shoe shop when I bumped into

Basil. He stood motionless and, without a word, he stared at me and my large collection of bags.

I stepped back and almost dropped the bags. But I quickly gathered my composure. I had to act normal: the last thing I wanted was to give Basil a reason to smile all the way to Punishment Square with me and Fiore in the back of his Jeep.

We looked at each other in silence.

I had to walk past him to get to my house. As I side-stepped him, he held me by the arm. Without looking at me, he said, 'And just what are you up to, dear Naser?'

I wish I hadn't responded but I did. 'Don't exhaust your mind thinking how to get back at me,' I said. 'Just drop it and leave me alone. I am not going back to your imam's mosque.'

He let go of my hand, and turning around slowly he sniggered, saying, 'We'll see.'

As I walked home, I couldn't stop thinking about my encounter with Basil: 'What is he going to do? Did he see what was inside the bag? No. I am sure he didn't.'

I reminded myself of the very thing that made me defeat my fear and accept Fiore's proposal for love, that life is temporary. If anything happens to me now, I thought, I am happy because at least I know what love feels like.

I lay on the bed, hardly able to wait for the next day and my appointment with the most beautiful flower in the world.

IT WAS THURSDAY morning, mid-November and almost four months since Fiore's first note dropped into my life. I was sitting on my bed, my veil spread out next to me.

The previous day, when we were at the Corniche, Fiore had shown me how to put it on. But when I stood up in front of the mirror that morning, it was much harder to do without her helping hands. I pulled on the black robe, which wasn't too hard because it resembled the gold-edged cloak that men wore over their *thobes*. It was the head *hijab* that was more difficult. I struggled to fix the layers of cloth with the safety pins just above my ears. I was going to need more practice. I wondered what would happen if it came loose in the street. I pulled it from the other side just to check that it all stayed in place. It seemed fine, for now.

I pulled up the socks, fastened the sensible flat-heeled shoes and put on my gloves. Then, finally, I attached the piece of veil covering the rest of my face. At first I gasped for air. Whenever I breathed in, the veil would stick to my nose, making the flow of air stop. I realised I would have to breathe softer and slower if I didn't want to suffocate. That worked better.

I looked into the mirror. Nothing of Naser was visible any more; even my trouser bottoms had disappeared. Before we left the Corniche, Fiore had told me, 'Naser, you grew up with women. You have seen how they talk. And I know you've not forgotten how they move when they walk, and how they dress. *Habibi*, you could easily be mistaken for a girl if you dressed as one.' But this, I thought as I stared into the mirror, is not what the women on Lovers' Hill looked like.

I squinted through the peep-hole of my front door to check there was no one in the hallway. As agreed, I left my flat dressed in full burqa at two in the afternoon to go to Fiore's house. The street was empty. For so long I had sat under my palm tree and watched the black and white film unfold before my eyes. But I never imagined that one day I would take the part of one of those mysterious dark shadows myself. 'It is so strange,' I thought as I walked down Al-Nuzla Street, 'that I am now in a woman's world, when just an hour earlier I was in a man's world.' I could switch between roles, and play both white and black.

I began walking faster when I saw the woman in Pink Shoes. I had to tell myself not to run. I had a desperate urge to pick her up and swing her around in my arms.

'It is me, Naser,' I said as I came close to her.

'I missed you, Naser,' she said calmly as she turned around and hooked her arm into mine.

'No kiss on your cheeks?' I joked. 'Don't I look like a woman to you?'

She chuckled as I tickled her. 'Naser. Stop it. That's enough. Naser!'

'OK.' I let go.

'Let's get going,' she said.

She opened the front door of the building.

The air-conditioned hall was spacious and decorated with shining surfaces. Facing the entrance were three lifts. The walls and floors were laid with beautiful Moroccan tiles. She squeezed my hand. 'Are you OK?' she whispered, as we stood waiting to go up.

'I have never felt better,' I whispered.

The lift arrived with two children and their mother. '*Assalamu alaikum*,' Fiore greeted the woman.

'*Wa 'alaikumu salam*,' she replied.

Fiore pressed the number three. I shook my head. 'So it is from the third floor that you see everything happening down there?'

She laughed and stood in front of me. I put my gloved hands round her waist and pulled her towards me.

'This is the women's entrance to our house,' she said. 'And that,' she said, pointing to the one further down the corridor, 'is for the men. My father arranged it like this the same day he threw out the television.'

She opened the door. The smell of incense hit my nostrils. There was a long hallway. 'Follow me,' she said.

The corridor was almost empty apart from a Syrian vase on top of a black marble table and shoes lined up along one of the walls.

At the end of the hall there were three small steps that glided down to a curved mezzanine. 'This is my room,' she said, opening the white door. 'Stay inside, *habibi*,' she said. 'I need to talk to my mother but will come back soon.'

The room smelt like the rooms of the women on Lovers' Hill: the smell of wet towels hanging by the wardrobe, and the jasmine-scented bra and clothes on the chair. I wanted to take my veil off but I was worried that her parents might come in.

It was a large room. The desk was situated at the centre of the wall facing the door. To the left of the desk in the corner, there was another vase on top of another black table; next to it on the floor was a radio and cassette player. Her bed stood in the far left corner.

Starting to the right of the desk and going all the way around the adjoining wall making a large letter L, stood high shelves that almost touched the ceiling of the room. The shelves were full of books. I took a quick glance and all appeared to be on Islamic literature. I walked closer and browsed through one of the top shelves. I picked out a book by a radical sheikh from Riyadh. 'Why does Fiore have this book?' I asked myself. It was called *A Muslim Woman's Role in Today's Society*. But when I leafed through it, I chuckled. The inside of the book was not what its title said it was. It contained erotic art illustrations with figurative explanations on how each drawing was done. So that's why she says she is good at drawing, I thought. I put the book back, still smiling. Clever girl!

I kept browsing and found more books on other subjects, like art, African culture, and the history of the Middle East. I found books by Nawal El Saadawi. It was at the bottom row of the shelves that I stumbled upon a novel which I had heard about from Jasim but never managed to read. *The Children of Gebelaawi* by Naguib Mahfouz. According to Jasim, it was considered a blasphemy because people thought it depicted the relationship between God and His Prophets, and it had been banned.

I remembered that Fiore had explained in one of her letters that it was her Arabic literature teacher who had given her those books, after she had smuggled them into Saudi Arabia. 'It is easy for her, because she travels with her friend, who is the wife of one of the princes, and the customs officials don't search the royal family.'

Fiore came back wearing her *abaya*, but without her face veil. Her headscarf was still tightly wrapped around her head.

After she had closed the door behind her, she raised her eyes to me. *Ya Allah*, I thought. This is it. We are finally alone.

'*Habibi*, why are you still veiled? Let me help you take that off.' I could feel her trembling hands. 'I am nervous,' she said in a low voice.

'So am I,' I whispered.

I had spent what seemed like a lifetime thinking of her. In my mind, I had thought of a thousand ways to touch her. In my room, during lonely nights, I had imagined her lying naked in my arms and making the world twirl around me. But now that the dream had become a reality, we were both overwhelmed by the moment.

But our fears, like blocks of ice over our bodies, soon melted by our desire.

I stretched my hands towards her waist, and then laid them on her hips. I squeezed them softly. I pulled her closer to me. She didn't have time to take off her headscarf, because as soon as she threw my veil on the floor, her attention turned to my lips. I was gripped by her face. I looked at her in long, adoring silence, taking in her deep brown eyes, her beautiful lips and her shining skin.

We stood facing each other for a long while.

It seemed to take an eternity before our lips met, but when they did, we closed our eyes and resisted the urge to touch one another with our hands; that freedom we gave over to our tongues.

'*Habibi*, let me take off the rest of my veil,' she whispered, turning around.

I stepped back to treasure every second. She undid her headscarf. I put my hand on my chest as she unpinned her hair and watched it unravel to her shoulders at the same time as her black robe slipped to the floor. She didn't move. Her posture looked like the women on Lovers' Hill: straight, tall, curvy and elegant. It wasn't a dream, going back to my village of the past to imagine a woman, to bring back the beautiful Semira. This was real. I was in a woman's room in Jeddah and she was standing in front of me looking gorgeous and confident.

I remembered the pink dress she wore last time, and how it loosely fitted the curves of her body. Today, she was wearing a knee-length black cotton skirt which embraced her buttocks tightly and a black shirt of the same material.

'It is so hot outside,' she said. Still with her back to me, she added, 'Naser, can you close your eyes?'

I knew why she wanted me blind for the next few seconds. So I said, 'OK. I promise.'

But this was a promise worth breaking.

She grabbed the towel and knelt to wipe the perspiration from her face and the back of her neck. She put the towel on the side, bent slightly and slipped her hands under her skirt. The pink nails rolled a shining red garment down her dark thighs and long legs; and as she straightened her back, her underwear plunged to her ankles; the red underwear with flower drawings ringed her Pink Shoes. The flowers of Eden were at her feet.

The moment she looked around, I quickly shut my eyes.

I heard her giggle. I smelt her breath. I felt her soft hand on my face. A shiver of excitement rolled down my belly when the tip of her wet lips tickled the loop of my ear with her words: 'So you kept your word? You can open your eyes.'

I did immediately, wrapping my arms around her waist. I kissed her. It was only when my hand found the zip of her skirt that I stopped. I knelt down in front of her, pulling her skirt with me, the last barrier between us.

I closed my eyes. I wanted to inhale her before I saw her. I moved with my head closer between her thighs. I breathed in deeply, and seconds later, I was still holding my breath making sure that this unique scent trickled to the depth of my lungs. I had drunk and smelt what Jasim called the most expensive and best perfumes the French had ever created. But this was different. This was so exotic, so mysterious.

'*Habibi?*'

She stroked my head. Her fingers crawled to the back of my neck; caressing the back of my ears, and then the lines of my jaw.

'*Habibi?*' She stretched her hand, I gave her mine and intertwined my fingers into hers.

Holding my hand, she led me to her bed.

Suddenly everything seemed so daunting. It wasn't like when we were on the Westerners' only beach. This was different. It was as if her bed was a foreign land, unfamiliar and frightening. Perhaps it was the weight of excitement. It could have been the nervousness of beginners, of not knowing when to touch and how. But I had never trembled like that day when I lay next to her in her bed for the first time; and nor had I ever seen someone look so tense as she did.

My body finally thawed and my hands and fingers grasped her breasts, only for me to let go when I heard a soft scream. Was she enjoying this? Did I hurt her? Should I stop?

I tried with my mouth instead, just softly I thought as I circled her erect left nipple with my lips. Again, I heard her gentle cry. This time, I stopped.

I stretched full length; lying on my side facing Fiore.

The feeling of her skin on mine paralysed me even more. I didn't expect that we would be so stiff next to each other that we couldn't even say a word.

My mind suddenly dwelled on the next stage, what would happen after the kisses, and after the touches. I remembered Omar telling Jasim and me at the café, 'When lovers, a boy and a girl, manage to somehow do the impossible and meet somewhere private and want to have sex, they have a term for it: "Making love like men make love to each other." A girl must maintain her virginity. Can you imagine what would happen if she didn't?'

I looked at her. Holding my hand, Fiore whispered, 'I am sorry. This is harder than I thought it would be.'

She then fell quiet. Small beads of sweat shimmered across her face, her neck and her chest in the low candle-lit room. We looked at each other without saying a word.

She pulled my leg and pushed it between hers. It felt warm and wet on my thigh. We stayed like this – my leg stuck between hers and my hands glued to her body for the rest of our time that afternoon.

It would take another three days before we talked about our first afternoon in her room. We kissed but we avoided going further. When we talked, it would be about safe things, like the book she was reading, or about my friends from Al-Nuzla, whom I hoped to introduce to her one day.

Then, on the third day, a Friday afternoon, we realised that we couldn't let the fear of physical love get between us. We had no time to lose.

★

That afternoon, as we entered her flat, she told me to keep my veil on and to close my eyes. 'I have a surprise for you,' she whispered.

The room was filled with the smell of food. She led me to the bed. I sat on the edge, waiting. I could hear her footsteps leaving and entering the room, backwards and forwards. 'Don't look yet,' she would say whenever she came back into the room.

After a while, I felt her warm breath through the light cloth over my face as she said in a low voice, 'Now you can take off your veil.'

I opened my eyes and saw her standing in front of me, towering above the bed. I looked down at the black high heels she was wearing. Her curly hair was pulled back. She was wearing tight jeans and a black shirt with its sleeves rolled up. The top buttons were undone. A long silver necklace dangled way down between her breasts.

'Enough looking at me,' she said, laughing softly. 'Look at this.'

Her table, which was usually piled with books and homework material, was now cleared and laid with two plates, a bottle of fruit juice, glasses, cutlery and candles.

I threw off my *abaya*. She switched off the light. Even though it was daytime, Fiore had drawn the thick curtains across the windows for safety's sake. Her room was as dark as night. I watched her as she moved around the room to light the candles. Soon, haloes of yellow light were spilling around her from all sides, as she floated by me.

She stretched her hand out and led me to the table. I pulled her back and drew her in tight until there was no gap between us.

I gently stroked her collarbone as if I were touching the only rose in the desert. I kissed her neck with the thirst of a pious Muslim who has sacrificed alcohol on earth for the rivers of red and white wine that run next to each other in *Allah*'s heaven. Then with her back still resting on my chest, she twisted her head towards me and gave me a quick kiss; she pushed against me with her buttocks and moved off to the table.

When I looked down, I saw the delicious food on my plate: rice and fried chicken, neatly placed with some salad leaves as decoration.

But my eyes were hungrier than my stomach. I thanked her for the meal but I couldn't stop looking. I wanted to tell her how beautiful she looked; how her neck would have carried all Nefertiti's golden necklaces and there would still be room for my kisses; how I loved the way she combined elegance with depth, love with strength, Egyptian blood with Eritrean.

But I couldn't say anything. It was like learning a new language, her language. And stuttering words would not be the trait of a dedicated lover.

She was wearing pink lipstick that stood out against her dark brown skin, which looked even darker in the dim light. I wanted to see more of her face, so I moved all the candles on the table closer to her until she looked like a goddess in a temple shrine.

Suddenly the *azan* was announced for the Friday prayer and the spell was broken.

Fiore spoke first: 'In half an hour the imam will arrive. Let's hope his sermon doesn't mess up our date.'

'We'll find out soon enough,' I groaned. She leaned forward, poured juice into the two glasses and passed one to me saying, 'For you, darling.'

We started to eat. This was the first time we had eaten

together, and we were both transported by the unfamiliar situation. I closed my eyes to listen to the way she chewed her food and sipped her drink. As she poured the last of the juice into our glasses, she glanced at me and looked away smiling.

'What?' I asked softly.

'It is strange,' she said, 'how good I feel at this moment. I am just happy that simple and beautiful things can exist in life. All it takes is to go out and search for them.' And then she added, like an afterthought, 'Patience and courage are the key to everything.'

After the meal, I complimented her on her cooking, and rested my hand on hers and looked at her in silence.

'Naser?'

'Yes.'

'Do you think less of me for what I did to get to meet you and for inviting you here to my room?'

I answered with a question, 'Do you think less of me as a man for answering your calls and for doing what you asked me to do?'

She shook her head emphatically.

'Then nor do I,' I said.

We looked into each other's eyes silently; only our fingers moved as they crawled on top of one another.

Then: 'We have worked so hard to destroy the distance between us; for us to be in my room, yet, there are still obstacles to overcome,' she suddenly said.

'I am sorry about what happened the other day,' I said, 'the first time together in your room.'

'I am sorry too,' she said. 'To be honest I thought it would be easier. I thought my desire would melt away my fear.'

'Do you think it was too soon?' I asked. 'Maybe we should wait . . .'

'Darling, I have been longing for you for so long and I worry that tomorrow might never come for us. Shouldn't we take each day as it comes?'

'But . . .' I stopped, struggling to finish my sentence.

'Do you want to tell me something? Please, *habibi*, say what's in your mind.'

I hesitated.

'*Habibi?*'

Holding her hand, I scratched her thumb. 'OK,' I said, telling her about what Omar told Jasim and me, about how single girls and guys make love in Saudi Arabia. She chuckled.

'Why are you laughing?' I asked her.

'Because it is funny. Your friend Omar seems to speak with authority as if he knows all the young people of this country. *Habibi*, maybe some girls do what Omar said, because they like to have fun with lovers before they are arranged-married. But I love you.' She stopped, as if she wasn't sure what she was going to say next. Then: '*Habibi*, I want us to make love like a man and a woman.'

She was biting her finger as she waited for my re-action, but I couldn't manage a word.

She tilted her head, holding my hand.

'Fiore, I am so . . . I am just so worried about you. If anything happened to us . . . Just imagine what will happen to you if your father finally manages to force you into a marriage and your husband finds out that he was not your first?'

'You are the only man I think and dream about. I am with the man I want and that's why I want to share all I have with you. I own my own body. My father doesn't. I choose who I want to sleep with, and I have chosen you.'

As I crossed my arms across my chest to temper the beating of my heart, the second *azan* sounded, announcing the start of the Friday sermon. We looked towards the window as if the imam was standing right there, and braced ourselves for his voice which would thunder through at any moment.

I stretched out my hand and caressed Fiore's face. The blind imam started his speech. We both fell quiet, absorbed in our thoughts. Only the imam's voice could be heard; his speech was about jihad.

'*Ya Allah*,' Fiore exclaimed, raising her voice. This was the first time I saw her agitated. 'He and his virgins! When is he going to stop using us women as bait for war?'

I wanted to tell her that the best thing to do during the imam's sermon is to think about beautiful memories instead. But I didn't want to be a preacher myself.

She rose from her chair and came towards me. She put her hands on my thighs. Her necklace dangled before my eyes, and the sight of her breasts beneath her black shirt hypnotised me.

She kissed me on the cheek and straightened up. She slowly undressed. She turned around and began to blow out the candles, those furthest from the bed first. It was like watching a lioness walking in a confined place, rattling the cage from one side to another. I stood up and followed her, a lit candle in my hand, lighting her way from behind.

She stretched out her hand, keen to extinguish the last candle in the room.

'No,' I said, 'a goddess should never be covered, not even by darkness.'

WE MET EVERY day after college and most of the days during the weekends. Fiore did her housekeeping early in the morning, so that she could spend the rest of the day with me. We were so wrapped up in our happiness that we didn't think about what was waiting for us if we made even the smallest of mistakes. But sometimes I wondered what would happen if we left the room unlocked and her father came in while we were silently lost in each other's world. But Fiore said that he never came to the women's section of the house when he was told there were female visitors around.

And her father never suspected a thing. Whenever we passed him in the entrance hall, he would bow his head. Her mother never came to the room either. When I asked her about it, Fiore simply repeated what she had said that day at the beach: 'My mother understands about love, because she never experienced it.'

We were obsessed with discovering one another's bodies; in Fiore's room with the curtain drawn against the daylight it was as if this was the sole purpose of our lives and nothing else mattered. We were taking our revenge on lost time. We would gaze at one another as if we were browsing through a never-ending picture book, which was magically different each time we opened it. With every *azan* that was announced, with every speech we heard from the blind imam, and with every sighting of the Jeep, of Basil and the religious police, I realised that the special world we had created together could be wiped out at any time. But we were determined not to be stopped by anything, not even by the fear of an uncertain future. We were intent that should they cut our love affair short, then they would not leave our bodies aching for more, our desires unfulfilled.

Maybe it was because she had been hidden from me for so long that I preferred her to be naked in the room. When she would complain, jokingly, that I didn't appreciate the clothes she had picked out carefully, I would teasingly reply that her own skin had long won the battle on the catwalk in my eyes.

We only had freedom in her room and we expressed this freedom with our bodies. And we had much in our armour to inspire each other's creativity, as we found out.

One afternoon, when the sun was blazing outside and we had shut out the world as usual, I told her that I had an idea that could make every bit of her body glow like Scheherazade.

'Have you got henna?' I asked.

'I'll bring some from the kitchen,' she whispered and tiptoed through the candlelight to fetch it.

'Naser, where did you learn this?'

'Did you already forget? My mother worked as a henna artist. You have such delicate lines in your hands. They branch out so narrow yet I would like to follow them to their very end.'

'That might take a long time.'

'Not as long as it will take me to draw pictures here and here.' I stroked her legs and feet.

Hours later, and with her head propped up on a pillow, she watched as I sketched henna flower patterns on her thighs. Then I slowly crawled around her on all fours inhaling her body's fragrance mixed with the earthy smell of the henna then exhaling my warm breath on her skin to dry the little wet rounds of pigment.

I pulled her up and sat on her chair, drawing her closer until she sat on my lap, spreading her legs over mine. She wrapped her arms around me. And with her buttocks anchored on top of my knees, I wrote my name in henna down the inside of her thighs, a letter at a time. ناصر

It took a while for the henna to dry. We lay on her bed, waiting patiently. But when the henna was fixed we made love and her thighs, hands and feet glowed, like a Fiore blossoming in eternity.

Some days all we did was play games, like foolish lovers. Her favourite was when I pretended to be a detective, tasked to find a mystery object.

'Thank you for coming at such short notice,' she would say, bowing her head.

'Always at your service,' I would reply. 'You have told our department that there is a mystery object somewhere in your kingdom that needs to be found. I am the best detective in the world, better than Holmes the Inglesi. I will find the object, my Queen.'

'Come in,' she would say. She would turn around and walk into her empire.

I would follow her in and standing next to her bed, I would say, 'My Queen, the mystery object can be anywhere in your kingdom, it might take a long time to find and therefore you have to be patient. Please lie down on the bed and wait.'

Then I would start the search, my lips hovering over her feet and kissing her toes; I would look up to see what lay ahead, and would see her kingdom lying stretched out in front of me.

DURING THOSE BLESSED few weeks, I spent the afternoons with Fiore and the evenings at the Pleasure Palace with Hani, Fahd, Yahya and their friends. I didn't want to raise Jasim's suspicion that I was up to something, so I made sure to visit him now and then. But he complained that I had changed. 'I am regretting that I have introduced you to books,' he would say with a smile. 'I have turned my dearest into a hermit.'

In the absence of a phone in her house, Fiore and I had devised a routine to contact one another: I would be in Al-Nuzla Street dressed in my *abaya* by late afternoon on school days and early afternoons on Thursdays and Fridays, Saudi school holidays. I was to approach when I saw the Pink Shoes.

But that routine was almost blown one day in December.

That afternoon, I looked through the peep-hole in my front door just as I always did before I left fully veiled to go to Fiore's. There was no one in the hallway. I opened the door and rushed down the stairs. But just in front of the building's main door, I bumped into Yahya. I was knocked back. I held the wall and steadied myself. 'I am sorry,' he said, bowing his head.

I watched him as he made his way up the curved stair-well to my flat on the first floor. I heard him knocking on the door. I stood still and watched him through the gaps in the balustrade. But when he turned his head to look at me, I hurried out of the building, sweating more than usual under my *abaya*.

Later that evening, when I got to the Pleasure Palace, there was a gleam of happiness on Yahya's face. He was playing a drum. Hani was clapping his hands and Fahd, dressed as usual in striking colours, was dancing. He was cutting the air with his hands as he rotated, and made little jumps up and down.

I joined Fahd on the dance floor. We stood in front of each other, our left hands behind our back, waving our right arms in the air.

'I wish we had swords,' Fahd said, laughing. 'Then we could have done the sword dance.'

Yahya started singing in his throaty voice. 'Soon I will find love. Soon I will find love.'

He stopped singing and clicking his fingers. He then opened his mouth and rolled his tongue to emit a long and loud ululation like a cheerful high-pitched cry of happiness.

After a few more songs and dancing, Hani and Fahd started racing after each other in front of the palace, and Yahya and I sat on the pavement.

Yahya suddenly said, 'I will fall in love soon.'

'Who is the lucky boy?' I asked.

'It is a girl,' he said.

'A girl?'

'Why are you surprised?' he asked.

'Well, weren't you laughing at me every time I told you I would find a girl in this country?'

'I know, but today I have realised that miracles can happen,' he said.

★

He told me about a woman he had bumped into in my hallway earlier that day. The moment she touched his chest, he said, his heart was reawakened. With a smile, he added that the girl was so affected that she couldn't move and she kept watching him. She was nervous, he told me, he had seen her hands trembling. 'Naser, I swear to you even though she was wearing a veil, I know she was smiling underneath it.'

He took my hand and added with a serious tone, 'From now on, I am going to camp outside your door. She might drop me a note and things could develop from there.'

Think of something quickly, I panicked. You don't want him stationed outside your house all the time.

'But Yahya,' I said, 'there are no single girls living in my block.'

'How do you know?' he asked. 'You are just being jealous.'

'No I am not,' I said. 'I live in the building. There are two women and both are married. Do you want to get involved with a married woman?'

'Why not? I need love like anyone else,' he said.

'But think about the consequences. What will happen if the religious police find out . . .'

'So? What can they do?' he barked.

'They could lash you in Punishment Square and even deport you.'

'No, they will not deport me. I will just be lashed and even if they want to deport me, they will not. I have good contacts.'

I needed to try a different strategy. 'Yahya, wasn't it you who once told me that you believe in love that is unselfish.'

'Yes, and? What's your point?'

'Well, if this woman is married and the two of you are discovered then she will be stoned to death. *Ya Allah*, they will put her in a hole up to her neck, with her hands handcuffed, and people will smash her face with stones. Not only will the one you love die, but she will die slowly after every feature of her beloved face is flattened and destroyed. There are blood-lusting men in this city waiting by Punishment Square, ready with big stones to beat her because she is married. If this is not selfish then I have no idea what is. I think you should walk away before anything starts.'

Yahya stood up without saying a word and drove off on his motorbike.

I knew I had managed to fend off Yahya, and stop him from pursuing his crazy idea of coming to my house to look for the girl he was convinced had smiled at him, but it made me realise just how far I had gone with Fiore. I felt uneasy. I thought once again about the risk we were running. While men and women lived totally separated lives, Fiore and I had managed to bring ourselves together under everyone's nose. When we lay naked on her bed, we sometimes heard the blind imam through the tannoys cursing the girls who dropped notes at the feet of boys. 'They will go to hell,' he would say.

But I was more concerned about the earthly punishment that might await us. 'What if we get caught? Will we be caught? What would happen to her? What might happen to me? What will they do to us in Punishment Square? What would her father do to her if he knew she was in love and brought shame to his honour?'

But being caught by the religious police wasn't the only thing Fiore and I had to look out for. Her father still wanted to marry her off.

Fiore said that her mother generally stayed quiet and would not challenge her father, but when it came to defending Fiore's future, there was nothing that could hold her back.

She would shout at her husband and tell him that she would never allow him to marry their daughter against her wish.

'We will see about that,' he would say. 'Your daughter is getting old. If she hangs around for much longer without accepting one of these offers, no man will want her any more. She will be too old, and she will die as a pensioner in my house. I will do whatever I can to prevent that.'

IT WAS MORE than a month since I had left my job at the car-wash. I counted the remains of my savings. I worked out that I had just enough to live on for two more months, until the beginning of February.

That morning, I had tea with Jasim in his café. He was in a good mood. 'Because,' he said, broadly smiling, 'when new customers come to my café and get a glance of my new waiter, they are hooked and always return. They don't want to live a day without seeing that boy.'

Since I had left his café, he had hired many boys, of all complexions and nationalities. His latest recruit was a Palestinian who had come with his mother and sister from a refugee camp in Lebanon.

Jasim gloated about the services his café offered in a society like Saudi Arabia. 'I am so privileged because I see men coming here burdened by lust, but leaving relieved and smiling, as if they have had a day in a paradise.'

I had long stopped believing in his ridiculous claim that he was a prophet sent to desperate men by the god of desire. As Mr Quiet once told me, 'Jasim is just a good businessman who found a lucrative niche in the market and exploited it fully using young boys and his smuggling business.'

But I could never tell Jasim what I thought of him. I always wanted to keep him on my side. You couldn't make an enemy of him, because he had so many links with powerful men.

'You never know,' I would tell myself. 'He might also be useful one day.'

LATER THAT AFTERNOON, after my tea with Jasim, I was due to meet Fiore in Al-Nuzla Street and as I had promised the day before, I was due to bring her Tayeb Salih's *Season of Migration to the North*, which had been given to me by Jasim ages ago. I was about to put on my veil when I heard a knock on my door. It must be Yahya, I thought. I quickly hid my *abaya*, and the rest of my disguise under the bed.

I opened the door and saw Basil. He was leaning against the wall with his hands inside his *thobe* pockets. As I regained my breath, beardless Hamid appeared from behind him. 'Go and search his house. I am sure this boy, like all corrupted boys in Al-Nuzla, has heaps of pornographic materials lying around,' Basil ordered Hamid.

'There is no porn in my flat,' I said, blocking Hamid's way.

Hamid pushed me aside, hissing, 'Move, *ya* apostate.'

I held my ground. I was suddenly fearless. I had no choice, with all the women's clothes and Salih's forbidden book in my room. I tried to shove Hamid back, but as I was about to shut my door, both pushed against me and they managed to force their way in. Basil quickly pinned me against the wall, screaming, 'Go, *ya* Hamid, get the stick from the Jeep.'

Basil thumped the door shut with his foot.

'I swear to *Allah* I have no porn magazines,' I screamed.

He pushed me harder, the side of my face scratched against the rough wall. 'Liar,' he said, 'I used to be a street boy myself and I know boys like you have dirty porn, ah? If you don't tell us where they are, we'll find them. Where are you hiding it? Your kitchen cupboard? Your wardrobe? Or under the bed?'

I had to beg him. 'Basil, I am sorry. I am really sorry I don't know what was wrong with me then. Please forgive me. I promise I will come back to the mosque if that's what you want me to do.'

'*Ya* apostate,' he said. 'How can you leave the imam and make a mockery out of him?'

Hamid banged on the door, screaming, 'Basil, are you all right? Basil? Answer me.'

'I am fine,' Basil shouted his reply to Hamid.

'Let me in and I will crush this cursed boy,' Hamid pleaded.

'Wait, *ya* Hamid,' Basil responded, 'I am making him confess.'

'Why don't you leave me alone,' I said to Basil. 'I told you I am sorry.'

'Shut up,' he said, pushing my head harder against the wall. 'Speak quietly.'

'What do you want from me?' I asked him.

He pressed his lower body against me and then I felt his hand squeezing my backside.

'Go to hell,' I said, trying to push him. 'How can you call yourself a religious policeman? You are nothing but a desperate freak.'

He shouted towards the door, 'I am going to open the door now, Hamid.'

'Wait. Wait,' I said. 'OK. Just let me go now. I will come to the park.'

He immediately yelled out, 'Everything is all right, Hamid. I am satisfied this boy has no pornography.'

He pressed his hand tight against my backside, and as

he caressed my bottom, he said, 'Meet me tonight at the park at 11 p.m. or I will come back to get you.'

He let me go and as he turned to leave, he smiled.

Before I went to Fiore's house that afternoon, I went outside the flat and walked down Al-Nuzla Street to make sure Basil's Jeep was not around.

The street was clear, so I went back and dressed up to go to the nine-storey building.

I had no idea what to do about Basil. But I knew that my magical time with Fiore couldn't go on for ever. I had to talk to Fiore or deal with it myself.

As soon as we entered her room, I ripped off my disguise and pushed her on to the bed. I pulled off her veil more roughly than I intended. She was wearing a white T-shirt, her bra glowing through the thin fabric like underwater lilies.

I was still sweating from the walk from my house to hers dressed in the full *abaya*. I was never going to get used to it. As I joined her on the bed, she wiped the sweat from my face with the edge of her T-shirt. She moved over a little, and drew her long hair to one side of her face, and started braiding it into a thick plait.

I caressed her elegant straight back and her wide hips.

I gave her Tayeb Salih's novel. She thanked me like an excited child given a beautiful and long-awaited present. She thumbed through the novel and then turned to me and looked at me with intense eyes; saying nothing. She suddenly pushed me back on the bed and lay on top of me kissing me passionately. After each time her teeth bit my lips, she used her tongue to soothe them gently.

★

'Thank you, *habibi*,' she said a while later, pulling away and leaving my mouth on fire. She sprung to her feet, saying, 'Wait, I've got a book I want to show you.'

She walked to her desk and came back holding a heavy-looking volume. 'Here, take a look at this and you will see what I wanted to be.'

Fiore threw the book into my lap. It was bound with an Islamic cover. She had already told me that all her books were bound abroad.

She fixed her pillow and lay down on her back. She stretched her legs out and the book she had just given me was pushed off my lap with her feet. She had immediately taken its place.

She then reached out and wanted to grab the book she had meant to show me. But I took it back and opened it. It was a book with large photos. Did she want to be a photographer? I looked at a picture in colour of a Japanese woman in a white dress, sitting on a bench with her legs crossed and staring at the wide still blue sea in front of her. How beautiful, I thought.

In my mind's eye I gazed far into the future. I saw Fiore as the most successful photographer of her time.

A flicker of happiness shone across my face but then I thought, what about me? *Ya Allah*, I had lost track of my own dreams. For a second I just couldn't remember what I had wanted to be when I was younger; before school where the dream of the afterlife was so imposed on us that dreams on earth were forgotten. What did I want to be? Who did I want to be with?

My mood plummeted.

I flicked through the photography book once again.

I heard Fiore breathing deeply. I turned and stared at her in silence. We were behaving just like any couple might act in any other bedroom around the world. But we were not just anywhere. I was in Jeddah – and I was in a woman's room. I was in Saudi Arabia, where love had been erased from the dictionary, and yet somehow I had found a way to express my passion for another.

I couldn't dispel the thought that I was living a dream. Everything was getting so blurred that I could no longer work out where the reality began and where the illusion set in. In a country like this, what could Fiore and I seriously expect of our future together? Where did we go from here? How would we live, and where?

I pushed Fiore's legs aside and covered my head in my hands.

'Naser, are you all right?' Fiore asked.

I nodded.

She now rested her head on my thigh. I looked down at her. Our eyes met and she winked at me. I bent and kissed her. Twirling a lock of her hair in my fingers, I whispered, 'I was just thinking about our future together. How nice it would be if you were to be a great photographer and I –'

'*Habibi*, let's not talk about this,' she said, sitting up on the bed.

'Why not? You gave me the book. I thought you wanted me . . .'

'I just wanted to show you something I had dreamed about in the past.'

'Past? You are only nineteen. It sounds like you've already buried your dream.'

'*Habibi*, I have been buried all my waking life, let alone my dreams. Now, let's read,' she said.

I kept quiet. But as I continued to flick through the photography book, I became more agitated. The pictures that had made me joyous only moments earlier now seemed to create only envy in me. I looked at the photographer's name and thought, if this woman can do this why can't *habibati*? I put the book aside. I didn't want to be reminded of a dead dream.

I gazed at the bookshelf stacked with books from all over the world. She, like me, was living someone else's life through what she read; breathing and eating from pages written in a faraway land. We were living an imported life. Why are we here? It felt as if the bookshelves were leaning towards us trying to push us out of the room, as if to say: life is out there. The books were our transport, their covers flapping, ready to fly us away to where we really wanted to be, in a place where we could be together and live our dreams.

As she shifted on the bed, my veil slid on the floor. I picked it up, thinking, '*Ya Allah*. I have to wear this *abaya* and make myself invisible just to be with her, just to see her face, just so that I can touch even only one tip of her finger. I have to schedule my caressing her breasts at a time when her father is praying at the mosque or out with his friends: even her moans have to fit a man's timetable.'

I was angry, I knew that now. I wanted to tear down the thick curtains, and break her window; then I would strip off her clothes, kiss her body all over and we would make love so freely that the whole world would hear our cries of pleasure, and the men of Jeddah would know that my woman was not a mute.

I turned back to the book and tried to read the introduction, but no matter how much I tried to quieten my thoughts, they quickly stormed into mutiny. I looked across at Fiore. She was immersed in Salih's *Season of Migration to the North*. She wasn't yet ready to face up to the truth.

And that was the tragedy, I thought. When she went out her beauty was covered by a piece of cloth, and at home her intelligence and knowledge were shrouded by the walls of her room. All her great qualities were concealed.

I knew we were alone at home because her father was out in the shopping mall, so I shouted, 'What is the point of your life?'

'What?' she asked. She sat up and stared at me. I looked away.

I didn't say anything.

'I am sorry.'

She stood up and said in a soft voice, 'I think you better leave. I need to be alone.' She got up and walked to her window and pulled back the curtain to let some light in.

'Why?' I asked her. 'I said I was sorry. It was a slip of the tongue, that's all.'

'I am not feeling well.'

'I want to be with you. I don't want to leave,' I said firmly. 'Why are you upset by what I said?'

'Sometimes you can be so naïve,' she replied. Her voice was calm, but it had a tone that was unfamiliar to me; slightly mean. 'Please, leave me alone now.'

But I was adamant. 'Why am I naïve?'

Without saying anything, she shook her head as if to imply that I couldn't understand anything. For a moment I thought of leaving her in her own closed world. But then I did exactly the opposite.

'What about me?' I hurled the question at her. I was not sure if it was meant for her, but I asked it anyway. Instead of waiting for an answer, I went on: 'I am tired of my life in this country. I am tired because I feel we are all trapped in a prison.' I lowered my head as if I was ashamed to ask, 'Fiore, what about you? Are you not tired of this life?'

Nothing. I turned my head towards her. She was standing by her window gazing out on to the street. She was frowning, and her expression was slightly comical, as if she was thinking of a quiz question which she wanted to answer but didn't know how.

Then, finally, she moved. She walked to the desk opposite the bed and stood there in silence. This was the first time since our early encounters that I had felt this tension between us. Had I gone too far? Maybe I was mistaken in thinking that she and I could talk about anything and that there would be nothing out of reach for us. Maybe she preferred to deal with some issues privately; maybe I should have listened to her when she asked me to leave her alone.

But instead of storming out, I found myself sitting back on her bed and saying in a clear voice, 'Fiore, I need to know what you're thinking. After all, we are sharing this moment together, even though we have been on a separate path all our lives. Now that our paths have crossed and we have managed to find each other, I need you to talk to me. You are my love and it is important for me to know what is on your mind.'

She looked at me with piercing eyes. She sat on her chair at the study table. I pressed on, over her silence, 'You must have something to say.'

Nothing.

Her failure to respond convinced me it was time to go. I put on my veil. As I stood up to leave, I caught Fiore looking at me. No emotion was visible on her face. Her elegant lashes did not show a hint of the sadness I was convinced she must be feeling, her lips did not quiver in the face of my emotional onslaught, and even her shoulders refused to slump – she sat up straight and tall.

I shook my head in exasperation. 'What is the matter with you, Fiore? Can't you even cry?'

'What will tears bring me?' she said in her calm voice.

'I have cried so many that it's a wonder I haven't drowned. Tears never changed anything.'

I looked at her and shook my head again. If I could only make her know what I thought of her. If I lived to be a thousand years old, I would never meet anyone like this again. She was the one who was giving me the courage to experience a life I never thought possible. She had transferred her strength to me with her notes, drop by drop.

I decided to provoke her just as she had provoked me. 'You have been silent long enough,' I said, 'you have no voice in the street but you are like a shadow indoors now too. For how long?'

Her eyes suddenly welled up but she was too stubborn to let a single tear fall. I approached the chair and tried to take her hand.

She stood up, and raged: 'Do you want to liberate me? Do you want to open the door to the cage and set me free like a canary?'

'No. I want you on the street because our streets lack colour without you. Because our days lack meaning without you. Now that you are talking about liberation, let me tell you what I think. Everything I do in this world that makes me happy is tied to you. So yes, my darling, your freedom is my freedom.'

I stopped. She pulled away from me and walked to the window.

There was a long pause before she began to speak.

'This window is my way into the world,' she said. 'When I was young, I am sure I had the same dreams as you. Why shouldn't I, since I was your equal until a certain age. After that, I was directed towards a different life. But I didn't want to leave my childhood. I stretched out my fingers, like claws, trying to hold on to those early freedoms. I had already made dreams, I even had ideas of what I thought would make me happy. But I was leaving whether I liked it or not. Something was pulling hard at my feet, while my bleeding fingers were trying to hold on to the edge of life. I was forced to enter this new world, where I have to wear all black as if I am the widow of life itself.'

I sank down on to the bed.

'Naser, what is it about me that entices a man to pursue evil desires? Why should I worry about their destiny in hell or heaven, why should I suffer because of their weakness? I am just a woman who wants to live freely.'

She stopped. I stood up and walked over to her. She leaned against the window frame.

'*Habibi*, whenever I argue with my father about how he runs my life, he throws at me that I need to do all this because it is what *Allah* wants me to do and I will be rewarded for it in the afterlife. A long time ago I believed him, even though I had doubts about some of the things he said. But later, my doubts started growing so huge that I had to find answers. But the books we had at school supported what he said. I decided to ask one of my teachers about my role in life, and she gave me a tape of the blind imam's teachings. It was called "The role of a good Muslim woman in our society". After I listened to his tape, I was scared for having dared to even ask a question, because the imam promised that those who question the rules of *Allah* will meet with *Allah*'s vengeance. But I found myself waking up the next morning with the same doubts and questions. I couldn't be deterred.'

Fiore paused, smiling softly as if she remembered the moment, and said, 'Then a new Arabic literature teacher, who I told you about before, came to our college. She was from Mecca and was in her late thirties. Over time, I grew attached to her because in her face I saw kindness, courage and intelligence. And one day, after her class, I gathered enough courage to ask her what was on my mind. She took me aside and whispered, "It's wonderful to ask questions." Then the next day, she gave me three books. They were the first of her many gifts. They were fiction and poetry books by different Egyptian writers. But my favourite book she gave me only days before she was moved to another college in Mecca almost a year ago, and that was Mahfouz's novel.'

Fiore paused, sighed and as she wiped her tears, she tensed her jaw, adding, 'My teacher wrote me a note inside the novel, saying, "Life is beautiful. Don't give it up for anyone." And from this window, hidden behind these curtains, I watch the kind of life I dream about. I have often tried to imagine the life of a man. It must be full of challenges. Just the idea of being able to chase a dream is enough to make me envy you.'

Fiore turned and faced me. 'Naser, I had already convinced myself that the kind of life I want lies elsewhere. I want to leave for Egypt or Lebanon. Life is too short to spend much more time reading in this room. I wish I knew how to get away. I would even go back to my father's country, even though there is a war out there.'

I listened to her soft breathing, and watched as more tears welled up in her eyes.

'LET'S GO OUT,' I said to her a few hours later, as I pulled her on to my lap. 'I am going to introduce you to my friends.'

She wrapped her hands around my neck and sighed, 'Naser, you know I would love to meet your friends, shake their hands, laugh, and talk with them. But . . .'

'Isn't it normal to introduce the woman I love and respect so much to my friends?' I asked.

'You know that's impossible.'

'Don't worry. I will wear my veil and come with you to introduce them to you from afar. At least you should know who my friends are. You are my love, for *Allah*'s sake.'

'Naser, you're crazy.' A smile broke through her sombre face.

'The first person you should meet is Yahya,' I said to Fiore as we walked down Al-Nuzla Street arm in arm, dressed in our *abayas*.

'Why?' she asked, holding my gloved hand.

'Because he always drives around to show off his boys.'

She laughed. Even though I couldn't see her face, I knew her well enough to know that her laughter would be accompanied by a gentle smile.

We walked all the way to the supermarket on Al-Nuzla, just past Jasim's café. But Yahya wasn't around.

On our way back, I spotted him coming out of the bakery. 'There, there he is,' I said to Fiore, pointing at him.

'Please, *habibi*, put your hand down.'

He was with a boy I hadn't seen before, they were holding hands. Yahya's free arm was wrapped around two bags of Lebanese bread. He was wearing a T-shirt. He walked with his chest thrust forward, tensing his biceps with every step.

'Nice to meet you, Yahya,' she whispered, as he walked past us.

We stood outside the shop, opposite Jasim's café. I had told her how, when I needed help, Jasim had taken me in and given me a job as a waiter, but I hadn't told her what had gone on in that back room with the mirrored ceiling. I was too worried what she would think of me. But I hoped that one day I would be able to tell her, perhaps when we both found peace of mind and were not continuously watching over our shoulder to protect our secret.

I pointed Jasim out to her, he was sitting outside the café with his friend Omar, and she told me how much she wished she could go and thank him for looking after me after my uncle left me homeless.

She chuckled when she noticed how Omar was talking non-stop.

I gently squeezed her hand, saying, 'Let's find Hani.'

'I can't wait to see him,' she said. 'Is he really the strongest man in Al-Nuzla?'

'No, Yahya is the strongest. But Hani is the most romantic. He is a poet. With a bit of practice, he would defeat even Antara Ibn Shaddād. But the great thing about him –' I interrupted myself and pointed across the street.

'Look, there he is, eating *shawarma* outside the Lebanese restaurant.'

'Stop pointing, Naser. You'll get us into trouble,' she

whispered. 'He looks nice,' she said, 'but who is the boy next to him in the bright colours?'

'That's Fahd, Hani's cousin. He is from Riyadh. He is only here for a few months. Wait, I have an idea.'

'Naser, don't be mad. What do you want to do?'

'Just wait and see. It's just a joke. I have some paper in my pocket. Have you got a pen?'

She gave me her pen. I looked around and when I was confident no one was looking, I took a piece of paper from the pocket under my veil, and quickly wrote a one-sentence note to Fahd: 'What lovely colours you are wearing, handsome boy.'

I crumpled the note and we walked towards them.

'You are mad,' whispered Fiore. 'Poor boy, he is going to think a real girl is after him.'

As we approached, we started walking a bit slower. Fahd was wiping the dust from his sunglasses.

As soon as I dropped the note, both Hani and Fahd scrambled for it like two hungry pigeons being given a grain of maize, like I used to do with her notes. Fiore pinched me and hissed, 'Look what you have done now.'

Hani won the battle for the note, but I could see him quickly passing it to Fahd. 'Fahd has a beautiful smile, look,' I said.

Fahd's face lit up and he shook his head, laughing. Hani and Fahd looked at each other and clapped their hands, laughing loudly.

'Now we should go and try to find my dear friend Hilal,' I said, beaming with happiness.

I had told her a lot about Hilal, since he was the one who helped us to go to the Westerners' beach. Without Hilal, we might never have met face to face.

★

Fiore laughed when she saw Hilal gesticulating furiously at some men unloading furniture from a van, as he limped around them.

'Is he moving house?' she asked.

'No. His wife is arriving from Port Sudan in a few weeks' time.'

'I hope I will be able to get to know her,' she said.

Then: '*Habibi*, let's go,' she said. 'It looks like it is going to rain. What's happening to Jeddah this year?'

'I like walking in the rain,' I said. 'Shall we go to Mecca Street? Please?' I dragged her by the hand and we scurried past Hilal and the removal men.

As we walked towards Mecca Street, I heard the familiar sound of a roaring engine going at full speed. I turned my head and saw the Jeep was now slowing down. I looked at Fiore. We held each other's hands. 'Let's walk faster,' I urged her.

'No,' she whispered. 'Let's be calm. Just don't talk. You don't want them to hear your voice.'

We squeezed each other's hand tightly and sweat was drenching our gloves.

The Jeep was getting closer, its engine now rumbling more softly. 'Why is it slowing down right next to us? Would Basil know it is me under this veil?' I asked myself, recalling that he had seen me coming out of the shop when I bought my veils and women's shoes. But he couldn't have seen what was in the bag. I was sure of that. Maybe they had already caught a man wearing a woman's *abaya*? Maybe the religious police had been ordered to look out for girls holding hands in case one of them was a man in disguise? I let go of Fiore's hand. But she grabbed my hand once again and clutched it.

I wanted to tell her not to hold me. I couldn't talk, fearing they might hear my voice. I released my hand from her grip. This time she didn't take my hand again.

Everything under my veil felt so dark. I felt hot and suffocated, as if I was trapped in a dark, airless lift. I wanted to scream for help, tear off the veil over my face and run for fresh air.

Suddenly I heard a loud crack. Instinctively I turned my head towards the Jeep. It had run over a bottle and broken it into a thousand pieces. I saw Basil in the passenger seat. I almost slipped on some wet litter. 'Naser, for *Allah*'s sake, pay attention,' Fiore hissed.

I steadied myself. The Jeep suddenly increased its speed before slowing down again, and then turned off its engine. It parked a few metres ahead. Why are they stopping? Are they waiting for us? Basil got out and stood next to the Jeep, a stick under his armpit.

'Let's go back,' I urged Fiore.

'No. If we go back and if they are suspecting something then that will just confirm it to them. Let's just go ahead.'

I mumbled a prayer, 'Please *ya Allah* help us.'

We walked slowly. We were like deer walking towards a trap set by seasoned hunters. And we couldn't run back because there might be hungry lions behind us. There was no way out.

I REGRETTED NOT having given Basil what he wanted from me in the park that first time. Had I done that, he might have gone back to his street life because he wouldn't have wanted to hang around with the imam after that. And if Basil was gone, I wouldn't have had a religious policeman breathing down my neck. 'But maybe now I have a second chance to get rid of him?' I thought, remembering my promise to see him later that night in the park.

Hamid joined Basil next to the Jeep, and both stood in our path. Would they notice Fiore's Pink Shoes? Would they see them as out of keeping with the black and white movie, and pull *habibati* away from my side for ever?

We got to where they were standing and Hamid and Basil moved aside to let us through. I held my breath. I was almost side by side with Basil. As he turned, he dropped his stick. It fell in front of me. I wished I could have stamped on it with my foot to break it into pieces. But I stopped short to avoid running into him as he knelt to pick it up. Fiore had already walked ahead. I was trapped.

Hamid was on my left and Basil took for ever to collect his stick and move out of the way. Was he checking under the hem of my *abaya* to confirm his suspicion that I was a man? I couldn't remember if my *abaya* was long enough to hide the tracksuit I was wearing underneath.

I looked down.

Basil straightened up and took a lifetime to turn and move out of the way.

I felt my veil sticking to my face, sucked in by the sweat, and by my gasping for air.

I caught up with Fiore.

We safely turned into Mecca Street.

I couldn't take it any longer. He was always out on the street. How many close encounters did I have to have with Basil before my luck ran out? I had to act before I was left face to face with this man.

It had to be either me or him in Al-Nuzla Street. And I would do whatever it took to make sure of that.

The best solution was to leave Jeddah. Fiore and I had already talked about leaving when we took the walk along the Corniche and sat on the bench looking out to the sea.

Even without the threat of Basil, what did our future look like if we stayed? Everything around us was run by men. The shops were owned by men, the cars were driven by men, all of the offices, government departments and banks around us were staffed by men, and all ministers were men. Where did Fiore think she might fit? I asked her. There wasn't a role for me in such a place either. The best of everything was kept for Saudis. No foreigners were allowed to attend the universities. The best jobs were for Saudis. Even dignity was reserved for Saudis.

Fiore had said in the past that she wanted to leave for Egypt or Lebanon. And now as we walked parallel to the flyover, down to Mecca Street, I told her that this couldn't go on any more and that we had to be serious about leaving rather than just dreaming about it. I told her everything about Basil, about the park and about what I had had to do to recruit the blind imam as our love-letter courier, to prove how serious this was.

'He wants to meet me in the park tonight because he wants sex, Fiore,' I said.

'What? *Ya Allah* . . .'

'I know your life in this country is hard because you are a woman. But I can tell you if you are a certain kind of a boy, it is also . . .'

'I am not . . .'

'I don't want to talk about what happened to me. I am telling you this thing about Basil because I want you to help me think about how to get rid of him. I can no longer do it myself. And I want us to escape.'

'*Habibi*, I will never be judgmental. *Ya Allah*, Naser . . . I am sorry . . . I am sorry about whatever happened to you.'

'We are both hurt in different ways. Let's help each other by getting out of this place. When we are somewhere safe, we will have a lifetime to heal. Fiore, we can't go on living like this. Look how scared we are every time we see the religious police. We need to make a decision fast. Because if we don't, Basil will make the decision for us.'

She stayed quiet for a while.

I wondered why she didn't say anything. Maybe she didn't love me enough to leave for real and put our dreams into practice. Maybe she thought I was just a restless young boy, maybe she wasn't ready to make such a big move. But I wasn't going to give up on her. I loved her too much.

As I walked by her side down Mecca Street – lined with palm trees and bright lamps – I told her, 'Fiore, look at us, we are barely twenty and we have effectively retired from life already. Outside Saudi they say life starts at our age. There, we can love freely, we can focus on life instead of finding ways to dodge arrest when we want to be together.'

Finally, she talked. 'Naser, I told you many times that I wanted to leave, but it is just impossible. I don't have any money. I don't have a passport. How would I get out?'

I held her hand and said, 'I know a way.'

As we continued walking, I laid out my plan. I told Fiore that we could get to Europe; that Hilal had told me about Haroon, the servant of my *kafeel*, who had been smuggled to Germany by a businessman, and that I knew where to find more information.

But it wasn't leaving Jeddah that was bothering Fiore. She wanted to go to Cairo instead of Europe. But even to get to Cairo, I told her, we would have to be smuggled since she didn't have a passport and she needed her father's permission to get one.

Then she said in a low voice, 'I am scared, Naser. How can I leave my mother?'

I pressed her gloved hand and whispered, 'Don't be scared, my darling. Goodbyes are always sad, but I will be with you. We will make it easier for each other.'

I told Fiore how I used to ask myself, how can a mother send away her children whom I know she loves so much? But slowly I realised that the ultimate responsibility of a parent is to seek out life for their children and to do what's best for them. I understood that it was my mother's love for her children that made her give the camel men everything she had to smuggle me and my brother out of Eritrea, while she stayed behind to live under the bombardment. She wanted us to find life elsewhere, because she feared if we stayed, our lives might be cut short. How could I not admire my mother for this ultimate sacrifice? I knew that Fiore's mother would also understand because she would realise that her daughter was leaving her to search for a better life.

We got back to her building with the rain dripping

from our *abayas* and our face veils, like infusers, filtering the rain water into our mouths.

In her room I gave her a quick hug. I reached for her hand, pulled her closer to me. I knew how she felt. But we had to put aside our feelings for now. We had to deal with Basil first. We couldn't have him around, popping up all the time as we tried to execute our plan. What was I going to do if he ever came to my room again? How was I going to explain to him the banned books, the veil, the woman's shoes and socks and the gloves? But if I threw away the *abaya*, how on earth was I going to get to Fiore's house?

I WENT SEARCHING for the Jeep in Al-Nuzla Street.

It didn't take me long to find it parked a few blocks away from the big mosque.

I looked down both sides of the road. In the distance I saw a new boy guiding the blind imam to his house; the late afternoon prayer had already finished. I wondered if he was genuinely a *mutawwa*, or a desperate lover like me, who had fallen in love with a girl from the college. It is possible, I thought. Al-Nuzla Street must be full of thwarted lovers.

I took a deep breath and walked a few yards towards my tree in front of my old house. I had abandoned it and had stopped watering it for a while because my heart was too preoccupied with Fiore. The branches that once crowned it were now dry and without life. I touched the trunk, and remembered how I used to bring my brother here to sit with me in the tree's shade. This had been a safe place to tell him about our mother, because my uncle forbade me to mention even her name in his house.

It had been five years since he had been taken by my uncle to Riyadh. I wondered whether I would still recognise him if I bumped into him. I wondered whether he'd become a *mutawwa* like my uncle wanted, and whether he still counted me as a brother even though in my uncle's eyes I was an apostate.

I straightened up, put my hands in my pockets and looked over to the Jeep. Basil was standing next to it. I saw Hamid leave the Jeep and go into the Yemeni shop. I crossed the road and walked towards Basil.

'Make it quick,' he said, as I approached him. 'I don't want Hamid to wonder why I am talking to an apostate like you.'

Me an apostate? I wanted to tell him how disgusted I was by his hypocrisy, but I couldn't show a sign of it. 'If you want me to come to the park with you tonight,' I said, 'you will have to make more of an effort.'

'What do you mean?'

'I want you to shave your beard,' I said.

'What?'

'Do you remember your life before you converted to the right path? The pretty boys? You never had a beard then.'

'I won't shave and if you don't come, I will take you in.'

'Basil,' I said brashly, hoping that I was right, 'you can't hold anything against me. Where is your proof? I am not afraid. I have nothing to lose.'

'You know I can't shave my beard. What will I tell the chief of the religious police?'

'It's your choice.'

'OK. OK,' he said. 'I will shave. Come to the park at eleven o'clock. No one goes there at that time. We will jump over the fence.'

I arrived at the park and waited under a light post just to the right of the gate. I could see two cars driving side by side, racing each other into the far distance. It was eleven o'clock exactly. I heard the sound of a motorbike. I turned around and could see nothing but a stark yellow light moving closer. The noise of the engine shattered the silence and the motorbike screeched to a stop in front of me. I jumped away. The first thing I saw were the feet in open sandals. Moving up, I could see no *thobe*, only a yellow tracksuit and white T-shirt. The face had no beard. I looked at him, stunned. 'Good, you came,' Basil said.

Now the beard was gone I could see signs of his earlier life that I hadn't noticed before: a big knife-scar across his right cheek, a long cut over his chin. But I recognised the expression of hungry lust.

He got off the motorbike and parked next to the gate of the park. He turned around and stood in front of me. For a moment I forgot that this tall boy, who now trembled in excitement as he took my hand, was the same Basil, the religious policeman who terrorised me in his Jeep. As he turned around to lead me to the park, I could hear the sound of another bike approaching.

When I returned home from the park a couple of hours later, I took a shower before I went to bed. I stayed awake most of the night thinking about the escape plan.

The following day, a warm Thursday morning, I set out for the only Eritrean café in Jeddah. It was the place where one could get the latest news about the war, and it was the place where smugglers came to do business.

The café was full of Eritrean men sitting around the blue tables. I walked to a waiter and spoke to him in Tigrinya. He pointed to a man sitting at the back of the café. The man was wearing a two-piece suit, with an Eritrean *gabi* draped over his right shoulder. His *gabi* was as white as his hair and moustache. He saw the waiter direct me to him and he stretched out his hand as I got to his table. There was another man sitting with him.

'*Assalamu alaikum*,' I said.

'*Wa 'alaikumu salam*,' both replied.

'Sit down please, son,' said the man wearing the *gabi*. 'What's your name?'

'Naser,' I replied.

'My name is Hajj Yusef. This is Mossa,' he said, introducing me to the man next to him, who was balding and had a heavy black moustache.

I pulled up a chair and as I sat he asked me, 'How are you?'

'*Alhamdulillah*.'

'The time has come to leave, ah?'

I nodded.

'Don't worry, son, *Allah* said that after hardship comes ease. Where do you want to go?'

I shrugged my shoulders and said, 'Anywhere. I want to leave this country. I can't go back to Eritrea, so any safe country that's far enough away from here.'

'We'll find a way out. Everything will be OK,' he said. I noticed his wrinkles, the scarf draped on his shoulder, and a newspaper in Tigrinya by his side. He turned to Mossa and said, 'Please remember him in your prayers. It hurts me to see someone moving from one country to another prolonging their exile by going even further away. But it is what *Allah* wished for our son, Naser.'

'It is not *Allah*'s wish,' Mossa said sternly. 'Forgive me for saying this, Hajj, but it is the people in this country who have the power who are responsible.' He paused before adding, 'Two boys I knew were caught last month without papers and are now in the Jeddah detention centre waiting to be deported. They are still kids, *ya* Hajj, who came to this country fleeing war. Who would send people back to a war zone, especially when they are so young?'

290

'No, they are not going to send them to Eritrea, they will send them to Sudan, most probably,' contested Hajj Yusef.

Mossa shook his head. 'That's if you have a United Nations passport issued from Sudan. If not, like these two boys, who smuggled themselves from Eritrea to Jizan in the south, then the government will send you back to Eritrea in exactly the same way you came in: on a fishing boat.'

I tensed my jaws. I wasn't going anywhere on a fishing boat.

Then Mossa turned to me and said, 'Go to Europe, son. I sent my children to Sweden. They treat them with dignity there, and they understand the suffering of people like us, so they support us until things get better in our own countries. In Jeddah, they tell us that education is for Saudis only, but in Sweden my children are encouraged to study. Oh *ya Allah*, just look at the difference. I know it is a cold and lonely place for them out there, but at least they will not see their father being humiliated day after day by his *kafeel*, beaten up, spat at, with the threat of deportation hanging over him day and night.'

'You can trust us, son,' Hajj Yusef said. 'I am an old man and I know a lot of things. I want to help my people. That's what gives me joy. I can give them advice and put them in contact with people who will find them a better place.'

Every wrinkle of his face seemed to carry a story hidden in its fold, and his kind face made me feel comfortable around him. So I said, 'There are two of us.' Without going into detail about Fiore, I told them that we both wanted to leave the country as soon as we could.

'I presume both of you have UN passports,' Hajj Yusef said.

'I have, but she doesn't have any passport,' I replied.

He raised an eyebrow when he realised that I was

going with a woman. He smiled and asked, 'How come?'

'She was born here,' I responded.

'Even better and cheaper,' Hajj Yusef said. 'She will have no problem going with a Saudi passport.'

I explained that she had never travelled and that even though her father was born here, he had been denied citizenship. Mossa yelled, 'How can they forget that in the past they needed other people's help? How can they forget the first *hijra* when Prophet Muhammad ordered his companions to immigrate to our land to escape persecution by his tribe? Didn't our King of Abyssinia offer them sanctuary, give them land to build their houses, and provide them with everything they needed? They even married our daughters, and yet they treat us like this.'

'Calm down,' Hajj Yusef ordered Mossa. 'Don't carry so much hatred. Hate is like fire and will burn your heart.' He turned his head to me and said, 'OK, Naser, let's talk business.'

'How much will it cost to get to Europe?' I asked him once again.

'It all depends on luck,' he replied. 'If the way ahead is smooth, that is, if the businessman is good, the fake passport he gives is good, the visa he fakes won't raise suspicions, and his business partners on the destination side are not too greedy, then it will cost around two to four thousand dollars. But if he, as sometimes happens, forgets to include a small detail in the visa stamp then you might be caught, jailed or told to go back and check with the embassy. The business of smuggling is unpredictable and can be dangerous, so you should be prepared to pay seven thousand dollars each.'

'Fourteen thousand, oh *ya Allah*,' I said, burying my head in my hands. 'How about Egypt? Can we go there instead? It must be cheaper to get us there, no?'

Mossa intervened once again. 'Son, Egypt is a beautiful

country. But the country doesn't have the capacity to look after its own, let alone take any more. Egypt receives aid from America. Plus, I am not sure they will grant you asylum.'

'If I get the money, are you sure the businessman can help me?' I asked Hajj Yusef, holding his hand.

'We are not sure of life itself, son,' he said. 'But if you get the money I will arrange everything with the businessman. But prepare yourself for the way ahead. Europe is not as easy as before.'

'Thank you,' I said, as I kissed the back of his hand.

After I left the Eritrean café, I walked around the neighbourhood in despair. I had thought it was going to be a lot cheaper – hundreds rather than thousands. Where was I going to get such a huge sum of money? All I had left since I gave up my job was four hundred riyals.

There was no one who could help us. Hilal had spent all his savings to bring his wife over from Sudan and to furnish his new house in preparation for her arrival. Fiore couldn't get any money from her mother because it was her father who earned and kept all the money.

I must have walked for a long time, because eventually I found myself outside the shopping mall, a long way from the Eritrean café. I went inside and sat by the fountain, silently gazing at the tinkling water.

I looked around. It was so quiet that I could hear the hum of the air conditioning. I saw the reflection of the chandelier on the tiles and my gaze alighted on the jewellery shop and stayed there. I stood up. I slowly moved towards the shop, one step at a time. I slipped my hands into my pockets. This will be easy, I thought. I'm a quick runner. I know all the little alleyways around here. I will have disappeared before the police even get into their cars.

I had promised Fiore I would succeed. This is the only chance to flee with her and be with her for ever. It will be easy. Very easy.

Please help me *ya Allah*.

The sales assistant was standing behind the glass counter and was speaking on the phone. Everything glowed a sparkling yellow. I walked over to the section where there were watches. I picked one up. Twenty thousand riyals. Two of these would be enough.

'Can I help you?'

I didn't move. I bit my lip. I looked ahead. Maybe three just to be sure, in case the businessman gets greedy.

'*Ya* boy, can I help you?'

Slowly I turned around. Our eyes met. The assistant was clutching the phone receiver to his shoulder like a baby.

'Don't worry, brother,' I said, 'I am still browsing. Please finish your call.'

He fixed his head-dress and said, 'Sure, go ahead.'

As he sat down, I got a glimpse of myself in the mirror behind him.

'Mirror?' I exclaimed. I remembered my first friend in Jeddah. Of course. How could I forget him? I turned to the man and said, smiling, 'Thank you, brother, for allowing me to look around. Thank you.'

And with that I ran to catch the bus to Jasim's café.

Jasim was my first, last and only option. If he didn't give me the money, there was going to be no escape from Jeddah. I swore to myself that I would do whatever was necessary to get the money from him.

★

294

Jasim was sitting at a table near the kitchen counting the day's takings. I grabbed him by the arm and pulled him to the small room in the back.

'Hey, what's the hurry, my dear?'

I shut the door behind us.

'I need your help,' I said, looking him straight in the eye. His face almost disappeared behind the smoke from his cigarette.

'Are you all right?' he asked, scratching his chin with the back of his hand.

'Jasim, you are the only person who can help me.'

'In the name of *Allah*, Naser, what is wrong?' he asked, throwing the glowing cigarette butt on the carpet.

'One day you'll burn this café down,' I said, stamping it out with my foot.

'Oh, so you do care about me then,' he said playfully.

I ignored his comment. I took his hand in mine and said, 'Jasim, I hope that you will be kind and will remember that I never complained about the things you did to me. In return, I hope you will help me.'

'Anything, my dear,' he said, kissing the back of my hand.

'I need fourteen thousand dollars,' I blurted out.

'*Ya Allah*, that's a lot of money. You're not thinking of opening a rival café, I hope, are you?'

'No,' I replied and without further hesitation I added, 'I am going to Europe.'

'You are joking, right?'

'I swear I am serious,' I replied. I could feel my eyes widen as I said this.

'*Ya Allah*, I can see that,' he said, as he went to sit on his bed. He looked at me and wanted to say something, but signalled with his hand that I should come and sit next to him.

'Jasim?'

'Shush,' he said.

He leaned his back against the wall, and closed his eyes.

'Where do you want to go?' he said.

'I told you, to Europe.'

'Yes, but where in Europe? It's not one big country, you know.'

I shrugged my shoulders and after a pause, I replied, 'That will be up to the smugglers. They will know which country is best.'

He sighed and asked, 'They asked for fourteen thousand dollars just to smuggle you out of here?'

'I am not going alone.'

He jumped up and said, 'What? Did you find your brother?' He hugged me, exclaiming, 'Oh, I am so happy for you. So he's had enough of your uncle, has he?'

'Jasim,' I whispered, 'I am not going with my brother.'

'Who are you going with then?'

I looked at him and for a second I wondered whether I was doing the right thing to trust him with the truth. Then I said, 'I am going with someone I love.'

He spat in my direction and turned to sit on his bed. He looked up at me and asked, 'Who is it?'

I rubbed at the trace of his spittle on my shirt.

'Who is it?' he screamed.

'Shut up for *Allah*'s sake,' I yelled, 'just listen to me, Jasim. Why don't you give me time to explain things to you? Just listen.'

I was breathing heavily. He stood up, bringing his face close to mine and asked, 'Then tell me quickly, who is he?'

'I am in love with a woman, Jasim. And I want to take her to Europe.'

He laughed loudly. Then suddenly the laughter caught

296

in his throat. He shook his head and looked at me, curled his lip and looked away.

After a while I took his hand and said, 'Please, Jasim, help us.'

He pushed me away, shouting, 'What about your brother? Are you going to leave him behind? You can't really be that selfish?'

'My brother chose to live with my uncle years ago and as far as I know the two are happy together. I don't know where they are, they never told me. I can't go to Riyadh and search from door to door. My uncle admires him. I know he will look after him.'

He sat on his bed and looked at me, slowly shaking his head. 'Who is this girl? *Ya Allah*, where on earth did you find her?' he asked, crossing his legs and pushing aside the pillow next to him.

'I'm sorry but I can't tell you.'

'And why not?' he shouted, kicking the box next to the bed.

I watched as he stepped up to the TV and swiped all the videotapes off the top. Breathing like a horse, he turned around. 'Oh, my dear, how much I have loved you, but you never wanted to see it. And now you are hurting me.' He caressed my face, but I pushed his hand away. 'Where did you find her?' he asked.

'I can't tell you.'

'So forget the money. Go and wash your cars and spend fifty years saving. Get out of here. Go on, leave and don't ever come here again.'

He shoved me towards the door. 'Don't push, I will leave by myself,' I said.

As I turned to walk out, I got a peek of one of Jasim's men magazines from Germany on top of the box by the bed. I looked up at the mirrored ceiling. I closed my eyes and saw my past racing towards me, my past in this room which I had been trying to forget for a long time. *Ya Allah*, I thought as I stopped.

'What?' he screamed.

'No,' I insisted. 'I will not leave without the money or . . .'

'Or what, my dear? Ah?'

'I will go to the religious police and I will tell them everything about your smuggling business, I swear to *Allah*, and I will tell them about what you made me do. Everything that happens in this room.'

'What? You dare do that and I —'

'I will,' I replied firmly. 'But I know you are sensible, Jasim. I don't want to give you any problems. I just need the money. Plus . . .'

'Plus what?'

'You always go to Europe, so you can come and see us.'

He laughed wryly. But then he turned his back to me and seemed to bow his head in thought.

After a few moments, he turned to face me, his eyes red at the rims.

'OK,' he said.

'OK, what?' I asked him.

'I will give you the money,' he answered. 'Now leave me, please. I will have to think how to get hold of such a big amount. I will give you a call when I have found it. OK?'

I couldn't believe it. I wanted to run to Fiore's house to tell her the good news, but I would have to wait for the following day to find the Pink Shoes in Al-Nuzla Street. So instead I went to Hilal. I knew exactly where to find him at this time of the evening.

298

I FOUND HILAL, as I expected, sitting outside his house. He was talking to his friend who was selling fried dough balls. Hilal was helping by putting small pieces of dough into the massive frying pan. When he saw me approaching, he stood up and limped towards me waving his walking stick. He hugged me and extended his hand, wet with flour. I declined with a smile.

'I need a big favour from you,' I said.

'If you want a new job, I have nothing at the moment,' he said, shaking his head.

'Hilal, I need your help with something else.'

'What? Another drive to the Corniche with your beauty? I always want to come and ask you about her, but love is private and belongs to the heart deep inside.' He poked my chest with his finger as he said that.

'Can we go somewhere private? I know a place.'

When we arrived at the Pleasure Palace, Hilal looked around like a young boy taken to a mysterious forest and left there alone: his mouth opened wide and he was shaking his head in disbelief.

I chuckled and sat on the pavement watching him. He looked up at the wall behind me. 'Oh *ya Allah*,' he exclaimed, 'this looks like the middle of nowhere and yet we're only ten minutes from Al-Nuzla Street.'

He laughed and staggered towards me. As he sat down next to me, he asked me, 'What do you call this place again?'

'The Pleasure Palace.'

I pulled a cigarette and a lighter out of my pocket.

Hilal threw his stick at a passing rat. 'Rats, I can handle,' he said, 'but are there ghosts around here too?'

'They say the King loved women and that he had lots of them. Can't you smell their lingering perfume?'

'Oh, yeah, now that you mention it, I agree with you. A woman's scent is eternal.' He put his arm around me and laughed. 'Let's hope they are around us now as we speak.'

The usual spell of muteness when a woman was mentioned fell over both of us. We set off on our separate dreams. I imagined I was looking up at the nine-storey building through the darkness. I focused on her third-floor window, and could see her sitting on her bed, as she told me she did at night, feeling lonely and longing for the next afternoon when we would lie together, warming each other's faces with our breath and enjoying each other's closeness.

My whole being flew back to that building, my heart gliding in front of me like a kite swinging in the air. I imagined that she was getting ready for bed; that for once she had thrown her window open, that she was taking off her clothes, combing her hair and rubbing oil on her neck, and caressing her breasts with her long damp fingers.

Hilal nudged me and asked, 'Are you all right?'

He took out his small box of chewing tobacco, put some in his palm and slowly rolled it into a small ball. He carefully placed the ball on the inside of his cheek and then, using his tongue, he moved it around and put it between his lower lip and teeth. The ball of *toombak* pulled out his lower lip and exposed his yellow teeth.

I looked at him for a long moment without blinking. 'Hilal, I am so happy that your wife is coming to Saudi. I was starting to wonder how you could manage to live without her for so long. I mean, you must really miss her.'

'Of course,' he said. 'But her letters keep me going.'

'She writes you letters?'

'And she writes beautifully,' he replied. 'I do miss her. But our letters give each other hope. If it were not for her letters, worries would be wound around my heart like the turban on my head.'

I laughed at his expression.

'But I am a lucky man,' he said, beaming. 'She is coming soon. When I was in Port Sudan, we arranged everything. Now, it is just a matter of small details. I hope it will take no longer than a month or two now. I am sure everything will be fine.'

Hilal heaved his shoulders forward and stretched his hand out to his healthy leg to massage his knee. 'Anyway,' he said, 'I am sure you didn't bring me here to show me the Pleasure Palace. I have a feeling what this could be about, but do you want to tell me first, my dear friend?'

'OK,' I said. 'Please listen carefully.'

THE NEXT AFTERNOON, after we laughed and talked about our planned escape – telling each other how unbelievable it all was – Fiore suddenly fell silent.

'But what will happen if our plan fails?' Fiore asked. Her warm voice dropped to a whisper. 'What will we do if Jasim doesn't keep his word?'

I could feel her anguish. I wished my embrace could calm her fears, or my kisses convince her that everything would be fine.

Jasim was our only option. We had tried to think of alternatives, but the reality was that there was no one else to help us. The only other choice we had was to stay in Jeddah and continue our lives the way they were. But we were both convinced that this was bound to come to an end. We were living like two fugitives in Jeddah. All we had was Fiore's room, with her father just yards away, the religious policemen patrolling Al-Nuzla Street, and the blind imam preaching about the evil sins. The small kingdom we created in her beautiful room was as weak as if it were a castle built of sand.

'It will be fine,' I tried to reassure her.

Fiore buried her face in her hands. I reached out to her and lifted her chin.

I feared going back to my lonely room. I didn't want to leave her. I wanted to be with her for ever. I didn't want to let go of her pink painted nails, her parted lips. I loved looking at her eyes; the fact that one was slightly smaller than the other gave the impression that she was eternally searching for something, for her life. As I caressed her delicate lips with my finger, and gazed at her wild hair, I was happy that she was my woman and I was her man. It felt right. We belonged to each other, I thought. We deserved to grow old together because we had made the impossible possible. I hoped fate would be kind to us.

Later that night, I went to the Corniche to say goodbye to my mother.

I sat for hours staring at the sea, until it turned as black as the sky.

Then, I stepped into the cool water of the Red Sea, wearing only my shorts. I had not felt this good for a long time.

Only swathes of darkness lay ahead of me. But when I looked behind me to the Corniche, I saw the street lights flickering and they reminded me of the oil lamps hanging from the camels when my mother sent me away to Sudan.

Now it was my turn to say goodbyes in the darkness.

'Mother, Semira, I'm sorry that I couldn't make my brother love me as much as he loved our uncle. And now that I have decided to take my life elsewhere, I am sad that we will all live in different parts of the world. Where I am going is a long way from here but if, as they say, all the seas of the world are connected then I will pray that the country which takes me will be surrounded by the sea on all sides, so that I can talk to you from wherever I am and you will still hear me as clearly. So this is not a farewell. I love you. Please keep safe from the bombs until we meet.'

DECEMBER WAS COMING to a close and January, the month of new beginnings, was only two days away.

It was almost three weeks since Jasim had agreed to give me the money for the smuggler businessman. He called to say that he would have the money ready later that evening.

Before I went to meet Fiore, I went to my tree with a bucket full of water. I had started to look after it again – as well as watering it, I would sit underneath it just as I used to. It was returning to life as if its thirst was not only for water but also for a friend's company. I wished I could tell Yahya and Hani about my imminent departure so that they could look after it in my absence.

The Jeep was parked in front of the big mosque. Hamid was standing beside the Jeep next to another shorter man. He had a white beard and was wearing a red and white chequered *gutra* and a white *thobe*, which fell slightly above his ankles. He had a stick in his hand.

For once, I was relieved to see a new policeman. He must be Basil's replacement, I thought.

After Basil led me inside the park that night, Yahya had arrived on his motorbike. He jumped over the fence and went for Basil.

It was Fiore's idea that the best way to get rid of Basil was to strip him of his beard since it was that which gave him religious authority over others; then to threaten him with such an earthly force that fear would spread in his weak heart for the rest of his life.

When Yahya held Basil by his neck, he yelled at him, 'It is not enough that you have recruited two of my best friends and sent them to Afghanistan? Yes, do you know them? Faisal and Zib Al-Ard? But I promise you this. If you come near Naser ever again, I will make sure you will die in Al-Nuzla Street and not Afghanistan.'

Later that afternoon, I was in Fiore's room celebrating the good news of Jasim agreeing to help us. We were in bed dreaming about our future life in Europe. Over at the mosque, we could hear the blind imam delivering his sermon. We lay naked next to each other on her bed, facing the ceiling, with one of her legs between mine. The room glowed under the candles. We both closed our eyes and thought about what was coming. We were silent for a while.

'Quick, close your ears,' said Fiore, sitting up and putting her two fingers on them.

The imam was about to end his speech and as always he finished off with the supplication: 'Oh *ya Allah* destroy the infidels' lands, as they are destroying our lands. Oh *ya Allah* tear down their towers and their houses.'

As the *amens* of the faithful rang through the street, Fiore lay back on the bed and hissed, 'He is praying for the destruction of our future home.'

'We are going to Europe,' I said to Fiore.
'But . . .'
'But what, Fiore?'
She whispered, 'It still scares me.'
She took away her hand from my chest and caressed my

305

face. She turned on her side and looked at me. Her lips on my neck felt like rose petals. My hand slipped down from her waist to the top of her hip. My hand pressed on her hip bone; her body was getting warmer. I could feel her warmth as she rested her chin on my chest. I looked at her parted lips, and her half-shut eyes. 'Will the Europeans accept us?'

'I hope they will,' I said to her. 'Fiore, no place in the world is perfect. But at least we are going to a place where we can fight to achieve our ambitions. Mossa said it won't be easy. He told me life as an immigrant can be tough, but you are a daring woman. You will tame the place.'

I could feel her warm breath as she laughed.

Like a scarf, she pulled her long curly hair to one side and spread it out across my chest.

'I couldn't believe it when Hajj Yusef said that some of the people he helped smuggle five years ago to Sweden came back to visit Mecca with Swedish passports. Five years and they let them be citizens of their countries.'

She turned back to lie on her back and was now staring at the ceiling. She closed her eyes.

'Fiore?'

'Yes.'

'I know it will depend on the smuggler, but where would you like to go?' I asked her.

Without hesitation, she said, 'To where I can be whatever I want to be. But if I can choose, I would want to go to Paris.'

'Why?'

'My favourite Egyptian photographer studied there. Plus I want to go and see the River Seine. I read it is the Mecca for lovers. Its water ripples with lovers' laughter. If we don't end up there, we should visit it at least once. Oh, *habibi*, I feel like I am waiting for heaven. Heaven is for people

306

resurrected from their death, and I feel a spark in my soul.'
She stepped out of bed and walked through the room.

She sat straight down on the chair, facing me. She crossed
her legs, and rested her left hand over her right thigh. Her
painted fingernails hung like pink flowers next to her dark
skin. She tied her hair up in a ponytail, all the while with
her eyes fixed on me, but not really looking, as if her mind
was somewhere else. Her fingers played with her dangling
earring. The light from the candle flames darted around her,
painting golden spots on her skin.

I moved towards her and sat by her feet.

'*Habibati?*' She moved her hand to my face and caressed
me silently.

'What are you thinking about?' I asked.

'I am trying to imagine every possibility, everything that
could go wrong in our plan and come up with alternatives.
Believe me, *habibi*, I am a woman in a man's world and I
find it hard to trust anyone.'

'Fiore,' I whispered, caressing her hands. 'Don't worry.
I already told you, everything is taken care of. Trust me. OK?'

She nodded her head. 'OK.'

That evening, I was lying on my bed waiting for Jasim's
call. The breeze wafted through the trees and drove a leaf
or two through the open window. I watched as they landed
on my legs. I looked at my watch, it was half-past seven.

The phone rang. I rushed to pick it up. Jasim asked me
to come to his café to collect 'the best present you will ever
receive'.

Al-Nuzla Street was glowing. The street was packed with
boys playing football, kids whizzing up and down on their

307

bikes, and men strolling along the street as if they were on the Corniche. A group of older men, some of whom were holding strings of Islamic prayer beads, were sitting outside the Yemeni shop.

A sudden wind hit the street. It looked as if we were all about to be blown away: everyone was pulled back by the wind, the men bowed their heads, white clothes were whipping up, some *gutras* were stripped off heads and were gliding like kites above the street, and even the stiff front garden trees on both sides of the road were bending more than was normal.

I folded my arms over my chest and continued to walk against the wind: two steps forward before I was pushed back one step. My arms were like swords slashing against the dirt flying in the air. I turned around and stood against my tree, leaning my back against the wind and waiting for it to pass.

When things calmed down, I continued on my way to Jasim's café.

A familiar smell of musk was in the air; the blind imam was up ahead being led along by a young boy. The imam was talking, the boy listening intently. I didn't need to see his mouth to lip-read, nor catch his words on the wind, words he had repeated so often that they now echoed continually on Al-Nuzla Street. I put my hands over my ears to shut out the past. I was looking to a new future with *habibati* instead.

As I entered the café, the men's eyes followed my every stride, and then switched to the boy coming out from the back holding a teapot and a few glasses. A man slipped a note in the back pocket of his velvet trousers. I looked around and saw Hilal sitting at the back, at the only table with a single chair. His face almost disappeared behind the coiling smoke of his cigarette. He nodded in my direction, and I smiled back.

I strode forward. 'Naser, I am here,' Jasim called from the other side of the café, waving his arm. I went over to Jasim's table and he stood up, took my hand and pulled me towards the back room. In the corridor, he leaned towards my lips. I pushed him away. 'Stop it, Jasim.'

He looked me straight in the eye, whispering, 'Come on, my dear. I have been waiting for that kiss for years. Just once.'

I dragged him inside the small room and shut the door behind us.

'I will miss you, *habibi*,' he mumbled.

'Is everything ready?' I asked.

He stepped aside and coughed. We looked at each other. I bit the inside of my cheek. He stroked his chin, looking at me with his lips pressed together.

'Jasim, is everything ready?' I asked again.

'Yes.' It was the only thing he said. Nothing else. I hated it when he fixed his eyes on me like that, wanting to melt me with his stares. I was so tired of it. His continuous attentions made me tired. His cheesy words about love made me tired. He had turned me from a boy into a toy for his customers. That infamous day, minutes before he allowed Rashid into the room with the mirror ceiling, he was sitting next to me on my bed. He stroked my thighs, saying that he wanted to help me get used to a man's hands. At the same time, he told me how sorry he was about Rashid but that the imam was to blame because if women were allowed to be around us, boys like me would not have had to endure these hungry men of Al-Nuzla. 'If these men really love women, why don't they turn their keys in their own doors and set the women free?' I asked him. 'Why don't they tell the imam to stop telling them what to do?'

'You don't understand,' he replied, trying to unzip my trousers. 'The imam is very powerful. His influence is immense. He has *Allah*'s ears as well as the government's.'

I stopped him from pulling down my trousers. I pushed him away. 'Don't worry,' I said, 'my body is already used to a man's hands. Just leave me alone.'

Now, four years later, I was in his room again. This time, I hoped it would be my last. The mirror was still cracked, and nothing else had changed. Jasim was still telling the same things to the new waiter: 'You are the perfect substitute for a woman . . .'

I looked at Jasim. 'Where is the money?' I asked once again. He turned away and gazed off into the distance. After a few long minutes, he finally pointed with his index finger to his bed. There was a white envelope on top of the sheets. A flicker of a smile overpowered my anxiety. I sighed with relief.

He went to sit on the bed and crossed his legs. 'The cheque is in here,' he said. He waved the envelope in my direction. 'I hope this will make you love me, even if only from a distance.'

I remained quiet.

He asked me to sit next to him but I stayed where I was, motionless, looking at my watch, my feet tapping on the carpeted floor.

'You have to go,' he said.

'Yes.'

'Can you at least give me a hug?'

I didn't move.

'Please, Naser. A friendly embrace, that's all I am asking.'

I could see him coming towards me. He leapt at me and quickly caught me in his arms. He sighed and whispered, 'Oh, Naser, I am sorry.'

'What for?'

He didn't say anything. I felt his tears on my cheek. His hand moved quickly from my back to my waist, and he held me tight.

I tried to release myself, but he strengthened his grip. After a while I stopped resisting. He pushed me away. I stumbled backwards but I steadied myself. He sat on the bed and picked up the envelope.

'Are you really in love with this girl, Naser?'

'Yes,' I replied, firmly.

'Can you give me my lighter, please? It is on top of the TV.'

I looked at him, then at the top of the TV. I saw his black lighter next to a pile of porn videos. I wanted to bring it to his bed, but he told me to stop. 'Stay there and throw the lighter,' he demanded.

I did as he asked.

Without moving his head, he caught it with his left hand.

'Why didn't you try to love me?' he asked, his voice breaking.

I didn't respond.

'Were you really planning to go to the religious police and tell them about this place?'

I gritted my teeth. I stared at him, then at the envelope in his hand.

'This is not the first time you betrayed me,' he said.

'What are you talking about? Jasim, please give me the envelope. I need to go.'

'You should have realised by now that I know about everything that happens in my café,' he said. He spat on the floor. 'How could he do that to me? How could he betray me? He knew I loved you. I thought he was my friend.'

'What are you talking about? Which friend?'

'I am talking about Abu Imad, the man you used to call Mr Quiet. I helped that illegal man and he went behind my back to come to your room after early morning prayer to have sex.'

'Jasim, you are being ridiculous. He was only a friend.'

'Wasn't it me who gave him money when he first came to this country and he had no one to help him. Ungrateful piece of dog.'

'*Ya Allah*, so you are angry because you think I slept with Mr Quiet, but you . . . *ya Allah*, you don't feel any remorse for selling me to Rashid?'

He jumped out of his bed and screamed, 'Shush. I don't want to hear it. You are cutting me to pieces. Why are you cruel to me?'

'Cruel? Me? Because I mentioned that you sold a young boy for sex? How do you think that makes me feel?'

He sat back on his bed and grabbed the envelope. 'It's strange that you would be prepared to sell me out for a girl,' he said.

'You sold me to Rashid. Please, Jasim. I found someone who is giving me the love I want. Now let's move on. I don't want to look back. I have a future to live with her. Give me the envelope, please.'

'Oh, Naser, my sweetheart. Why did you decide to threaten me? You are naïve. You have been in this country for ten years and you still don't know how things work?' He slit the envelope open, took out the cheque and started fanning himself with it.

I approached him, almost creeping. 'This country, my dear, is all about who you know. Have you ever heard of a prince being beheaded or flogged, even though we all know they are just as capable as the rest of us of committing crimes?'

312

'Jasim, I need the money. Just give me the cheque please.'

'I am well connected to my *kafeel*, the police chief of Jeddah, the Blessed Bader Ibn Abd-Allah,' he said, pulling the ashtray towards him.

Jasim's *kafeel* was mine too. What? Did Jasim know what he had done to me?

'I am sure you know him, ah?' he asked.

I had had a suspicion that it was Jasim's *kafeel* who had helped him smuggle in illegal books, pornography and everything else that was forbidden in Saudi Arabia. I knew he must have been particularly powerful, because customs officers never searched their luggage, so Jasim could get anything past the gates at the airport.

But now I could see why the religious police stayed blind to what happened in his café.

'I am a well-connected man,' Jasim shouted his importance once again. 'That's how I got rid of Mr Quiet.'

'You deported your own friend?' I stuttered, holding back my tears.

He placed the cheque in the ashtray and set fire to it. I lunged at him to try to save the burning cheque, but he punched me and pushed me away with his foot. I landed with the side of my head on the TV. Immediately a stream of blood dripped from my nose and forehead. I turned to look at him. The flames of the burning envelope swelled behind him. I begged him, 'Jasim, don't do that. I can't love you but if you want anything else, then tell me. I just need the money. Please.' He calmly picked up a perfume bottle from the box underneath his bed. The cheque turned into grey ashes. He broke the tall glass bottle in half. Some of the perfume splashed on the carpet. 'Come closer and you know what I will do,' he threatened me.

He lifted his arm, holding the broken bottle to his face. He let the red perfume drip into his open mouth. 'You shouldn't have tried to mess with me. You know I have a lot of contacts. So I asked the religious police to go after you, my dear. And you know what, my dear, I have told them you have committed adultery. Whether they find evidence or not, you will be stoned in Punishment Square and I will be there to throw one at your filthy body with your black heart.'

Jasim laughed a loud, sneering laugh: 'Well, what are you waiting for? They'll be here any minute.'

I ran out of the room. By the time I got out of the café, the familiar Jeep with shaded windows was already approaching. I dashed to the left and heard the sound of tyres screeching behind me. Without looking back, I sprinted down Al-Nuzla Street towards Kharentina and away from Fiore's house. But the Jeep was faster than me. At the big supermarket in Al-Nuzla, they caught up with me. I stopped. It was over.

I stood there panting and defeated. Three men jumped out of the Jeep and grabbed me by the arms. I recognised Hamid and the short man with the white beard who had taken over from Basil.

Hamid cuffed my hands behind my back and bundled me into the Jeep. The other two walked to the front seats. The seats at the back were like those in an ambulance, two long benches facing each other. Hamid was sitting in front of me. The Jeep drove off. 'Why am I calm?' I thought. 'Why am I not screaming? Why am I not kneeling to beg them to have mercy?'

But all I did was whisper: 'Why *ya Allah*?'

'Don't pronounce *Allah*'s revered name,' Hamid shouted.

'Fiore,' I screamed, beating my head against the window.

He punched me under my ribs. 'Take this, *ya* apostate, *ya* cursed. Don't you dare mention a woman's name,' he yelled. 'And now you will suffer for making a mockery out of the imam.'

I looked up at Hamid. 'Forgive me,' I mumbled.

'It is too late to ask *Allah* forgiveness, you will be lodged in hell, *inshaAllah*.'

'Please forgive me, *ya habibati*.'

'*Ya Allah*, and now you are asking forgiveness from a woman instead of *Allah*,' he wailed. '*Ya* Sheikh Abdul-Aziz, in the name of *Allah* pass me the stick.'

I screamed at him, 'Go on, hit me, *ya* future sheikh. But I tell you this, I did not commit a crime, and *Allah* is my witness. All I did was love, and love is heaven sent.'

'Don't you ever say that, *ya* dog. Tell us who this woman is.' He cursed me again.

'Never. I will never let your hands touch her.'

'Don't be a hero,' he said. 'Tell us who this evil woman is, for the sake of *Allah*, or I will break this stick on your head.'

'Never. She is more blessed than you.'

The man with the white beard, turned around and slapped me from the front bench, shouting, 'Shut up *ya* cursed, *ya* heartless.'

'Oh Fiore, I will miss you.'

Hamid swung his stick in the air. He lashed at me, creating lines of fire with every swipe on my shoulders. In all his agitation, his *gutra* fell off, but he continued hitting me.

He finally sat down, breathless. I lowered my head and felt tears rolling down my face. Hamid smacked me on the head, saying, 'We don't have a lot of time. Where does this apostate live?'

'You call her an apostate because she loved me? What is the use of a heart?'

He threw his stick away and started punching me with his bare fist. I begged him to stop. 'I'll tell you who she is.'

He looked at me with his dark eyes. He bent down to pick up his *gutra* and adjusted it on his head. '*Ya* Sheikh Abdul-Aziz, stop the car. He is going to tell us. We know she is from Al-Nuzla. So we might as well pick her up while we are here.'

Through the shaded window, I could see the nine-storey building. This was the first time I hoped she wasn't at home.

I bowed my head. With tears rolling down my face, I started talking: 'I will tell you who she is, for I am proud of how she looks, talks and thinks. I will describe her for you from head to toe and then it is up to you to find her. You will need to knock on every door in Al-Nuzla and break down the men's sections to reach her. You will need to stop every woman in the street and unveil her face. You might want to cram yourself into the women's section of the bus, the amusement parks and the shops. And you will have to break the walls in the mosques that divide the women from the men. I promise you that if you do that, you will find her, for she is special. Her intelligence shines like the marble of palaces, and her eyes are different to the rest because in hers you will find it is the determination and strength that make them beautiful and glowing. For this woman is a true lover.'

I watched as Hamid rolled up his sleeves and put his *gutra* and his white knitted skull-cap on the seat next to him. I knew what was coming. Still, I looked him straight in the eyes, mumbling her name. 'Fiore.' He picked up his stick. 'Fiore.' And when he pushed me on to my knees, I repeated her name to drown out his yelling and suppress my own pain. 'Fiore. Fiore. Fiore.'

The Jeep drove all the way down Al-Nuzla Street and through Mecca Street then turned left towards the centre of Jeddah. From there it took a few more turns before we arrived at the central prison of Jeddah, where my friend Mr Quiet had once been imprisoned.

Inside the prison, I was shadowed by the three policemen. I looked around. We were passing many closed doors and some open ones. I could see men looking through the bars of their cells, staring at the empty space before them. I bowed my head, and saw that many of the floor tiles were broken like everything else in that place.

When we reached the end of the corridor, I glanced back. It was a long corridor and it felt like an endless black hole, with no light and little air.

Hamid un-cuffed my hands and threw me inside a small cell saying, before closing the iron door, 'I hope you will be stoned soon, *inshaAllah*.'

An African-looking man sat at the back of the cell. When he saw the state I was in, he stood up and with his handkerchief wiped the blood off my face. 'Be patient, son,' he said, 'here, drink some water. You look like a man who has a story to tell. And I have all the time in the world to listen to you. But first you must take a rest.'

The cell was very small with fluorescent lighting and a tiny window near the top of the wall. It stayed bright during most of that night and was boiling hot, as if we were sitting in the middle of the desert. Most of the floor tiles were missing and spiders crawled everywhere. The stench of vomit was fixed to the walls of the cell like mouldy wallpaper. There were two mattresses on the floor. Both were thin and reeked of urine, where terrified men had been reduced to wetting their beds like babies.

The next day, after having listened to my story, the man, who turned out to be a Nigerian Muslim named Mustafa, exclaimed, 'What a wonderful woman your lover is, Naser. A woman who orchestrates a love affair with such godsent power can only be a love prophet. Now hold your head high. You are lucky and privileged to have enjoyed the company of such a strong woman. And don't despair, Naser, life is short and you must be happy that a woman like Fiore has given you nearly six months of her life.'

IT IS EXACTLY five days since I was caught by the religious police and brought to this place. It is now five in the morning. I am obsessed with time, counting the seconds, the minutes, the hours, the days, because I am inventing my own calendar, starting with the day in July when my life with Fiore began.

I am sitting on the thin mattress on the ground, opposite Mustafa. He is lying down, facing the wall. He is asleep under the harsh glare of the fluorescent lighting.

I am sitting with my arms wrapped around my legs, rocking back and forth. I am constantly fighting my mind, not wanting to think about the punishment awaiting me. Mustafa told me that there is no point thinking about that day. 'They will try you in your absence,' he said. 'They won't allow you a lawyer or even for you to defend yourself. They won't tell you when you will be punished. When they decide it is time, they will come to your cell and take you to Punishment Square.'

Instead, I try to think about Fiore. Soon, a prison warden will arrive to take us to pray in the prison mosque. In the beginning I refused and was dragged out of my cell all the way to the big mosque in another wing of the prison. But Mustafa told me that I shouldn't resist, that the beating is not worth it. 'Remember that *Allah* is not theirs alone. Anyway, don't miss the chance of going out from this cell to that mosque.'

The mosque is a beautiful, spacious place. It is bigger than the grand mosque in Al-Nuzla. The walls are painted in glistening white and the light is soft and calming. The musk floats around. Mustafa is right: once there, I feel like

I am on a day out – I breathe the nice scent and can escape from my cell, where the walls seem to be closing in on me by the second.

Once I overheard a man cry in the middle of a prayer, 'Why do you make a mosque as nice as this and our cells as filthy as a donkey's barn? Why make all this effort to please a God that may or may not exist and neglect us, your brothers in humanity? Don't we exist for you?'

No one heard of him again.

'It's ironic,' Mustafa tells me. 'They force us to pray, thinking they are doing their duty entrusted upon them by *Allah*, but they don't know that He, the Almighty, in the end will answer the sufferers' prayers.'

But I have no time to think about the guards.

When I line up behind the prison mosque's imam and face Mecca, my heart leaps to Fiore, hoping that *Allah* will listen to the prayers of my heart along with the calls of His believers.

Mustafa has never told me how he ended up here. Whenever I ask him, he replies that he will tell me one day and that now is not the right time for me to hear other people's stories. 'Naser, you are still tender with Fiore's love. I don't want to be the one who disturbs her in your heart.'

When the fluorescent lighting is switched off for a few hours every night, I lean against the wall, and while listening to Mustafa's deep breathing, I recite Fiore's notes and letters, all of which I have memorised. When the memory of her eyes, lips, thighs, and her breasts get too much, I lie on my back and I imagine that her face occupies the ceiling of my cell and brightens my loneliness.

★

It is Friday, a week has now passed since I was brought here. It is eight in the morning.

A stocky, bearded guard enters my cell.

It must be time. I turn to the guard and ask him, 'Are you taking me to Punishment Square?'

He grabs me by my hand and pulls me out of the cell. I want to turn to say goodbye to Mustafa, but he is sleeping.

The long corridor is empty. My hands are trembling as I am imagining being put inside a hole in the earth and stones bouncing off my face.

I am in a small room with no furniture. It is as small as my cell. Its white paint is fading. The only remarkable thing about it is that it has a big glass window in it. But I can't see what's behind it. Three police officers are standing in front of me. The stocky one in the middle is flanked by two larger men. It is he who first asks me a question. 'Where does this apostate live, *ya* dog?' the officer asks in his sharp voice.

'Who?'

'Don't waste our time. The religious police said you were calling a name. Fiore. We have checked the database of residents and no one exists by that name in the whole of Jeddah.'

I smile despite myself. Hearing her name reminds me how special she is. 'Because,' I responded to the officer, 'her name is very simple. Very elegant. Very unique.'

'I am going to ask you one more time,' he shouts, spraying his spit all over my face. 'Where does she live? In Al-Nuzla? Mecca Street? What is her real name? Who is she married to?'

The two large officers move closer and are now by my side. They both have trimmed black moustaches and large ears.

More spit covers my face. The stocky police officer is yelling.

'I will not tell you anything about *habibati*. And I vow that I never will, whatever you do to me.'

Each of the two large officers lands a fist on each side of my ribs. I fold in two; soon I am on the floor. When I see their boots lift off the ground, I close my eyes.

My back, chest and stomach burn with pain. I can't breathe properly because my nose is bleeding. I can't open my mouth, because my lips are too swollen. I can only just about see with one eye, the other seems to be blinded. I am being dragged by the two large officers into the corridor. With my good eye, I can see blood dripping in front of me. My chest is pounding. Where are they taking me now?

They open the cell door and throw me inside. I manage to see Mustafa running towards me. 'Oh *ya Allah* what have you done to him?'

'Shut up,' says a sharp voice, the voice that was cursing me as the two large officers kept beating me up. The voice of the stocky officer.

I feel Mustafa's hands on my cheeks. 'Please, officers,' he now begs. 'Blood is streaming from this wound in his forehead. Please help him. Can't you see that he has injured his head?'

'Don't worry, your time will come soon, *inshaAllah*.'

'What has this man done to you? He fell in love. How can that have caused you so much pain that you are making him suffer so much? Look, officer, this is serious. Please take him to the hospital.'

'Take him to a hospital to treat him and then smash his face all over again in a public square? Don't make us laugh. It is good he is wounded, he is now half-way there.'

I hear a loud roar of laughter.

IT IS FRIDAY again. This is my third week in prison. I have almost recovered from the beatings I received again last Friday. I am expecting a visit from the stocky interrogation officer and his two large assistants.

'Mustafa, do you think today they will take me to Punishment Square?'

He doesn't answer.

'Mustafa, I hope they will be merciful enough to behead me instead of stoning me.'

He bows his head.

The door opens. Two officers wearing black armbands stand there and ask me to stand up. I can see the same passiveness in their eyes that I saw in Abu Faisal's eyes. 'This is it,' I mumble.

As I walk towards them, Mustafa holds my hand, rolls up my shirt sleeves. He embraces me tightly. I am lost. I don't react. I don't know what to say. I am shaking but I am not able to say a word. I just look at Mustafa. He squeezes my hand firmly and, with his eyes unflinching, he makes me swear never to regret what I have done because 'Life is temporary, and there is no shame suffering the consequences of love.'

He turns his back and sobs.

The two police officers handcuff me. I try begging one last time, 'Jasim lied to you. I am not married. I was in love with a girl. She was not married. I swear to *Allah* this was the

323

first love for both of us. I should be lashed, not stoned to death. Look, doesn't the law talk about witnesses? Where are they?' I close my eyes and see myself being buried in a hole up to my waist, and men hitting my face and my head with stones until I die. I start screaming. I beg the officers, 'Why don't you take me to the judge? I have a lot to say to him. I swear on the Qur'an that I was in love with a single girl and that I am not married.' I am pushed out of the cell and into the corridor. I beg them one more time. 'Please, if you want to kill me, then please ask them to behead me. *Allah* will reward you. Have mercy on me, please kill me quickly.'

Outside the prison, I see the model of the plane, sitting still, even though its front wheels are ready to take off into the sky, into no man's land. I wish a miracle would happen and the plane fly away with me.

When I lower my head, I see the officer kneeling down to chain my feet. My tears drop on the ground in front of him. He looks up. I shut my eyes and tilt my head backwards. I exhale hard. I think about Fiore, how much I miss her, how much I want her to be with me, to give me my last hug in this world.

I am loaded into a truck with the two police officers. I am sat down on a metal seat, and I am blindfolded. But I know where I am going, so I lean my head back and wonder what Fiore is doing now, whether she is in her room writing a letter that I will never receive, dreaming about our life together, a fantasy that will soon die with me.

I AM STANDING barefoot on smooth warm tiles. Someone takes the blindfold off and I am in a familiar place. Punishment Square. Ahead of me is the shopping mall where Fiore and I first met. I look down and remember the story I heard in school about the Pakistani man from 'I Am Innocent' Street. I am innocent like him, I think to myself. Will my blood write those blessed words on the tiles?

The crowd is gathering, forming a circle around me. I look at their hands to see if they are holding stones ready to throw at my face.

I don't see any.

Just as I am about to give a sigh of relief, I see Abu Faisal storm into the circle. My knees buckle and I plunge to the ground.

I have so much pain inside me. I want someone to hold me, comfort me, to tell me it is all right, that beheading is more merciful and this way it will be quicker. I look to the crowd for that someone. I have so much to say. I want to tell them how I am feeling right now.

But the crowd is oblivious to my sorrow. Some are holding hands and whispering to each other, I see some bending double as they laugh at each other's jokes, and I see others looking at their watches as if to say, 'Come on, get on with it, we need to go soon.'

I bow my head and fight my tears. I don't want them

to hear me or see me cry, because they will never understand. Love is a foreigner in this square.

I raise my head and take a glance at Abu Faisal. He is inches away from me, still looking at the crowd, pumping up his chest. He slowly turns his head towards me. Our eyes meet. I think of his son, my friend.

Abu Faisal must be waiting for the sword. I search for women in the crowd. I see four at the far end to my right. They are wearing the full veil. I look down at their shoes. She is not here.

Suddenly a loud voice beams through the tannoy. I look over my shoulder. It is the announcer. I brace myself.

'We are here, brothers, to witness justice being served against this apostate,' he says. 'This man has committed the ultimate sin: fornication. And a man who commits such a shameful felony in the land of Prophet Muhammad, peace be upon him, must be a man void of a heart, and soul. This man kneeling before us on this wretched ground is nothing but a traitor who sold his religion for lust, a man who substituted praying to be in the arms of a cursed creature, a man who instead of reading the Qur'an, spent his precious time on this earth with a woman, who will *inshaAllah* be his path to hell. And this man refuses to ask *Allah*'s forgiveness for his crime, kneel before the Almighty and beg His clemency. He lives his life like Satan, who acts as if he has done nothing wrong and lives his days empty of guilt. How can this man face *Allah* without regret? How can he breathe the air of the Almighty without a hint of remorse? He has deviated from the right path, but our judge has ruled that mercy is not worth a dog like him, and it is our hope that a punishment of a hundred and ninety-nine lashes will bring the fear of *Allah* into this apostate.'

I break down and weep with happiness. I am not

going to die. I am not going to be beheaded. I stand up. I want to snatch the tannoy from the announcer's hand and shout to Fiore, hoping she will hear me wherever she is. '*Habibati*,' I want to yell, 'I am alive!'

Suddenly I feel the hands of someone ripping my shirt off. I look up. It is Abu Faisal. He is holding a cane. I hear the roar of the crowd cheering at the same time as I feel a swishing sound of the cane landing on my back. Some in the crowd begin to count. Others are shouting, 'Hit the apostate harder, may *Allah* burn him in hell.' I feel warm blood on my back. The cane is stripping into my flesh. But nothing matters any more, because I am thinking about my love, my life. 'Now what will happen? What other forms of punishment will they think up? Will they deport me? Will Fiore still love me, even at such a long distance? What will happen to her?'

I collapse.

I AM BACK in my cell in the same prison. I cannot stand so I am lying flat on my stomach on my mattress. They just threw me here and left me with nothing. It feels as if someone is pouring boiling liquid on the wounds across my back and bottom. I can only pray that the pain will gradually subside. For now my only remedy is to bite the greasy sheets on my bed.

It is a week since I was flogged in Punishment Square. The wounds are still healing, but I know they will leave great ridges of scars on my back. I can barely sleep, because whenever I try, I keep having nightmares about the Square and Abu Faisal.

I still don't know what is to happen next, what they will do to me, and whether all this will come to an end. Even *Allah* seems not to know. My prayers are not answered. My fate is firmly in their hands.

I am on my own in this cell. Mustafa is not here. He was taken away last Friday while I was in Punishment Square. He never told me why he was in prison. I don't know if he was deported back to Nigeria or taken to the Square as well. I grieve for his absence. I grieve for my love.

I have been refusing their two meals a day. I only eat and drink once a day to have the required strength to think about her, while waiting for whatever they will do to me next.

And all I do in this lonely cell is remember again and again the last time I told her I loved her.

A policeman enters my cell and asks me to stand up.

'Come here,' he says, standing over me. He adjusts his black gun-belt and joins his hands on top of his belly. I stand up.

He points to the exit. He steps backwards and pushes me out.

I shudder when I realise it is Friday. He leads me out as we zigzag our way around other police officers in the corridor. I follow him as if I were his tail.

We go into an office with three tables and a stack of papers and files and he orders me to sit down. He points at the wooden chair. He walks around the table and passes the phone to me. 'Here, you have a phone call waiting,' he says. He stands up and leaves the room.

I hold the phone receiver and without understanding I stare at it silently for a while.

'Hello?'

It is Hilal on the line.

'Hilal? *Ya Allah*, Hilal, I am so happy to hear your voice. What –'

'Listen, Naser. Listen carefully, my friend, I only have a few minutes on the phone. Boy, my heart sank when I saw you running out of the café and I knew your plan had failed.'

'They took me to Punishment Square. They flogged me. I really thought they were going to execute me. What are they going to do to me now?'

'In the name of *Allah* the merciful, listen. It was my *kafeel* who managed to reverse the execution ruling.'

I wipe my tears, thanking Hilal and his *kafeel* over and over again. 'It's OK, Naser.'

'How can I ever thank you?'

'By being strong. I am sorry about you and Fiore.' He pauses for a second, giving me some time to let his words sink in. 'But you will have a lot of time to grieve. Now listen to me. OK? They will deport you to Sudan. You are going to Port Sudan. The religious police raided your flat but I made sure I got there first and took all the letters, the notes and your mother's portrait to my house. Thank the Lord, you never used her real name.'

'Why are they doing this? Hilal, tell me why? I miss Fiore. How is she, Hilal?'

'Naser, be strong. You took a risk when you went to Jasim. I know you had no other option, but now that you are caught you will be sent away. This is no time to feel sorry for yourself. My wife is here. She met Fiore in Al-Nuzla Street; she knew to look out for her Pink Shoes. My wife told her what happened to you.'

'Are her shoes still lighting up Al-Nuzla Street?'

'Fiore told my wife she doesn't need them any more.'

I bend over, my arms pressing deep into my belly to stop the pain.

I remember my diary. I ask Hilal about it.

'Yes, I found your diary too, I asked my wife to give it to Fiore together with the notes.'

I drop my head in despair, embarrassed by the secrets from my past described in the diary which Fiore now has. But Hilal is oblivious to my worries.

'Now, pay attention. My brother will wait for you in Port Sudan and take you to our house in the city. It will be your return address for Fiore from now on. Once I get your letters, my wife will take them to Fiore. Please remember that I lived in Jeddah for so many years without seeing my wife. Letters were all we had between us. And letters are sometimes all lovers need. The barrier that separates you from Fiore will crumble into the Red Sea with your words. Because no obstacle is big enough to keep the feelings of lovers apart. And whenever you want to talk to Fiore, walk to the beach of Port Sudan and the waves of the Red Sea will take your message to Fiore. Naser? Naser? Are you listening?'

'Yes. Yes.'

'Make sure you hide what the police officer will give you really well. You don't want anyone to take it away from you. May *Allah* be with you, my friend. I will see you in Port Sudan very soon.'

He puts down the phone. My fingers lose their grip and the receiver falls on the desk, my head follows and my hands clutch my stomach.

The officer comes into the room and closes the door behind him. He puts his hand into his pocket and quickly takes out a folded envelope. 'Here,' he says, stretching his hand.

I stare at him, confused. I snatch the white envelope out of his hand and know it is a letter from Fiore. I can smell her perfume.

The officer taps my shoulder and says, 'Hide it quickly. We have to hurry.'

I tuck the envelope deep in the pocket of my shirt, close to my heart. He holds me by the arm and leads me away.

Three police officers – wearing khaki trousers and green shirts – join us in the long corridor. The prison gate opens and the sun welcomes me with its intense heat. I struggle to open my eyes against the white light. I am taken to a waiting police car and pushed inside.

I think about the letter pressed against my sweating body. I badly want to rip it open and read it now.

I AM IN a police car speeding down a wide, tree-lined avenue. I am looking through the car window. I know we are on a flyover, but I can't exactly pinpoint where we are as the car is driving so fast and all I can see are flashes of buildings and trees as they get swallowed by the speed.

But I know where I am going. I lean my head against the seat and look through the window, thinking about Fiore.

The car is now driving down the bridge. I see long cranes dominating the sky above the sea.

The smell of the sea is coming in through the car window. I want to do what I did ten years ago, when I first arrived in Jeddah, when I hung out of the window and I inhaled the breeze, full of beautiful dreams. Instead, I shut my eyes, press my knees together and drop my head.

So is this the port I have heard so much about? How come my legs aren't trembling? I take a deep breath. I smell the silt in the air. I want to look around, but a policeman drags me into an office where a decorated officer sits on a leather seat behind a brown desk full of papers and passports. 'Take him to terminal seven,' he says.

I am back in the police car. We drive past the livestock terminals, and the container terminals, before reaching the passenger terminals. The car halts and as I step out I see a large boat. Just yards away, there is another anchored ferry with an Egyptian flag. That ship is loading with vehicles and hundreds of passengers.

'Curse on you, *inshaAllah*,' one of the customs officers swears at me. It is only when he says this I realise that I have planted my feet firmly on the ground. They pull me by my collar and throw me behind a man in a grey suit in a long queue leading to the large boat with two decks.

I see the women's queue to the right, parallel to us. I look at them, hoping for a miracle, that Fiore is one of them. Not all the women are veiled. Most women just look down, some watching their tears fall down on their feet. There are children screaming, but the men stare at the sea in silence.

All of us are being deported.

My queue starts moving. I still can't walk normally; the places where the stick landed still burn my back, my legs and my arms. I can see the boat rocking, flexing its muscles, daring us to ride on its shoulders.

Allah is called upon constantly by the women and the men in the queue, and even by the Saudi officials, who mention one of *Allah*'s ninety-nine names in every single sentence, even in their curses and beatings.

'Come on,' I mumble to myself, 'move it.' I want to go to the upper deck of the boat and watch the dock. Hilal told me that he would be there to wave goodbye.

THE GATE OPENS and we start embarking. There are security guards watching our every step, but we are free to move between decks. I go up to the second floor of the boat to get a good view. I look at Jeddah and as the boat rocks on the waves, the Bride of the Red Sea tilts from left to right as if in a slow dance.

I hear someone shout, 'Men and women, listen to me.' I turn my head to see a light-skinned man wearing a Sudanese turban standing up on a bench. I catch his eye and he grins and adds, 'My dear people, let's not give them satisfaction. We are proud people. We have a proud history.' Some of the group start to sing songs about their homeland. I turn back to watch the dock.

The boat's engine roars. I battle against my tears, leaning over the railing and looking over at the dock. Nothing is moving. I hold my shirt pocket, and I press my hand against the letter. I want to read it now but am scared about what it might say. I will wait a little longer, until we are far away from the coast.

I look out over the sea. There is a sudden and strange calm on the surface. It looks like a still blue carpet. Just before we depart, a flock of black birds flies over us and heads to the dock. The birds linger in mid-air for a few seconds, flapping their wings frantically, as if hesitating to land. Then like a theatre curtain opening, half of the birds fly one way and the other half go the other. Beyond the cloud of birds I can see the gathering of women on the dock, and in the midst of them, a pair of Pink Shoes.

'*Habibati*. Fiore.'

Her *abaya* quivers like the feathers of a bird. When she raises her hands to quieten her flapping cloth, she is like a black flamingo ready to soar.

'I love you, *habibati*,' I whisper.

The Pink Shoes stand out against the white stones of the dock. She kneels: her head bows first, her shoulders follow and her elegant body folds double. The birds return and cackle around her. She takes off her Pink Shoes and stands motionless against the wind. She brings the shoes to her chest and hugs them tightly. The boat blows its horn and starts its journey. Fiore bends down and throws the shoes into the sea.

The Sudanese group sing on but I cry, silently. I only whisper 'Fiore' once, but the ripples of the Red Sea echo her name a thousand times.

I wave. 'Fiore, I have your letter. Look . . .' I take it out and wave with it at her. 'I will always love you.'

She blows me a kiss with her gloved hand and turns.

As she walks away from the dock and joins the lines of other women waving at those departing, it is only her *abaya* which is beating a sad goodbye in the air. As the boat pulls out she is lost from sight, she looks just like everyone else. But I can still pick out the shoes on the blue water. They too are leaving Jeddah, the swinging city, and dancing with the waves like two pink lights flashing in the Red Sea. The tide carries them higher and higher before burying them deep in the waves. Jeddah returns to the black and white picture it always was.

Habibi,

I rehearsed this moment a million times inside my head. Even long before I proposed my love to you, when I used to dream about falling in love, I would imagine what would happen if my lover and I were taken away from each other.

Sometimes in moments of weakness I wish I had never interrupted your rest under your tree. I often held back from approaching you. I would pass your tree, with you sitting underneath it like a fallen apple, and a flash of love would tickle my heart and I would want to come nearer, but I didn't.

For many months, I studied your face every time I saw you, and by the time I had finally overcome my caution, I was convinced that my love for you would be matched by your solidarity. It comforts me to think I was right. I was right to show my love for you whatever the consequences. And it makes me the luckiest girl in the world.

Habibi, Hilal told me you will be given this letter by your guard. I don't know where you will be when you read my words, you might be in your cell or on the boat in the middle of the Red Sea, but I know you will be far away from me.

When I am in my empty room, I look for your memory. When I lie on my bed, I close my eyes to capture the aroma of our love-making, still lingering on my sheets. I press my face into one of my pillows, imagining that your silhouette is imprinted next to the embroideries of unicorns on its cover, hoping that your lips will suddenly surface and kiss me. And I take the other pillow, as if it was your hand, and place it on my heart, because that is where it is hurting most.

I close my eyes to look for your laughter and words that are still echoing across my room. Sometimes, I stand in front of my mirror all day long, hoping to go back in time. It is then that I feel I am standing in front of you, my back glued to your chest and my hands reaching behind so I can bring you closer to me still. I feel you filling my ears with the words lovers say to each other tirelessly, but when I turn around to say I love you too, I find that my dream has vanished.

I cry at the emptiness. I scream over the loneliness. My mother comes to my room and wants to embrace me. But I tell her she mustn't because my body is still tender with your last touches. I try to search for that last spot where you stood, the last place your body occupied. And when she leaves, taking her sorrow with her, I crouch on my bed. Then night falls and when the morning comes I go over it all again. I feel iron bars forming around me, trapping my soul and my heart in the prison of the past.

When the pain becomes too much, I go out. I walk on Al-Nuzla Street, the same street where I once felt like a queen when you looked down at my feet, as if my shoes were the most beautiful thing in the world. But now all that too is gone with you. My shoes are ordinary now, they mean nothing to anyone around here.

I find myself walking on and on, my Pink Shoes passing blind onlookers, and a bus ride brings me to the Red Sea.

I am now sitting on the 'oud player's bench, writing this letter to you. It has been a month since you were arrested.

I have come here to tell you that I have finally taken the decision I have postponed making. I have lost hope that a miracle will bring me closer to you; that someone will bring us back together. Hilal told me you were going to Sudan and I did my best to try and borrow money from my friends to pay for a forged passport and a ticket, but they all said they couldn't help because their fathers and husbands kept their money. I even tried to look for work but my father shut the door on my face saying that no woman in his house works. I even started doubting whether we would ever meet again.

But yesterday afternoon, habibi, I made up my mind. I was sitting here, with my back to Jeddah, looking out to the sea over which you had looked out so many times. I felt the spirit of the 'oud player, whom you told me so much about, sitting next to me, silently staring at the sea. I closed my eyes, fearing the fate that lay ahead of me when I reopened them.

With my eyelids cast down, like the shutter of the window in my room, I saw the life that was waiting for me in Al-Nuzla. I knew that if I went back, I would be buried under men's rules.

I felt cornered between the raging sea and the men of Al-Nuzla. Which one would it be? Death awaited me in both directions.

I kept my eyes screwed shut, taking myself deeper into the hollowness of my life.

When I opened them, I looked to the sea, and the high tide.

I wanted to rip off my veil and run, run so fast into the water, the mesmerising waves, where I would be like an excited child, naïvely waving about, shouting, yelling and laughing at the brief freedom, at the short-lived beauty of life, before all of it came to an end once I reached the depths.

But I didn't move. My feet felt heavy, as if my Pink Shoes had grown roots deep in the sand.

I remembered the promise I made to you the last time you were in my room.

I felt like howling, matching the sea's roar. But in silence, I found my hand moving to my bag next to me on the bench, containing your diary, your memory. I put it on my lap and bent over it, crying.

I tried to hold back from reading it ever since Hilal gave it to me, but yesterday I needed to hear your words, I needed you close to me to help me out of my situation.

I saw page after page about your life in Jeddah, from the moment you arrived, to the day when you were fifteen and you were sent by your uncle to your perverse kafeel, and your time in Jasim's café. I saw so much pain, so much suffering chained to the pages and your striving to break free. And when I finished reading, I bowed my head and could think of nothing else but my aching desire to hold you tight, and to tell you how much you mean to me.

I hurried to Hilal's house, thinking about nothing but being with you. I begged him to help me with my plan. He was shocked and tried to change my mind saying that I shouldn't trade my dignity, and that patience was the hope of lovers. He offered to ask his aging kafeel Jawad Ibn Khalid, who had left suddenly for medical treatment in America, to help me when he returned from his trip in a few months' time. But I told Hilal that I could not be sure whether his kafeel would be able to assist, and that I had no time to waste, since my father had recently announced that he had found a husband for me and that this time he wouldn't let even my mother stop him. What would a husband do to a wife when he found out he wasn't her first? I had to act now.

He reluctantly took my proposal to your kafeel, Bader Ibn Abd-Allah, who you told me has the power to get me a passport and order customs officers to wave me through without question.

Habibi, as I get ready to give your kafeel what you had to give him when you were fifteen, I know you won't judge me. I have to do what it takes to get a life that is rightfully mine, I have no regrets whatsoever. I don't want to think about what will happen. Instead, I only think about when I will see you and remind myself of the promise I made you on our last Friday afternoon together. Can you remember that afternoon, habibi? We had just one candle glowing in my dark room. We were standing naked in front of each other. Half of your face was covered by the darkness, half of you glowed in the candlelight.

'Fiore?' you whispered.

I didn't respond.

'Fiore?'

I reached with my hand to the table and grabbed

the candle, and held it with both my hands. I examined your face in silence. Our faces came closer, near to the flame. The fire turned your lips a stark yellow. Sweat trickled slowly, like tears, down your lower lip. We became a mirror of each other in our sadness, and love, pain and longing.

And when the candle dropped between our feet, when the darkness claimed the room, when your lips fell on mine like a lid, I wanted to tell you, before you left, that I had no regrets because life is priceless, because I am too young to die, because I will never let them bury me alive, not when my heart still loves you and has so much left to give, not before my eyes that adore you, but still have so much to see, go blind. 'Habibi,' I wanted to begin, as your teeth bit on my lips, as your breath accelerated the beating of my heart, as your tongue hypnotised mine. 'Naser? Habibi?' I had so much to tell you, but my words were dispersed just like your hands moving over my body. And when we began to twirl around each other as if we were on a sacred dance floor, dancing in tandem, joined from head to toe, and as we continued to move in a circle breaking everything in our path until we finally found the bed, we stopped. I wanted to scream, 'Naser, listen to me.' But you put your right hand under my left thigh, your left under my right, and you lifted me off the ground so high that I felt I was about to touch the stars, and when you swung your body, we fell on to the bed like two birds from the sky. My hair fell over your face, my breasts pressed tight against your chest, and when I plunged between your thighs, I whispered a promise in your ear, 'Habibi, if Jasim betrays you, and I am left behind alone, I will not succumb. I will not be another

anecdote in the imam's sermons to frighten future lovers.
I will not protect my father's honour, because this is my
life. No. I will take myself across the Red Sea just as I
brought you to my room. Whatever happens, I will not
die. I'll do whatever it takes, because I haven't lived yet,
because I lust for life. And life, I know, is beautiful.'

Acknowledgements

I am indebted to three very special people: *habibati* Lies for being a companion, a tremendous supporter and the first reader. To *sadeeqi* Kevin Conroy Scott, my agent, for believing, guiding and for his unstinting enthusiasm. And to *sadeeqati* Clara Farmer for combining superb editing with generous support.

Also, to Juliet Brooke and Susanna Porter (my editor in America) for making great contributions; to everyone at Chatto & Windus for being brilliant; to the four ladies at A.P. Watt for their excellent comments.

To David Gothard, Binyavanga Wainaina and Kadija George for showing confidence in my work in those very early days.

A special mention of my brother, Saleh. The journey somehow goes on.

Finally, to the mysterious girls in Jeddah who made love possible with their secret notes.

Thanks to you all.

Glossary

Abaya: veil – the large, black cloak dress worn by women in Saudi Arabia

Alhamdulillah: thanks be to Allah

Allah wa Akbar: Allah is great

Assalamu alaikum: a greeting – Peace be upon you. See *Wa 'alaikumu salam*

Astaqfirullah: May Allah grant us forgiveness

Azan: call to prayer

Bismillah: in the name of Allah

Eid al-Fitr: festival of fast-breaking marking the end of Ramadan

Gabi: traditional white cotton scarf worn in Ethiopia and Eritrea

Gutra: a traditional Arab head-dress

Habibi/Habibati: My love

Halal: permissible under Islamic law

Haram: forbidden under Islamic law

Hijra: migration

InshaAllah: if Allah wills it

Iqama: residence permit

Jallabiyah: a long robe worn by Sudanese men

Kabba: building located within the Great Mosque in Mecca which houses the Black Stone. Muslims all over the world turn towards the Kabba when they pray

Kabsa: classic Saudi Arabian dish made from rice, meat and spices

Kafeel: a sponsor. Every non-Saudi living or working in the country has to be sponsored by a Saudi. The *kafeel* system gives full control to the Saudis over the lives of the foreigners they sponsor. The *kafeel* has the power to withhold the passports of those under their control and deport them whenever they choose

Krar: (*Tigrinya*) a traditional Eritrean musical instrument

Mahram (pl. mahaarim): unmarriageable kin with whom sexual intercourse is forbidden

Majlis: reception room

MashaAllah: what Allah wishes. Often used as a compliment for something good

Mihrab: a recess in a mosque that indicates the direction of Mecca

Minbar: where an imam delivers sermons

Mutawwa (pl. mutawwa'in): a term used to describe those who follow the strict interpretation of Islam. It is also used to refer to a member of the Saudi religious police

Ogal: a black band fastened around the *gutra* to hold it in place

'Oud: a musical instrument similar to a lute

Outer: (*Tigrinya*) a clay pot to keep water cool

Salat Al Asar: the prayer in the last part of the afternoon. It is the third of five daily prayers

Shahada: declaration of faith to Allah

Shawarma: Middle Eastern meat or chicken sandwich

Shisha: a water pipe used for smoking tobacco

SubhanAllah: Glorified be Allah

Sunnah: to follow the religious actions instituted by Prophet Mohammed

Sura: chapter. The Qur'an is composed of 114 chapters

Tagiyah: a white knitted skull cap

Takbeer: to call the name of Allah – it is said at the start of a prayer and every subsequent set of prayers

Tasleem: saying *Assalamu alaikum* to close the prayer

Thobe: a long-sleeved one-piece garment that covers the whole body

Tigrinya: the language of Eritrea

Toombak: a rolled ball of chewed tobacco

Umma: a community or nation. It is used to refer to the community of believers

Umra: little pilgrimage, performed at any time except the days of the main pilgrimage

Wa 'alaikumu salam (in response to the greeting *Assalamu alaikum*): And upon you is the peace

Ya: exclamation. Literally, the word means 'oh'. A prefix before calling someone

Yallah: hurry up

Zib Al-Ard: Dick of the Earth!